W9-CFL-622

Some Bitter Taste

BY THE SAME AUTHOR

Property of Blood
The Monster of Florence
The Marshal at the Villa Torrini
The Marshal Makes His Report
The Marshal's Own Case
The Marshal and the Madwoman
The Marshal and the Murderer
Death in Autumn
Death in Springtime
Death of a Dutchman
Death of an Englishman

with Paolo Vagheggi
The Prosecutor

Some Bitter Taste

Magdalen Nabb

Copyright © 2002 by Magdelen Nabb and
Diogenes Verlag AG Zurich

Published in the United States in 2002
by Soho Press, Inc.
853 Broadway
New York, NY 10003

All rights reserved.

The characters and events in this story are fictional. No reference is
intended to any real person either living or dead.

Library of Congress Cataloging in Publication Data

Nabb, Magdalen, 1947-2007
Some bitter taste / Magdalen Nabb.
p. cm.
ISBN 978-1-56947-339-9
1. Guarnaccia, Marshal (Ficticious character)—Fiction.
2. Police—Italy—Florence—Fiction.
3. Florence (Italy)—Fiction.
I. Title.
PR6064.A18 S66 2002
823'.914—dc21   2002070579

10   9   8   7   6   5   4   3

For invaluable help, as always,
on matters regarding the Carabinieri
the author wishes to thank
Generale Nicolino D'Angelo.

Some Bitter Taste

The young man, Gjergj, just disappeared. From one day to the next his few possessions vanished from the little room in the villa and that was it. The marshal often had occasion to wonder what became of him. But the Albanian problem . . . you could only do your best. At least Dori was off the streets. In a sense, you could say that was more important because there was a child involved. It would be . . . what? About three months old by now. Coming back to his carabinieri station in the Pitti Palace after a fine spring afternoon in the country, the marshal hoped to goodness this coming summer wouldn't be as hot as the last. He still remembered the day they returned from their holidays back home in Syracuse to be hit by the suffocating heat and the crush of tourists. Florence in July . . .

The Pitti Palace dominates the neighbourhood of Oltrarno, the left bank of the river Arno; it stands just a stone's throw from Ponte Vecchio and its huge bulk, spread out horizontally, is like a stone barrier that, from the square, closes off the view of the Boboli hill behind it . . . It is difficult to imagine, behind the severe, rusticated facade, rhythmically spanned by arcades, the hidden garden rising up the hillside which the visitor

**discovers only after crossing the threshold of the palace, as the
large courtyard opens up before him . . .**

Marshal Guarnaccia flipped the pages of the guidebook.
Pretty pictures. Cost a pretty penny, too. He was willing to
bet that the woman who had left it behind when she came
in to report her lost or stolen wallet had left that on the
counter when she bought the guide. Once you started forgetting things in this heat . . .

He leaned back in his leather chair with a sigh. You come
back from holiday, fresh and hopeful, and you think everything will be different. Then you walk back into your office
and everything's the same.

A young carabiniere knocked and peered in at Marshal
Guarnaccia's door. He looked up. 'Has that woman come
back for this book?'

'No, she hasn't. Can I send in the next one?'

'How many more of them are out there?'

'Just four in the waiting room but there's that prostitute—
I told her to come in this morning.'

'Oh.'

'Did I do wrong? She won't talk to anybody but you, and
Lorenzini said—'

'You did quite right. And if she turns up I want to see her
straight away.'

'Yes, Marshal. So shall I . . .?'

'Just give me two minutes, son, will you?'

What good would two minutes do? Well, he could take his
jacket off, for a start. Only nine-thirty and it was sweltering.
It was true that down home in Syracuse the temperature
often reached one hundred and two, one hundred and four,

even one hundred and five degrees, but there was always a breeze from the sea. Florence in July . . . He flipped through the rest of the brightly coloured guidebook.

The slope leading up to the fountain of Neptune from which one has one of the most beautiful panoramas of the city.

It was true and what's more, here he was inside the Pitti Palace and that view was right outside his window. Only he couldn't open the window or even the shutters because it was too hot. There were no words to describe Florence in July. If only the Arno valley weren't so stagnant. Breathing the same soup of evaporating river, car fumes, sweat, and drains day after day made you long to stay indoors where it was cool and clean. Every evening on the news they told you that children, invalids, asthmatics, and the elderly should avoid going out during the hottest hours of the day. Marshals of carabinieri were not a protected species, it seemed.

'Poof!' He hung his uniform jacket behind the door beside his hat and holster. In his shirtsleeves he felt a little better and, with any luck, he would have no cause to go out today at all. It crossed his mind, as he slid his bulk back between desk and chair, that it might be easier to bear the suffocating heat of Florence if he weighed less. Thinking about it, part of that unreasoning postholiday buoyancy was a vision, after the overeating excused by the visit home, of a renewed and lighter self, to be achieved by wishful thinking alone.

'No, no . . . That's not it, at all.' He knew now what that after-the-holidays feeling came from. From school days. Cooling weather, new shoes, new teacher, new start. Satisfied that he had pinned it down, and reminding himself that each new school year had resulted in nothing but dismay and confusion for himself and irritation for his teachers, he addressed himself to the present. He was overweight, overheated, and overworked, and there were two more months of heat to get through. But at least he was behind the big desk now and no one these days accused him of not paying attention. Except his wife.

'Marshal?'

'What?'

'It's her, Marshal. That prostitute . . .'

'Bring her straight in and tell the rest they might as well go home and come back this afternoon. Anybody who insists on waiting can wait but this is going to take a long time.' It had already taken the marshal two months of patiently whittling away at the Albanian girl's natural diffidence in the face of uniformed authority to reach this crucial moment and he didn't intend to lose her now, for her sake more than his own. Arrest and convict one pimp and a dozen others are ready to take his place, but for the girl the story could have a happy ending.

'Sit down, Dori.' She was a fabulously good-looking girl, tall with lovely long legs; short, very blond hair; blue eyes; wide, painted lips. The face of a porcelain doll. She could surely have been a successful model if she'd had the luck to be born somewhere other than Albania. 'How are you feeling?'

'I'm all right.'

'No more nausea?'

'Not much. In any case, I'm working. Might as well keep earning as long as I can.'

'In another month it'll be showing.'

'So what? Some men go for that. It's happened to plenty of the other girls. You know what men are like. There's plenty of them want you when you're menstruating. Being pregnant's not that big a problem.'

'Who's running things now Ilir's inside?'

'His cousin, Lek.'

'I thought as much.'

'Makes no difference to me, does it? He's okay . . .'

'But?'

'Nothing . . . that friend of mine—you know, the letter and money you found—well, he made me give him her address.'

'I see. It doesn't surprise me. I suppose he thinks she's as good-looking as you, and Ilir's inside.'

'You're wrong. He's not trying to pull one over on Ilir. He's his cousin. That's why Ilir trusted his girls to Lek instead of the rest of his gang. He's looking after Ilir's interests, that's all. He's not interested in running girls, anyway. He's got a building firm. He's making plenty.'

The marshal knew all about the man and his building firm but he didn't say so. He only said, 'Does she know what she's getting into?'

'She knows what she's getting away from. D'you know what they say about women in that arsehole end of the earth where she comes from? "Women should do more work than donkeys because donkeys live on hay and women eat bread."'

'All right, Dori. Just remember that not all these girls have your luck. So, what about this man Mario? You can't keep him waiting indefinitely. I thought you were here because you'd made your mind up.'

She opened her bag and fished out cigarettes and an orange plastic lighter, then hesitated. He pushed a big glass ashtray towards her. 'So what's it to be? Have you made your mind up?'

'D'you mean about Mario or that other business?'

'It's all one, Dori. Marriage or prison, that's what it comes down to. If you shop Ilir you'll have to disappear from the streets. If you don't shop him, you go down. We may need you for proof against him but we've already got proof against you. Do you want your baby to be born in prison? There's another person to think about besides yourself.'

He could see that this child had no reality for her yet but once it was born she'd have to come to her senses, and though a girl as good-looking as she was might pick up more than one client willing to marry her, a man who'd take on a child too might not be so easy to come by.

Ilir Pictri, her protector, had been caught collecting money from her, which he did at intervals during her night's work, afraid of her stashing a bit away for herself or being robbed. She could make two million lire in a night with no trouble at all. He had her go into a phone box at the entrance to the Cascine Park, pretend to make a call, and slip the money under the phone book. Ilir would go in after her, pretend to make a call in his turn, and pick up the money. It had been easy enough for a couple of carabinieri in plain clothes to work this manoeuvre out. They arrested him during a 'phone call'. Ilir was inside now, awaiting trial, and they needed Dori's testimony to convict him of pimping. When they'd searched the flat after Pictri's arrest, they'd found a letter written by Dori to a friend of hers back in Albania. A translation revealed that she was encouraging the girl to join her, telling her what she could earn and enclosing money for the journey with details and contacts for a clandestine passage. This letter made her guilty of pimping along with Ilir and she'd been offered a deal. Testify against him and charges would be dropped against her. Now a regular client of Dori's, Mario B., had offered to marry her. The marshal had called him in and had a quiet talk with him and it seemed that he was willing to go through with the marriage even though the girl was pregnant. He had even said, 'You never know, it could be mine. Besides, she told me herself, you know. It's not as though she tried to hide it from me like some girls would have done. She's a good girl who's had a bad time.'

And, the marshal thought, she's tall, blond, and sexy, and you, though honest and respectable, are an office worker whose face is as dreary as your job. So he didn't try to dissuade Mario. He just listened to him. He was going to need luck to make such a marriage work, but then who didn't?

And now he listened to Dori. She was a lot more realistic than her prospective husband, and her fears were well grounded. If she'd ever had any hopes or illusions, they'd been crushed out of her long before Ilir's money paid the exorbitant fee that brought her across to Puglia, wet and starved in a rubber dinghy.

'Besides, how long will he get? Whether I'm married or not, he could still come after me when he gets out.'

'You can afford to pay him off.' He wasn't being strictly honest and they both knew it. The average price of a girl was around twenty-five million lire. A girl with Dori's looks wasn't easy to come by. She couldn't afford to pay him off.

'So get married. You'll be living in Prato. A different city, a different world . . .'

She lit another cigarette, thinking about it. The same image was in both their heads. Neither of them wanted to put it into words. Black nights on the motorway. Girls who refused to play ball, girls who thought they could set up on their own account, beaten, tortured, abandoned. The most recent had got off lightly with fractures to shoulder, arm, and knee. She was eight months pregnant. The baby had survived.

And even so, after their experiences in Albania, it was authority that they feared, uniforms that they hated. So it needed patience.

If only that Mario had a bit more oomph, he'd threaten to change his mind instead of hanging around bleating like a sheep. That might shock her, make her realise . . .

The marshal himself had a card up his sleeve but he didn't feel justified in showing it. One that would link her, probably unjustly, to an organized crime investigation. Better wait and see. He had a job to do, when all was said and done, and Captain Maestrangelo, his commanding officer, wouldn't be any too pleased if he risked blowing an important case in the hopes of getting a good-looking prostitute safely married off. There was nothing for it but to play Mario's part for him. He stared at the map of his Quarter on the wall behind the girl's head and said, 'I didn't really want to say this.' Which was true enough.

'Say what?' She tensed, swallowing smoke, coughing.

'I've been talking to Mario—'

'Talking to him? Putting him off? Is that what you mean? Telling him to find some nice little respectable Italian girl who works in an office—'

'No, no . . . nothing of that sort. No . . .'

'What then? What?'

'Just the opposite, Dori. I've been doing my best for you but you've let him go off the boil, you know. By this time, he'll have talked about it—to his mates at work, to his mother even. Can you imagine the fuss a mother would kick up?

What she'll be saying to him? The tears and tantrums, day in, day out?'

'He's never mentioned his mother to me. Anyway, why tell her? Why tell his friends? What business is it of anybody else's?'

'He was bound to tell them at some point.'

'He didn't have to tell them I was on the game.'

'But he couldn't avoid telling them . . .'

'That I'm Albanian. Go on, say it! So I can't be anything but, can I? Fucking racists!'

'Yes, but in your case it's true, isn't it? So they'll all be trying to put him off. I doubt if he gets a minute's peace, at home or at work, and it's bound to be having its effect. Get him while the going's good, Dori, before you get AIDS, before Ilir gets out because you haven't given evidence, before your baby's born.'

It worked. An hour and a half later he had the signature of Dorina Hoxha on a statement, typed up by Lorenzini, that would keep Ilir inside for a few years. Now that Dori had talked, she would have to get off the streets and throw in her lot with Mario, who, fortunately, was an orphan.

The next time the carabiniere put his head round the door, the marshal, with a little sigh of pleasure, said, 'Lunch . . .'

Two

'It is almost one but . . . you said if anybody insisted . . .'
'Who is it?'
'A signora . . . Hirsch—'
'No, no. Don't send a foreigner in if Lorenzini's gone off.'
Lorenzini could manage a bit of English and could redirect people to Borgo Ognissanti Headquarters in French and German when communications failed. He was considered the station linguist.
'He hasn't gone and she's Italian. Passport is, anyway.'
'All right. Show her in.'
Some people came through the door with their complaints tumbling from their mouths; others had trouble knowing where to start. He watched this woman glance discreetly round the room as she smoothed her linen dress beneath her and tried to gather her thoughts. She wouldn't find much inspiration, he thought, in the row of army calendars behind his head, the photocopier, a filing cabinet. Her hair looked very white against olive skin, her eyes almost as black as her elegant frock. He noticed a gold necklace, yellowing diamonds in her ring. No wedding ring, though. The poor people of the San Frediano Quarter were voluble. They called a spade a spade. They had no resources outside their own

families and they came to him to tell all and invoke his help. Women with old diamonds usually had influential friends to help them, and if they came to him it was to demand action and tell him as little as possible. He stared at her with his large, slightly bulging eyes. She met his gaze for a second then shifted her glance to the right and upwards. The tips of her varnished fingernails touched her necklace. He waited. She changed her mind about lying to him and met his gaze again, saying, 'I've come to you because I'm frightened.'

'I see. And who are you frightened of, Signora?'

But her eyes flickered up and right again. 'I don't know. I—someone has been in my flat while I was out. Naturally I have no way of knowing who.'

'Was anything stolen?' He was reaching for a sheet of lined, stamped paper to take her statement.

'No! No, nothing was stolen and I don't—do you have to write this down?'

'Not at all, Signora, if you don't want me to.'

He put the paper back.

'I don't. I thought that if I told you, in confidence, you could advise me. My neighbour, Signora Rossi, a young woman whose husband is an architect—they have a little girl who occasionally spends a little time with me in the afternoons if both parents are out at work—of course, this has nothing to do with the problem. I'm just trying to explain why I came here, even though . . .'

'That's all right, Signora. You don't have to explain anything.'

'Perhaps not, but I don't want you to think that I would waste your time. I mean, not reporting anything stolen, just wanting to talk to you.'

'That's what I'm here for.'

'You're very kind, but I remember. . . my handbag was snatched recently—you know the sort of thing, a youngster on a scooter. They say one should be thankful not to be injured as so many women are when they try to hang on to their bags and are dragged into the road. Anyway, I reported it at your headquarters in Borgo Ognissanti and, though they were perfectly polite, quite kind, in fact, I didn't feel I could go there with—I mean go there and talk about—'

'Being frightened? Well, you're right. They're very busy over there. You did well to come here. This neighbour of yours, do I know her?'

'From years ago, yes. She said you wouldn't remember her but you were very kind to her and her husband just after the little girl was born and they thought they were going to be thrown out of their house. Perhaps you do remember.'

'I can't say I do. I don't imagine it was anything much, whatever I did. So you told your neighbours about what's worrying you?'

Again her eyes left his, her fingers trembled, nose, mouth, throat.

'I mentioned it. In case they'd seen anyone on the stairs, near my door.'

'Very sensible. Now, are you absolutely sure that there's nothing missing?'

'Yes.'

'Were there any signs of a forced entry?'

'None.'

'What sort of lock have you?'

'A spring bolt. Six horizontal bolts and a floor-to-ceiling vertical one.'

'Not the sort of thing they open with a credit card. Well then, Signora, if no one has broken in and there's nothing missing, what makes you think someone has been in your flat?'

'I don't think. I know.'

'How?'

'There were things out of place. I'm not an excessively tidy person but one senses when things are not the way one left them. We all have habitual ways of placing things . . . I see you do think I'm wasting your time.'

'No I don't. I think that you're an intelligent and sensible woman and that you wouldn't waste your own time, let alone mine. I don't think you'd be here—I don't think you'd be frightened—because of a vague sensation. Was there something—a smell, a trace of some other person, cigarette smoke, for example, if you don't smoke yourself?'

She seemed to stop breathing for a moment. The wave of fear passing through her body was visible. His big eyes were still fixed on her and she seemed unable to drag her gaze away now.

'The first time.' He could hardly hear her.

'No one can overhear what we say in here, Signora. Don't be afraid to speak up. Was there cigarette smoke? Ashes? Just a smell?'

'Just a smell. Not cigarettes. More like cigars.'

'And the other times? Was there a smell?'

'A knife.'

'A *knife?*' Was she going to turn out to be crazy, like so many others with similar complaints? 'What sort of knife? A dagger? A hunter's knife? A bread knife?'

'Not a bread knife but it was a kitchen knife.'

'I see. And was this kitchen knife yours?'

'Yes.'

'And it wasn't in its usual position.'

'You don't believe me, do you? I wasn't going to tell you about the knife. I knew you'd think I was mad. It was lying in the entrance hall, right where I'd see it as I walked in the door! I'm not mad, Marshal, I'm in danger!'

'Now, now, Signora, nobody said anything about being mad.'

She had tried so hard to be composed but her face became red and blotchy now, her eyes bloodshot. The marshal stood up.

'Please! You're not listening!'

He'd spoken too soon about that, it seemed. 'I am listening. I'm just going to ask one of my carabinieri to bring a glass of water for you and then you'll calm down and tell me the rest of your story quietly.'

When he came back and sat down she was already quieter but her face had a collapsed look about it which the marshal had seen a hundred times at the moment of a confession. He was pretty sure that this woman wasn't going to confess anything that could be any business of his and he was right.

'I may as well tell you before I go any further that I have spent time in a psychiatric clinic. You would get to know, anyway I suppose. But it was only for severe reactive depression after my mother died. I'm very much alone in the world— but I'm not paranoid or anything like that. If you check they'll tell you.'

A carabiniere brought in the glass of water and murmured, 'There's nobody out there now. Can I go to lunch?'

The marshal looked at his watch and stood up. 'All right, but first see that this lady sits down with her glass of water in the waiting room until she feels well enough to leave. Signora, leave your address with my carabiniere and don't worry. I'll come and see you at home myself.'

'Wait. There's something else.'

There was always something else. When people wanted his help without the embarrassment of telling him the full facts, they went on tossing him titbits until they got his attention. She was feeling about in her handbag with a shaky hand. 'I've had a threatening letter. Here. Look at this.'

The marshal took it. It was a picture postcard, one of those joke ones that show an enlargement of the genitals of Michelangelo's *David*. Every bar in the city sold them. Rather than an anonymous letter, it looked more like something neighbouring kids might send to a tedious spinster who nagged about radio volume or the street door being left open.

The woman said nothing. He felt her eyes fixed on him as he turned the card over.

It was addressed to Sara Hirsch, Sdrucciolo de' Pitti 4, 50125 Firenze. It had been posted in the city in July. The postmark was too blurred to see the exact date.

It said, 'NOW WE KNOW WHERE YOU LIVE WE'LL BE COMING TO VISIT YOU. WHEN WE DO YOU'LL BE SORRY.'

The marshal looked at her hard. 'Signora, this is from someone you know.'

'How can you say that? How could I know—'

'No, Signora, you misunderstand me. Whoever sent you this is known to you. The writing is known to you so the writer has tried to disguise it in a very amateur way. Look here at the *N*, and then here, look at the *L* here and here. A different style each time.'

'But why? After all, I've done nobody any harm. Why should they threaten me? What do they want?'

'The message is clear enough, Signora. It means just what it says. "We know where you live." They intend to make you frightened of living there. I take it you're not the owner of the flat.'

'No . . . no.'

'Well, Signora, whoever it is wants you out. Unfortunately, given the length of time, sometimes twenty years, needed to obtain an eviction through legal channels, there are lawyers around unscrupulous enough to resort to terrorist tactics, especially in the case of a woman living alone. It's a bad business, Signora, and very unpleasant for you but at least you know the motive behind it now and it's something that you have every reason to be angry about but not afraid. I've known a few of these nasty lawyers but there's never been an instance of actual harm.'

She stood up. 'I must go. I must think what to do.' She held out her hand for the postcard.

'Just a minute.' He photocopied it before giving it back to her. 'You'll find that you have something in this person's writing at home, I think, something to do with your tenancy. If you have any further trouble we can have a graphologist take a look.' He didn't specify what sort of trouble, given that she herself hadn't gone back to the story of somebody's having been inside her flat. It was more than possible that the message had frightened her into imagining all that, but it was also possible that it was pure invention, something to get his attention. She showed no relief at his explanation of the message. People were strange about what they would admit to and what they wouldn't. Perhaps she felt that being evicted was something shameful that only happened to poor people who didn't pay their rent. In Florence it could happen to anybody and did. He kept quiet. Any attempt to comfort her would probably just embarrass her. He showed her to the door. She paused in going to look him in the eyes, her chin held high.

'Don't imagine that I shall allow myself to be bullied. I shan't.'

'That's the spirit, Signora. Why don't you have a talk with your lawyer and tell him what I've told you.'

'I will. I intend to make a number of calls immediately on my return home. I intend to defend my rights. I have more cards up my sleeve than these people know about. I am not weak, even when I feel weak.'

It could be, of course, that every word of her story was true and that she was crazy just the same. Things happen to crazy people as they do to everyone else. That last speech sounded like she rehearsed it to herself every day.

She seemed to him to be torn between her anxiety to get away and her anxiety to convince him. She jumped back to her earlier story as though reading his mind.

'Whatever you may think, everything I've told you is true. That knife was lying right inside the front door.'

'I see. And where's your kitchen?'

'Immediately off the hall, on the right as you go in—you're not trying to suggest I dropped it there myself?'

'I'm not trying to suggest anything. No, no. You don't have a cat? Or a dog.'

'No. I've always wanted a cat but until I'm more settled in life—what are you trying to say?'

'Nothing, except that—'

'Listen, there's something else . . .'

'If there's anything else you can leave a note about it with the carabiniere. I'll come and see you one afternoon this week when you've had time to talk to your lawyer.' He took the carabiniere aside to say quietly, 'Find out if she had her locks changed after her bag was stolen, will you? You know how it is with people living alone. They frighten themselves into hysterics and then you find out they haven't taken the most obvious precautions.'

She was watching, trying to hear. As the carabiniere approached her she fixed the marshal with frightened eyes and said, 'You'll really come and see me as you promised?'

'I'll come.'

The marshal was late for lunch.

'You're late,' Teresa said. 'I'll put some fresh pasta in. The boys have eaten your share.'

'Where are they?'

'In their room playing that new computer game.'

The fresh, buoyant postholiday feeling returned with the smells in the kitchen where Teresa was pinching big leaves of basil from a plant for his pasta. One of the rows and rows of bottled tomatoes was open on the marble worktop, and a crate of oranges and lemons, picked yesterday morning in Sicily, stood in one corner, their peel rough, their leaves smooth and shiny. The perfume filled the whole flat. The smell of his childhood. What was Teresa going on about?

'You're not listening to me.'

'What? Of course I am. No, I won't try and learn their wretched computer games.'

He had tried once but Totò got more and more infuriated with him.

'*Oh, Dad!*'

Giovanni had been more patient. He was a bit on the slow side himself and never won though he always wanted to play.

'I've got better things to do with my time, and so should they have.'

'It was your sister bought it for them.'

'They couldn't have talked Nunziata into buying a computer game if you hadn't talked me into buying the wretched computer last Christmas "because they need it for their studies".'

He let the blips and yells coming from the bedroom say the rest. He knew very well that Teresa was trying to cover the noise by an unnecessary clattering of pans. The spaghetti slapped into the colander. While he stirred a lump of butter into the glistening sauce she started the washing up.

'Aren't you sitting down for a minute?'

'I ate with the boys. You didn't phone to say you'd be late.'

'Couldn't interrupt.' He hated it when she washed up instead of talking to him.

'Well, neither can I. I've another two wash loads to do, not to mention all the ironing. I don't know which is more work, leaving or coming home. Besides, there's no point in talking to you when you're in this mood.'

'What mood?'

'This mood. If you ask me, you won't play with them because you're too slow and Totò loses his patience with you, like anybody would.'

And wasn't that what he'd just said? He was offended and not all that sorry to have to drink off an espresso standing at the sink and go back early to the queue of people he'd sent home in the morning. He nodded to them all as he passed through the waiting room to his office, muttering, as he closed the door behind him on his equivalent of the holiday washing and ironing, 'I don't know which is worse, setting off or coming back.'

In the end, Teresa got her workload back to normal within three days. On the fourth day he was just beginning to see over the top of his.

A girl from Brescia, worried to tears: 'It's the keys I'm worried about. I feel such a fool.'

'No, no . . . Signorina, you mustn't worry so much. If you say your friends' son can be contacted and a new set of keys made—'

'But the locks will all have to be changed! They'll never let me stay in their house again after this, I know they won't.'

'It wasn't your fault, Signorina. These bag snatchers are very fast. Now, try and remember: You said you were in Piazza del Carmine. Was it a moped or a scooter?'

'A scooter, dark blue.'

'Was he wearing a helmet?'

'Yes, he was. That was dark blue as well, with white zigzags on it, like lightning.'

Blast that boy. As if his mother, fighting a losing battle against cancer, hadn't troubles enough.

Domestic violence. A regular customer, immense, with lap-dog: 'Yap! Yap yap yap!'

'Baby! Poor Baby. Hush now, it's all right.'

'Yap yap!'

'Did you call your lawyer?'

'Of course I did. She said the case won't come before the judge until September. She says I shouldn't let him into the house in the meantime. You've no idea how violent he is.'

'I do know how violent he is, Signora. You called me out a number of times if you remember—'

'That was before I asked for the separation. You've no idea—'

'Yap yap yap yap yap! Grrr.'

'You know, I don't think she likes your uniform.'

'I'm sorry.'

'Shh . . . nice man, he's a nice man. Look, he's going to stroke you.'

'Not on the desk, Signora, if you don't mind. Keep the dog on your knee. And if your lawyer told you not to let him in, why did you?'

'Because Baby won't eat her dinner if he's not there.'

'Yap!'

A man of seventy-odd, stiff with rage: 'You and I understand each other! I did my military service in the cavalry, I don't know if I mentioned that.'

'Yes, I think you did.'

'A missing streetlight is an invitation to a mugger. I've written to the mayor but he hasn't deigned to answer so I'll leave the matter in your hands. You're a man of good sense.'

'Thank you.'

A stolen bicycle: 'Worth nothing so why steal it? That's what I don't understand.'

'You're sure it wasn't street-cleaning night? You should check that the municipal police haven't picked it up.'

A woman whose top-floor neighbour spent his evenings

leaning out of the window, smoking: 'With *my* patio as his ashtray. I've put a nice bit of matting down and what's going to happen if it catches fire?'

'Ah, ignorance, Signora, ignorance is an ugly beast. You tell him I know all about it, that should do the trick. If it doesn't I'll come round.'

The cat-shooter girl: 'There must be something you can do.'

'Yes, but we've already done it.'

'I just can't believe it.'

'But there it is.'

She lived in one of the little terraced houses down near the Ponte alla Vittoria, and one of her neighbours, she couldn't distinguish which, was regularly taking potshots at the local cats from his bedroom window with a shotgun. '*And there's an elementary school playground immediately beyond our little gardens! What if he hits a child? All you have to do is check which person in the street has a shotgun.*' So they had and it turned out that the young lady was the only person in the row who didn't have a shotgun.

'They all have regular licences, Signorina. If you could lean out a bit farther when the shooting starts perhaps you could manage to work out which house it is. Otherwise . . .'

'He shot two yesterday. One dead and the other with its spine full of shot. I found it and brought it in but it's paralysed and I know I'll have to have it put down.'

Another cat. This one lost: 'Didn't settle, you see. They don't, do they, in a new house? She must have got over the wall into the Boboli Gardens so, with you being right on the spot here, I thought I'd leave you a photograph—you can't mistake that black patch on her knee. I suppose your men patrol the gardens?'

'No, no, they don't. If you give the photo to one of the gardeners—they feed all the cats in there twice a day—I'm sure they'll find her for you.'

A stolen camera, mimed: *'Sprechen Sie Deutsch?'*

'Lorenzini!'

Nevertheless, when at half past five that afternoon he opened the windows and the outer shutters and turned off the light, he was able to congratulate himself since it looked as though he might just clear the backlog this evening. But wasn't there something he'd forgotten, somewhere he'd said he'd go this week? Later, as he was writing up the duty sheet for the next day it was still nagging at him. As he finished it, he remembered: the woman with the postcard. It wasn't urgent but he had promised her he'd go this week. If he didn't turn up she would be more frightened than ever because his reassurance had been false. He stood up and got his jacket from behind the door. The phone rang. Captain Maestrangelo at HQ.

'There's been a burglary at the Villa L'Uliveto, Sir Christopher Wrothesly's place up behind the Piazzale Michelangelo . . . Pian dei Giulari, so it's on your territory. Small stuff, I gather, but you ought to go up there so I'll pick you up in ten minutes. You've nothing on you can't leave?'

'No, no.'

The marshal buttoned his jacket and went to look in at the duty room door. 'Lorenzini?'

'Marshal?'

'I have to go out. If there's anything, you can reach me through Captain Maestrangelo's car. Minor robbery. Nothing interesting.'

Lorenzini looked sceptical. 'When did the captain ever leave his desk for a robbery, minor or otherwise?'

'Oh, important foreign resident. Bit of pressure to make a show, I suppose.'

'Hm.'

'You might finish the duty sheet.' Even so, thought the marshal as he locked up behind himself and stumped unwillingly down the stairs towards the furnace of the outdoor world, pressure wouldn't account for it. A personal favour maybe, but the captain . . .

Then he was outside on the gravel and the still-burning sun plus the stored heat coming from the great stones of the Pitti Palace overpowered him and melted down all thoughts beyond self-defence. He fished for his handkerchief and sunglasses and shifted from fiery exposure to simmering shade.

Three

Heat and silence. Too hot even for the birds to sing. And the rhythmic sawing of crickets only accentuated the stillness. Captain Maestrangelo and the marshal stood waiting by the smaller door on the left as instructed by the lodge keeper, who had opened up for the car and pointed the way along the cypress alley. A double-sided staircase led up to the central doors giving on to the first floor in the style of the Medici country houses. This one had been built by a banking family of almost equal fame. The captain gazed up at the balustrade, where statues and urns were silhouetted against a pale, vapourous sky. The marshal was looking down to his right at the layer of sulphurous filth that indicated the city. It was impossible not to feel pity for Florence, lying there beautiful and defenceless, unable to cough up the smog that was rotting and choking it.

'Until you come up to a place like this you don't realise . . . ,' murmured the captain, gazing up in admiration.

'That's true,' sighed the marshal, gazing down in dismay.

'I'm so sorry to keep you waiting. Please forgive me. Come this way.' The man who opened the door was Jeremy Porteous, Sir Christopher's secretary. When they introduced themselves he shook hands first, attentively, with the higher-ranking officer and briefly, without eye contact, with the marshal. They followed him into the coolness of a circular hall with a silent fountain at its centre. The marshal, taking off his dark glasses and trying to refocus in the dim light, only had time to glimpse a curving stone staircase and part of the pattern of a mosaic floor. They crossed a corridor where a feeble lightbulb in an elaborate chandelier made only itself visible and then reached a spacious room, where a stronger bulb illuminated plain painted cupboards and a big square table, obviously part of the kitchen offices. Here Porteous stopped and faced them, saying, 'Sir Christopher will receive you in the garden. I feel I ought to warn you that he is not well and that anything in the nature of a shock could be very dangerous for him.'

'Does he know about the burglary?' the captain asked.

'He does . . . but . . . we all feel that if possible we should not have him think that any member of his permanent staff could be involved. That would distress him a great deal more than the robbery itself—especially in the case of one young person—any disappointment in that quarter . . . So that, whatever your conclusions might be, we'd be grateful if you'd confide them to us in the first place. I'm sure you understand me.'

Are you indeed? And who's 'we'? The marshal already disliked this man. A handshake can tell you a lot. Not that it was limp, or damp, for that matter. It was too . . . elegant, somehow, and a bit too warm and clingy for the marshal's taste. And watching him now, as he gave careful instructions to the captain, he was altogether too nice-looking and, though he was tall and thin and his nose was sharp at the end, everything else about him was soft. Soft skin; soft greying dark hair; soft floppy suit, silk presumably; soft, delicate voice. And the perfume. The marshal took a small step back. His presence was irrelevant anyway. Porteous spoke exclusively to the captain.

'It was, as I said, a very tiny stroke—he remained confused for two or three days, couldn't read or tell the time or remember what he'd just said—but he was quite aware of his condition and it was very frightening for him.'

'It must have been,' said the Captain, 'very frightening indeed.'

The captain himself was an elegant man. A quiet and serious man. Certainly not soft, though. Quite the opposite.

'He's back to normal now. But the fear remains.'

'Of course.'

'So he must rest and avoid anything that would excite him. He is using a wheelchair as a precaution and it's parked out of his sight once we transfer him to a chair. He's very proud and doesn't mention the business at all, so I beg you . . .'

'You need have no fear,' insisted the captain. The marshal, who knew him well, heard the hidden impatience in his voice. Porteous, if he heard it too, cared nothing about it and tattled on about Sir Christopher's dislike of doctors and Sir Christopher this and Sir Christopher that and Sir Christopher the other. The marshal was reminded of someone, or so he thought. Then he got it. Those officious, unctuous priests who were always strutting and smirking with self-importance around the pope when you saw him on the TV news. No doubt, if they ever gave voice, it was the same story—the Holy Father this and the Holy Father that . . . after the shooting, how long ago was it . . . time passed so quickly.

'This way, please.' He opened the door. A brilliant rectangle of fresh gold and green. The marshal blinked and replaced his sunglasses. They walked between lemon trees, many of them as high as themselves, and again, as in his own kitchen, the marshal picked up the sharp scent of home and childhood. But these lemon trees were in decorated terra cotta pots, standing like guards all along a gravel walk at the far end of which was what must be the *limonaia*, its tall brown shutters open, its great doors ajar. Behind the lemons, to left and right, low razored hedges divided the various vegetables of the kitchen garden. The marshal, who was always interested in food, took a good look at what was growing there and was very curious to see, beyond the usual beans and salads, a patch of sweet corn. No doubt on an estate this size—and he knew it to be very big—there'd be a farm with hens. Odd place to grow your hen food, though. The man was a foreigner, of course, but his workmen surely weren't.

Halfway to the lemon house they turned left on a path leading to a high clipped hedge backed by young cypresses. They went through a narrow gap, a gateway in a lichened wall, and down some steps into a rectangular garden enclosed on the opposite side by a high wall with an arbour directly facing them beyond a lily pond. Once inside this garden, which looked to the marshal like a sort of outdoor room, they could see, to their right, the city under its cloud of pollution over a low balustrade flanked by tall cypresses. To their left, in the direction of the house, a stone staircase led up to a semicircular terrace, its curve enclosed by a high hedge with statues placed in niches. Two of the green niches were empty, the marshal noted as they were led across on a raised path to the arbour, a circular plinth, with a vine-clad wrought iron roof supported at the back by a curve in the lichened garden wall and in front by two stone pillars. There, in a deep wicker chair, Sir Christopher sat in leafy shade. Beside him were paints and a half-finished picture on an easel. There was no wheelchair in sight, though the marshal's eyes searched for it under cover of his dark glasses, and Sir Christopher rose slowly to greet them as they arrived. Perhaps it was the thought of a wheelchair, coupled with the memory of his mother after the stroke, but the marshal was expecting someone old, wrapped in rugs, perhaps even in bedroom slippers. Sir Christopher was pale and tired-looking but he was wearing a cream linen suit and a patterned bow tie. He didn't look particularly sick and he was younger than the marshal had expected, in his late fifties at the most. His hair was dyed brown. Porteous introduced them and the marshal noticed the way Sir Christopher shook hands with them, smiling and according equal attention to both. A gentleman, then, unlike the soft fellow who now left them.

'It's very good of you to come. I understand from Jeremy that we've lost nothing of particular value this time. He is preparing a typewritten list of the small objects which are missing. He'll bring it out to us in a moment, I'm sure, so perhaps you'd sit with me and drink something.'

They sat down. The captain declined to take anything and, though impressed by the variety of drinks, mostly alcoholic, set out on a low wicker table beside Sir Christopher's chair, the marshal said, 'I'd be glad of a glass of water, if that's all right. Hot day. . . .' And he'd better not drink much of that or he'd break out in a sweat again after having cooled off so nicely in the captain's car.

'Of course.'

The marshal expected a servant, perhaps a butler, to appear from nowhere and do the honours but Sir Christopher served him. He put a lot of ice in the glass, which the marshal didn't want, but he didn't like to say so. He'd have done better to take nothing because now he didn't know where to put his hat and so held it precariously on one knee as he sipped the freezing cold water.

'Do I understand from your saying "this time" that you've had other burglaries?' Nothing disturbed the captain's quiet gravity and one sunburned hand lay smooth and still on his perfectly balanced hat.

'One quite serious burglary, I'm sorry to say, though a great many years ago now. The distressing thing about that occasion was not so much the considerable value of the stolen artworks, which were part of my father's collection, but the fact that there seemed no doubt that someone in the house was involved. Someone who let them in and took them to the things they were interested in. There were no signs of a forced entry, you see, and there were two dogs in the house who didn't bark.'

As the captain asked his questions the marshal listened to the sawing of the crickets and the water trickling feebly in the fountain at the centre of the lily pond. He was worrying about what to do with his ice-cold glass since the table was out of his reach. It was becoming agony to hold. Would it fall over if he put it down on the pebble-patterned floor booby-trapped with creeping flowers? Sir Christopher saw his discomfiture and leant forward a little. 'Do let me . . .'

Like the marshal, he was a big man, a bit overweight, and the hand that reached for the glass had plump pale fingers. 'We were obliged to fire a young man we'd just taken on to help with the cataloguing of the collection here, which my father never kept up to date and which, I'm afraid, still is far from complete. The young man—a very diligent worker—was the only person other than my curator, who's been with us almost thirty years, and my dearest friend, Renato, an antiquities expert with whom I've dealt all my life, who could have directed the thieves to those pieces.'

'They couldn't have helped themselves to whatever attracted them?'

'Ah, my dear Captain, if you were to see the top floor of this house you would realise how impossible that would be. My father was a real collector. He didn't buy for this house, the house was just a receptacle for his collection, nor did he ever sell anything. It's a sort of Aladdin's cave up there. Not only that, but since things were being moved during the cataloguing process, pairs had occasionally been separated—in the case of one piece needing restoration, that sort of thing. Yet they made no mistakes and their choices were precise and, sorry though I am to say it, admirable.'

'And nothing, I presume, ever appeared on the market.'

'Nothing. Robbery on commission. Collectors, you know, have no scruples. They mention to their dealer that they are looking for a certain type of piece and ask no questions when, after a time, it is produced. Still, a very sad business, having to send the boy away. He had taste, and one tries to help the young . . . Jeremy came to me at that age, knowing nothing. He is now very expert indeed.'

'Sir Christopher . . .'

Jeremy Porteous, the soft, dark man, was back, flourishing a sheet of paper in front of him.

'Thank you, my dear. Captain, here is the list of stolen goods, nothing of great interest, as you'll see, but my lawyer will be dealing with the insurance company and they'll need a copy of our report to you.'

'Of course.' The captain took the list and passed it to the marshal without glancing at it. 'Marshal Guarnaccia will deal with everything. He'll transfer this list to one of our report sheets and bring it for your signature. Naturally, we'll circulate this list to all the Florentine antique dealers but I can't, as I'm sure you realise, offer you much hope . . .'

'I do, indeed, realise it and apologise for having to take up your time on account of the insurance. I don't expect to see any of these things again. And although I'm sorry for it, since the silver was from my father's bedroom, which has never been touched since his death, what I'm most concerned about is that poor boy, Giorgio.'

'I'm sorry?'

'I should really be very distressed and surely with fingerprinting and so on you can prove—'

'Now, you mustn't upset yourself,' Porteous interrupted. 'The boy assures me—'

'So did Alex assure us, and I'm still not convinced we were right to do what we did. I can't let young Giorgio be judged unfairly.'

Porteous laid a hand on the older man's shoulder, murmuring, 'Remember you mustn't get agitated.'

'I know.'

'The marshal will need to speak to all your staff, Sir Christopher, including this Giorgio. Did he replace the boy you dismissed after the other robbery?'

'No. Oh, no, since Alex there have been a number of . . . he's quite recent, has only been here a matter of months. A charming boy. You won't . . . ? I mean . . .'

'The marshal will speak to him just as he does to the rest of your staff.' The captain got to his feet. 'Sir Christopher, please believe me when I say that your preoccupation is perfectly comprehensible. You want to feel safe in your own home, among loyal people, and that is certainly more important than recovering a few pieces of silverware. If I might take a look at all access points of the house and then the room or rooms where the thefts occurred. The marshal here will stay with you and explain the procedures which will follow. I'm sure he'll convince you that you have nothing to worry about.'

The marshal's heart sank. Maestrangelo had an unshakable conviction that he was good at talking to people and getting them to talk to him. But in this case it was ridiculous. Why the captain had come here was still a mystery. The marshal had been a bit embarrassed to ask on the way here but, surely, if it was the usual thing of pressure from high places—important foreign resident—the captain should be sitting here making polite small talk while the marshal got on with his business, checking for forced entry, questioning staff, and so on. The very idea of leaving him with the job of trying to comfort a millionaire who'd had a few knickknacks stolen! And besides, to get people to confide in you, you had to edge into the thing gradually, chat about everyday problems until you found an opening or rather the other person did. People needed to talk, after all . . . what in God's name was he supposed to chat casually about to this chap? What could his everyday problems possibly be? He launched, instead, into an explanation about fingerprinting the staff—just to eliminate them, you understand—the examination of the outside of the building, the precautions to be taken in case this should be a trial run for something bigger once the flurry had died down. When that petered out and the captain hadn't reappeared he was back to wondering what the everyday problems of a rich man might be. He gazed about him, trying to think of something to say, avoiding the painting on its easel. He'd be sure to say the wrong thing there. It looked pretty amateurish but that was probably because he was used to the ones in the Pitti galleries and didn't understand modern stuff. He shifted his attention to the garden, a safer subject altogether. Pale pink and white geraniums spilled out of terra cotta vases and urns. A few white roses still bloomed on branches that scrambled up the walls and around the lower branches of other trees. There were low trimmed hedges, very neat and geometrical, enclosing all sorts of bushes and pale tangles of tiny, unimpressive-looking flowers.

'Your garden's beautifully kept.' Well, it was true of the hedges, anyway. For the rest, it seemed out of control, especially because every nook and cranny in the walls and pebbled paths was matted with growth of some sort or another. Yet the man must have an army of gardeners . . . shouldn't have spoken.

'It is beautifully kept and in the case of this particular garden I have reason to be grateful for it because I've neglected it myself for so many years. My first thought each morning is for the gardens. I like to spend an hour at least with the gardeners. But this garden . . . they've loved it and cared for it and they've changed nothing apart from moving out one or two things which were in need of restoration. I know it's not for me that they do it, but I'm grateful, even so.'

The marshal understood nothing of this but searched for another remark to make about the garden since it was evidently an everyday concern.

Behind the safety screen of his dark glasses, his eyes scanned the place for inspiration and saw with surprise an old friend who would serve his purpose. There was a statue down there on the left of a young girl pouring an endless trickle of water from a stone jar into a pool at her feet.

'Isn't that a copy of a statue in the Boboli Gardens?'

Sir Christopher followed his glance and smiled. 'No, no, it isn't, but your memory doesn't deceive you. The one in the Boboli Gardens is a Renaissance copy of this one, which is Roman, the second century A.D.'

Oh, Lord . . . Well, he had done his best. The captain had no business leaving him in this predicament and if they had to sit in silence listening to the crickets for an hour, he wasn't going to make a fool of himself again.

'You must know the Boboli Gardens well, Marshal, to spot that so quickly.'

'Well enough, yes. My station is in the left wing of the Pitti Palace. The Quarter under my care, the Left Bank, roughly speaking, includes this hill.'

'Then I'm under your care, too. I'm pleased to hear it. And are we a well-behaved little flock in this Quarter? I so seldom go down to the city these days that I'm quite out of touch. Do you have much serious crime to deal with? Florence always looks such a sleepy place from this distance.'

That was true. No traffic noise or fumes reached here. Alleys cluttered with mopeds, peeling shutters, prostitutes on the beat in the park, streets fouled with dog muck, bits of pizza in greasy paper, Coca-Cola cans, and hypodermics were all invisible, seething under cover of a serene pattern of red and ochre interrupted by domes and spires and blurred by a blanket of mist and pollution.

'Serious crime? It happens, but most of my time is taken up by . . .' He realised that Sir Christopher was trying to put him at his ease and if he was surprised to find the usual roles reversed he was also grateful. 'My biggest enemy, to tell you the truth, is the heat, and what with being a bit overweight—' Should he not have said that? After all, the other man was—

'And no doubt, as we all do, you intend to lose weight, sometime soon.' Sir Christopher smiled. ' "The triumph of hope over experience".'

A tiny plop interrupted their talk and circles widened on the surface of the pool in front of them.

'The frogs are waking up for their evening meal. I've loved that fountain since I was a tiny child when I wasn't allowed near it without a nurse. I had one nurse who told me that elves and fairies were born from the buds of water lilies and that if I was lucky enough to see one open I should see one of the little creatures sit up yawning and fly away. I never realised that it was one of many ploys for preventing me from running about. I'd had rheumatic fever, you see. It damages the heart valves. Still, her story kept me quiet for hours, and I find water lilies magical to this day. It's a pity to have the fountain trickling so slowly but they need the still water at the edges.'

'And aren't you bothered with mosquitoes?'

'Oh, no. There are the frogs, as you see, to eat them, and those little fish eat the larvae. This was my mother's garden. As you know, all great gardens have at least one secret garden. There are two here but this one was her particular favourite. The architectural elements and the statuary are original but she chose the flowers.'

In the marshal's opinion she hadn't made much of a choice. Wonderful perfumes reached him, but he liked plenty of colour in a garden himself, and here such flowers as still survived the July heat were white or so pale as made no difference. He could smell lavender, but even the lavender bushes, when he spotted them, were white. Very odd, that. 'Very nice,' he murmured politely. 'She must have liked white . . .'

'Ah, yes, the lack of colour seems odd to you, I imagine. You're a man who notices things, aren't you? I would like to show you this garden as it should be seen. She called it her Night Garden. It only starts to come into its own at dusk. My mother gave dinner parties—this would be in the fifties—on the terrace up there. There's an almost concealed "doorway" at the centre back, do you see? That's where the guests arrived, either directly from the main driveway through a wisteria arch or along a path, covered with climbing roses, from my mother's small drawing room. You came by a shortcut, I know, from the kitchen garden. There's another "doorway" at the back farther to the left which you can't see and which leads to the kitchens. The table was in a horseshoe arrangement and everyone sat behind it, for the view, you see. The moon rose over there to light the scene, and those cypresses at each side of the balustrade framed the view of Florence by night. Now you will understand her choice of flowers.'

'They show up in the dark?'

'Yes, but there are also flowers which give out perfume at dusk and at night.'

'She must have had a wonderful imagination, your mother.'

'She was a wonderful woman. Her name was Rose and she was, without question, the most beautiful woman I have ever seen. You think I say so because she was my mother but when you go into the house, look at her portrait in the long drawing room. There's a portrait of my father, too, of course . . . I suppose—I've been thinking about this almost daily of late—that we are all destined to disappoint one or the other of our parents.' He fell silent and his pale face, which had become animated as he described the garden, faded into lifelessness again.

The marshal, remembering the tears of joy in his parents' eyes when they first saw him in uniform, didn't feel he should speak. He waited, listening to the crickets, the plip-plopping of the frogs, the trickle of water. He stared over at the water lilies as if waiting for one to open, trying to imagine a childhood in this place. The only things their childhoods had in common were the burning sun and the scent of oranges and lemons.

'Are your parents alive, Marshal?'

'No, no. My mother died about six years ago and my father long before.'

Sir Christopher sighed, shaking his head. 'We don't understand until it's too late, do we? How we should talk to each other, ask forgiveness, try to understand each other, put everything in order before it's too late. It would be simple enough but we don't realise the necessity. My own father quarrelled with his parents and would never allow them to be mentioned. I remember on my first visit to England with him I tried to ask him about his home, his childhood. His only answer was, "My life began when I met your mother." Had he, in some way, let them down

just as I . . . I could never have been what my father wanted—
the English school, the sports, the riding to hounds . . .'

'Well, no. From what you've said of your ill health . . .'

'If you knew how I thanked God for my ill health that
saved me from being sent away from this dear place to some
dreadful boys' school and spared that unfortunate grey pony
from my unwilling attentions. I used to be sent down to the
paddock beyond the olive groves over there with titbits to
give him. I was very careful not to be seen tossing the stuff
over the wall so as not to go near him. Then I'd settle under
an olive tree with the book from my pocket and read for an
hour or so while the pony gobbled the bits of apple and car-
rot and then returned to his peaceful grazing. I wonder what
happened to him in the end? Sold, I suppose. Why did my
father want me to be so *English?* My dear mother did what
she could to protect me without ever contradicting him. At
least until she gave up and withdrew so deeply into herself
that no one, not even I, could reach her.'

Sir Christopher rested his head on the high back of his
wicker chair. His eyes were closed. 'Marshal, I really must
thank you.'

What could he possibly mean?

'I must thank you because, for some reason, I find myself
able to talk about this garden to you and some of the memories it evokes. Until today I have always avoided coming in
here. My mother turned against it and then . . . Nothing
romantic, I'm afraid. My mother died in a clinic. Of cancer.
Just in case you imagined something dramatic happening
here.'

'No,' said the marshal truthfully. He never imagined things.

'You were probably told that I'm ill and that I'm too proud to admit to it.'

'Something like that.'

'You are a man who notices things. I'm inclined to think you are also a man who understands things . . . people. At any rate, that's the impression you give me, the effect you have on me. What can I say? I know I won't live long and, unlike a drowning man, I am seeing my whole life pass very slowly before me. Every day my lawyer visits me and every day I find myself unable to make a final draft of my will. A will is a documention not just of a man's property but of a man's life. I suppose you're married, children and so on?'

'Yes. Yes, I am.'

'So the script is in many ways written for you. I must invent my own. I have no heirs. I have, thank God, some fixed points in my life, true lifelong friends. My lawyer is one of them. Dear Renato, too, whose taste for fine paintings and statuary has always guided my own—more so than my father's, I think. And, of course, Jeremy Porteous, whom you've met. He has been with me since he was nineteen and he never leaves my side.'

'You're lucky, then,' lied the marshal, who wouldn't fancy an arrangement like that at all. As for employing a nineteen-year-old as a secretary . . . well, the man's private life was his own business.

'Yes, yes, I am lucky. If my art had been appreciated as it deserved I would have little to regret and, of course, that happens to so many artists. Galleries these days are nothing but cheap commercial ventures, run by people with no cultural background, no aesthetic sense. My work, on the other hand, has been admired by some of the most important people in the civilised world for whom this house has been a meeting point. But—well, I mustn't burden you. I want to thank you, as I said. I got up the courage this very day to come into my mother's garden. An attempt to reconcile all the suppressed elements of my past. It's as if I knew that the coincidence of that minor theft would provide me with someone to whom I could talk about the garden and about its beauties instead of thinking only of sad memories. I must think over my life, I must examine every corner, dark as well as light. Reconcile everything, accept everything.'

'I understand. It's often easier with a stranger.'

'With the right stranger.'

The marshal muttered some incomprehensible politeness and then, as the other still kept his eyes closed, started reading the list of stolen goods to give him time to recover. Silver hairbrushes and combs, silver stud box, cuff links and tie pins. The marshal paused and looked around him. What could it feel like to own all this? The knickknacks on the list had approximate values beside them. His entire overdraft didn't equal the price of a pair of silver hairbrushes with JW engraved on their backs. The marshal had no romantic notions about money not buying happiness. It bought a great deal of comfort and security and for him it would have bought the presence of his wife and growing babies in those years of his mother's long agony after the stroke. Those years couldn't be retrieved. Teresa, stuck down in Syracuse helping to care for his mother, had lived without the comfort of her husband, bringing up the boys single-handedly. You need money in this life. But not too much of it or it starts up a whole new set of problems—fear of kidnapping, fear of a stock exchange crash, virulent family quarrels, distrust of

everyone around you. Sickness and death got you, anyway
. . . Was the man asleep? He was facing death and his best
friend was his lawyer . . . He was asleep. The marshal got to
his feet in relief at the sound of the captain's brisk footsteps
on some distant path. It wasn't quite as hot as it had been but
his ineptness at talking to Sir Christopher had made him nervous and he removed his dark glasses to put a handkerchief
to his forehead. At once the low sun attacked his eyes and he
hurriedly dried them before putting his glasses back on.

Sir Christopher was awake and getting up.

'I haven't in some way upset you, have I? I do beg your pardon.' He looked more puzzled than concerned.

'No, no. It's an allergy I have. Sunlight makes my eyes
water. That will be Captain Maestrangelo coming along now.
You must excuse me. No, please. There's no need . . .'

Sir Christopher walked a few steps with him as far as the
lily pond. It was typical of the marshal's clumsiness that in
turning to shake hands there he almost tripped on a tilted
slab of marble whose lower edges were obscured by a mat of
little white flowers.

'I'm sorry . . . I do apologise.' He'd stood on what looked
like a small marble gravestone near the base of the fountain.
This place was a minefield of embarrassments.

'Not your fault at all. Those charming flowers do obscure
the path, I'm afraid. "*Medio de fonte leporum*" . . . such true
words.'

'In the middle of the fountain . . . yes,' hazarded the marshal, recognising a couple of Italian words in the inscription.
The rest was Greek to him.

'Ah yes, I've always heard they teach Latin better in Italian schools than English ones. You obviously weren't as bad

a student as I was. I never went to school—my illness and so on—but my tutor was an Englishman and, I'm afraid, rather unimaginative. I'm sure I failed every Latin test he ever gave me. "Hamilcar Hannibalis pater, dux Carthaginiensis . . ." Why do they think all little boys are interested in war? Of course, you're a military man yourself. I beg your pardon.'

The marshal was still staring down.

'Was it a cat that died?' Bit small for a dog and too big for a canary.

'No, my dear Marshal, there is nothing buried there. Ah, Jeremy, have you shown the captain everything?'

'Yes, and he has already spoken to Giorgio.'

'I wanted to set your mind at rest on that score, if possible.'

'And is it possible?'

'As far as I can tell at this stage, yes. I understand you pay him more than adequately and he wants for nothing. He seems much attached to you and well aware that he would have everything to lose and nothing to gain by risking your displeasure for the sake of a few pieces of silver which he would necessarily be forced to sell quickly and badly. I believe him.'

Sir Christopher, who had hung on to every word of this speech as though his life depended on it, breathed deeply and held out his hand.

'I thank you, Captain, I thank you from my heart. And this good man, too. Will I see you again?' This was addressed to the marshal and the look which went with it was almost pleading.

It was Maestrangelo who reassured him. 'The marshal will be present during the fingerprinting and will bring your copy of the report for signature. He will talk to the rest of the staff.'

'And to me, too, I hope. I have enjoyed our talk today very much.'

It seemed as if he meant it and yet he turned and walked away from them to sink back into the wicker chair as though he had on the instant forgotten their existence.

He won't live long, the marshal thought, recognising that tired detachment. He's ready to go and can't write his script, as he calls it, can't find the exit.

They drove down the winding Viale dei Colli. The trees were lit from below, pink and gold like theatre spotlights. The captain said, 'A wonderful sunset . . .'

The marshal said, 'You were satisfied with the boy's story, then? Or did you just want to keep Sir Christopher calm?'

'I'm not altogether satisfied—oh, as to the boy, Giorgio, as they call him, his real name's Gjergj Lisi, an illegal immigrant—Albanian from Kosovo—but they legalised his status. He was a medical student. He's quiet, intelligent, and desperately grateful to be here. Besides, the robbery's for you to deal with—no, I'm not satisfied because what brought me up here was the idea of being in the house of a man who owns, actually owns, a Leonardo drawing.'

'He does? And did you see it?'

'No, I didn't, or anything else from the collection other than one or two portraits, this century and not interesting. I was shown the master bedroom and the interviews took place in the kitchen offices. Still, I was in the house where the drawing is and, besides, the villa and its garden are among the most famous in Florence. It features in a book my bank gave me last Christmas. There are five or six colour plates in it of L'Uliveto, and since it's not open to the public

I thought I'd take the opportunity. I hope I wasn't in your way but it's a trivial business, anyway.'

'Hmph.'

'You think there's more to it than meets the eye?' The captain looked hard at him. He always maintained that the quieter the marshal was, the more it was worth paying attention to him. The marshal couldn't see it. If he was quiet it was because he had nothing to say. To be quizzed only embarrassed him and sent him deeper into his silence. All he said now was 'No, no . . .' The captain was a good man, a serious man, an educated man. It wasn't right that he should expect as much from an NCO like the marshal as he did. 'No, no.'

And so, as they came down to the city, their talk turned to other matters—Dori's statement, Ilir Pictri's cousin Lek and his 'building firm', a lucrative line of business, based in a flat in Via dei Serragli, which the captain was investigating, the condition of the pregnant girl with multiple fractures.

'The case will come up in September.'

'You got them all then? But surely the girl is in no condition to testify? I heard she was still in hospital. Lorenzini mentioned it the other day.'

'Yes, but there was another girl involved. They threatened her, too, but presumably the intention was just to frighten her. They did that all right. She called the free phone number for help. The two girls made the journey here together, apparently, both seventeen.'

It was easy enough to say, as people generally did, so as to ward off any passing discomfort the fate of these Albanian girls might possibly provoke, that they knew exactly what they

were being shipped over here for and what dangers they
faced. After all, in Albania everybody watched Italian television. They saw the news. The trouble with this comfortable
idea was that people, especially inexperienced youngsters,
think themselves capable of anything to escape dead-end
poverty. They also think that they can make a bit of money
and then get out into a better life. They are wrong on
both counts. The pimps make the big money and the girls
don't get out. They are on a road with no turnoffs. Also, a
seventeen-year-old girl knows neither what she is capable of
nor what excesses might be demanded of her. Another girl,
in hospital with severe bruising and multiple fractures, had
been sick all over her very first client and his very new car.
As a punishment she was forced to perform the service
requested by the client for her pimp and two of his associ-
ates and beaten when she was sick on them, too.

'Let's hope, at least, that what happened to the pregnant
girl will be the saving of her friend.'

'You're very sanguine,' the captain said. 'I'll be content if
she turns up to testify.'

'She's in a safe place?'

'Oh, yes. In a convent.'

They were in Via Maggio and the marshal remembered.
'Drop me here, would you? I want to cut through Sdrucciolo de' Pitti. I've a call to make there.'

There are some things we can't explain to ourselves,
though if we knew how to read the signs they are surely there.
Standing in the exhaust laden heat with the evening traffic
of Via Maggio roaring at his back, the marshal looked up
the ginnel to a sliver of the Pitti Palace, its pale stones
rosy in the sunset. His stomach tightened and a thought

flashed through his mind. 'I'll need to call the fire brigade.' The thought vanished. He didn't react to it, much less act on it. He had to force himself to start walking up there. Torn between the urge to hurry and his reluctance to move at all, he walked at a perfectly steady pace, his face expressionless behind dark glasses. He felt as though he were walking in a cloud of cotton wool which prevented him from registering noise or movement. Yet there was noise and movement, he knew that. A child directing a tricycle towards him on the slope, mouth agape with excitement, a mother, hand held high, behind. A boy poised on a moped that wouldn't start, a blue cloud almost hiding him. Another thought flash: 'There's no use blaming myself.' He didn't know the numbering but the group that had collected outside an antique shop on the left drew him toward it. Only when one of the women there looked round and then touched the man next to her and pointed at him did the cotton-wool cloud dissolve. The moped roared away, the mother cried out, and the marshal stopped the tricycle as it came straight at him.

'Oh, thank you, Marshal! Thank you so—you little monkey! Just wait till I get you home!'

When he reached number 4, the woman who had pointed said, 'We called 112. We were expecting a car.'

'You did right. They'll be here.'

'Marshal Guarnaccia, don't you remember me? Linda Rossi.'

'Yes. Yes, I remember.' He didn't remember her but he understood. 'So, you live above Signora Hirsch, is that right?'

'On the top floor. I hope I did right but I was worried. You see, she—'

'Come in with me.'

It was a small but well-kept staircase. Dark. The marshal removed his sunglasses so that at least he could make out the yellow glow of a lightbulb in a small lantern if nothing much else. The second-floor door was fluted and had shiny brass fittings. The stink of decomposition was overpowering and the woman beside the marshal retched.

'I'm sorry, I can't—'

'Go up to your flat.'

She scurried upstairs, heaving.

The marshal peered at the door. There wasn't so much as a scratch on it, as far as he could see; entry would have to be made through a window so as to open up from inside, they would need a ladder crew. The rest was for Forensics to check. A snake of foul-smelling liquid was oozing from beneath it. He called the fire brigade.

Four

She lay on her back, head near the door, one foot pointing down the short tiled corridor, the other twisted beneath her torso. Her left arm was stretched outwards, her right hand clutched to her breast. Her chin was tipped up as though she were trying to see who was coming in the door behind her but the face wore a dark and iridescent mask that flickered in quiet concentration. There were tinier movements in the stickiness under the eyelids where already new life fed on her spent one. The flies rose from her, buzzing angrily as the marshal pushed the door with a gloved hand as far as it would go and stepped inside. Before they settled again he saw the bluish mouth twisted in a grimace and the throat wound alive with maggots.

The marshal stepped over her extended arm, avoiding the coagulated blood that had flowed as far as the skirting board and collected there and the thin stream of viscous liquid oozing towards the landing. The patch of blood was very large. A carving knife lay on the floor near the open kitchen door.

In the few moments of peace given him between the fireman's opening of the door and the arrival of squad cars, the prosecutor, photographer, forensics, the marshal superimposed other images on the one before him: Signora Hirsch coming in as he had done, looking down. '*A knife. Not a bread knife but it was a kitchen knife.*' Signora Hirsch sitting opposite him in his office, the fear that flooded through her body when he'd asked about a smell. Had she smelled it again as she opened her door for the last time? The only smell now was coming from her dead body.

He held a clean folded handkerchief over his mouth, remembering her pleading look as she told him she had been depressed but that she wasn't mad. He had known mad people in his time. The year when the asylums were officially closed down, people institutionalised for decades were thrown on the mercy of their families or of the world at large. He knew well enough that there were people capable of slitting their own throats, setting up a scenario like this to prove their own stories. They needed help and pity wouldn't help them. The marshal was under no illusions. He did wish he had visited her earlier in the week but only because it might have offered her a few moments of human comfort, not because it would have made any impression on whatever process was working towards its conclusion in her life.

'Evening, Marshal. Could you . . . ?' He stepped out of view as the photographer started taking his long shots from the doorway. The kitchen wasn't very big. A bit old-fashioned, very clean. The knives, excepting one, stood in a wooden block near the draining board. The sitting room had an old-fashioned air, too. Of course, she wasn't young, but still . . . The reason became clear soon enough. There were two bedrooms and she slept in the smaller one, book and tissues on the bedside table. The master bedroom was unused. A gold satin bedspread covering an otherwise unmade-up bed. Her parents' house, then. She'd mentioned her mother, her

SOME BITTER TASTE • 51

mother's death. Depression. *'I'm not paranoid.'* Might be worth finding out the circumstances of the mother's death.

'You finished? Turn her over then, will you?' A lot of clattering. 'Bag the knife.' 'No journalists yet! I said no . . .'

The precious moments of peace were over. The echoes of Signora Hirsch's voice faded. The atmosphere, suspended since the moment when the murderer shut the door behind him, evaporated. The house became a crime scene and the woman a corpse. Flash—a corpse showing position relative to door. Flash—close-up, corpse only. Flash—throat wound and surrounding bloodstain. Flash—close-up, wound only. Flash—decomposition signs—body orifices, mucous membranes. 'Rectal temperature . . .' The doctor's voice. 'Got to be at least forty-eight hours, probably more, but in this heat . . .'

The prosecutor appeared on the landing. He looked about fifty. He wasn't tall but there was something stylish about him. The marshal, running an eye over the striped short-sleeved shirt, pale linen trousers, and glossy shoes, put it down to money and to the jacket swinging on his shoulders, the fine leather briefcase, much battered, and the tiny unlit cigar in the corner of his mouth. He had never seen this man before, which made him apprehensive. He watched him as he spoke to the doctor. Then their eyes met.

'Ah, Marshal—Guarnaccia, isn't it? How did you happen to be here?' Oddly enough, the one reassuring thing about him was the little cigar. Reminded him of Prosecutor Fusarri, a strange and anarchic character but a familiar one.

The marshal, with his tendency to think he could only be in the way during any important investigation, gave a brief explanation and made to retreat back to his little office, stolen mopeds, and missing cats.

'Excellent. No reason why you shouldn't handle this—and, of course, it's your patch so no doubt you know her neighbours, valuable witnesses, and so on. Carry on, Marshal.'

The marshal sighed as he started up the stairs to the top-floor flat. He had no objection to carrying on but he had a feeling that there was more to this faith in his competence than a three-second encounter could warrant. The emergency call had gone to Borgo Ognissanti and he saw Captain Maestrangelo's hand in this somewhere. That remark about knowing the neighbours gave him away. He wasn't wrong. Neighbours it was, then . . .

'I suppose I shouldn't be surprised. You deal with so many people. We'll never forget your help, though.'

'How long have you been living here?'

'Just over two years. My husband's doing very well. You remember, he's an architect—no, of course, why should you—'

'I do remember now. He was a still a student back then.' He remembered the tiny flat where most of the space was taken up by the husband's drawing table. 'Do you own this flat?'

'Yes—or at least we will when we finish paying for it.'

'I'm glad to hear it.' He remembered now that there had been some trouble about an eviction, which in turn reminded him of Signora Hirsch's anonymous postcard. 'Do you happen to know if Signora Hirsch owned her flat?'

'I don't, I'm afraid. She was very pleasant and kind but a bit . . .'

'Reserved?'

'That's it, yes. Reserved. Not the sort to stop and gossip on the stairs. Lisa—my little girl—said she talked a lot to her, but perhaps she was more at ease with a child.'

'Ah, yes. I remember Signora Hirsch mentioning that you work, and that your little girl sometimes spent a bit of time with her.'

'Lisa's twelve but we don't like her to be alone in the house. Signora Hirsch always treated it as a social visit. She didn't want to be paid. She said once that since losing her mother she missed having someone to look after. Marshal, tell me the truth. She is dead, isn't she?'

'Yes, she's dead.'

'I knew it. I told Signor Rinaldi but he wouldn't listen to me—typical of that kind of man if a woman tries to tell them anything—said I was exaggerating, though the smell was strong enough on his landing—he has the shop on the ground floor and lives on the first. As if a respectable, refined person like Signora Hirsch would go away leaving her rubbish bag behind the door—that was his story—but he had a snooty attitude towards her. I think they had a bit of a row. Rubbish bag, indeed! Oh, I know people do but never in this world would she—in any case, she wasn't going away. She would have told me. I count on her for Friday afternoons, you see, for Lisa. I do freelance editorial work for a publisher so I work at home but I do occasionally have to go in, like this afternoon, so I went and rang her bell and saw—oh . . .' She covered her mouth and nose with her hand as though the smell still clung there. 'She was in some sort of trouble, you know. I told her to go and see you but I don't know whether she did.'

'Yes, she did, but I can't say I understood what was going on. When did you last see her?'

'Last Sunday.'

'You're quite sure about that?'

'Positive. We'd driven out to the country for lunch at the house of some friends of ours. They're doing a cottage up. It's nowhere near ready but they work on it on Sundays. My husband's helping them a bit so we sometimes join them for Sunday picnic lunch. We didn't come home until going on for seven and we overtook Signora Hirsch on the stairs.'

'Did she mention where she'd been?'

'Yes, to her brother's. She sometimes visited him for an hour or so in the afternoon, more often lately, I think.'

'Did she ever mention his name?'

'Not that I recall, no.'

'Did he ever come here?'

'I couldn't say. I never saw him. But what I wanted to tell you was that we'd no sooner got in and shut our door than the phone rang. It was Signora Hirsch in an absolute panic, saying there'd been somebody in her flat. It wasn't the first time. My husband went down and when he didn't come back right away I followed him. She was in a terrible state. I asked her if there was something she could take to calm her down. I've always noticed that she takes the stairs very slowly and wondered if there wasn't something . . . Anyway she took some medicine but she wouldn't go to bed, saying she preferred to be on the living room sofa with the television for company. I advised her to go and see you as soon as possible and she promised she would. I never saw her again.'

'And you haven't seen anyone, any stranger, on the staircase recently?'

'No, never. The flat just below us is empty at the moment and there's very little movement in this building other than Signor Rinaldi's furniture being shifted between the shop and his first-floor flat, where he sometimes stores things because he's so short of space. I've certainly never noticed any strangers on the stairs or hanging about on the second-floor landing.'

The marshal looked at his watch. 'I suppose I'll find this Rinaldi in his shop at this hour.'

'No, not today. When I saw him and we were talking about calling the carabinieri, he was on his way out. He works alone, you see, so when he goes out buying or visiting the antique fairs he has to close the shop except very occasionally when he finds someone to look after the place for him. There's no one there today.'

'I'll have to come back, then. Now, what about when Signora Hirsch's mother was alive? Did they have visitors then?"

'Oh, that was well before we moved in. We've only been here a couple of years and I gather that this flat, like the one below, was on short lets before, usually to foreigners, people here for the academic year, that sort of thing. I know that because it was Signora Hirsch herself who said she was glad we'd taken the flat and that now she'd have permanent neighbours, a bit of company. What—I suppose I shouldn't ask you but—I mean was I right about something being wrong with her? Was it her heart?'

'I can't tell you much. There'll be an autopsy, but it will be in the papers so you'd better know now: It looks as though she was attacked.'

'Attacked? You mean somebody really did get in? Was she murdered?'

'We don't know yet exactly what happened.'

'But is it safe? I mean for Lisa? I'm sorry . . . it's the shock, it's only just sinking in.' Her hands were shaking and she tried to cover her nervousness by affecting to tidy the sitting room, which was already tidy. 'Perhaps you want to sit down . . . I have to sit down. Feel a bit odd. Sorry.'

She sank into an armchair and the marshal stood beside her, holding her shoulder steady with a large warm hand. 'Will your husband be home soon?'

'He never gets back before nine.'

'Call him and tell him to come home. The little girl is in?'

'She's in her bedroom doing her homework.'

'Well, you get on with whatever you would normally be doing.'

'I should be getting supper on.'

'Then do that. You have nothing to fear. The second-floor flat is full of people and I shall certainly be there until your husband gets home and will come up later to see that you're all right.'

'Thank you.'

As she let him out, a voice on the stairs below was calling, 'Marshal? Is that you, Marshal? There's something you'd better have a look at!'

He hurried down, hat in hand. The men in Hirsch's flat were grouped round an open cupboard set in the left wall of the entrance. There was a coat rail in there but most of the outdoor coats which had hung there had fallen from their hangers. Whatever had taken up most of the space behind had been torn from the wall and the resulting mess of dust and plaster swept onto the piles of coats. A red-handled sweeping brush had been thrown in and had fallen out when the cupboard was opened.

'Makes the scenario pretty clear,' remarked the prosecutor, pointing at the gaping hole with his little cigar 'By the look of it I'd say there was a safe there. They no doubt threatened her in the hope of learning the combination but she didn't give it up.' He glanced around him. 'Wouldn't have thought she possessed anything worth her life. Of course, you know more about the victim, Marshal.'

'Not a lot . . .'

'They're still fingerprinting. Come out on the stairs. They've finished out there.' When they were out he lowered his voice. 'I wish I could light up. Would be an improvement on the smell at least. Right, tell me all.'

The marshal told all, including the kitchen knife story, the postcard, and the smell of cigars. The prosecutor removed his, looked at it with a brief smile, and popped it back in his mouth. 'Never mentioned a safe?'

'No, but the top-floor neighbours might be able to help there. It won't take a minute.'

'I'll accompany you.'

'I don't think . . . it's a child, you see—might be a bit over-awed by someone of your importance.' If the prosecutor had doubts about what he really meant, the marshal felt sure that he would choose to think himself important rather than imagine he might not be too good with children. The prosecutor let him climb the stairs alone. Signora Rossi must have recovered her equilibrium because there was a good smell coming from the kitchen.

Lisa Rossi, looking up from her exercise books, looked and acted nearer fifteen than twelve but the marshal assumed that meant he was getting old. Her figure was light and pretty and only a thickly concealed rash of teenage spots indicated her immaturity. Pop stars stared sullenly from posters all over the walls of the tiny room. Soft toys sat in line on the single bed.

'She's a bit weird but I like her.'

'In what way was she weird? Your mother has told you that she's dead?'

'She did but I forgot for a minute—I mean I liked her . . . do I have to do that?'

'Do what?'

'Talk about her like she doesn't exist anymore. It doesn't feel like she doesn't exist anymore. I've never known anybody who died before.'

'It's all right. You don't have to if you don't want. As long as you remember her she does still exist in a way.'

'My mum said robbers attacked her. She's really upset.'

'And what about you? Does it upset you?'

'No. It just feels . . . weird.'

'Weird like Signora Hirsch? Tell me why you think she was weird.'

'Oh, I don't know . . . like she was really old—like my gran. She never talks about now, always about things that happened years ago and people I've never heard of. I don't mind, only she's not that old, is she—I mean was she? She doesn't look it, doesn't wear old lady's clothes and stuff.'

He'd had the same thought himself, hadn't he? So perhaps it wasn't just a question of her mother's furnishings. 'Lisa, can I sit on the end of your bed a minute?' There was no room for more than her desk and chair and he didn't want to loom over her.

'All right.'

'I've got something important to ask you. There's a built-in cupboard in the entrance hall in Signora Hirsch's flat and I need to know if you ever saw inside it.'

The girl hesitated, twining a strand of long fair hair round her finger. 'Does a secret still count when somebody's dead?'

'It depends.'

'So how do I know whether I can tell you?'

'Don't worry. You can tell me because if it's the sort of secret that should be kept forever I'll tell you and neither of us will ever tell anyone else. Telling me doesn't count because of my job.' She seemed like a twelve-year-old now, a little girl venturing into adulthood and then retreating.

'There was a safe. She didn't say so but I saw. She got some things out and showed them to me.'

'What sort of things? Did they look valuable? Were they jewels, things like that?'

Lisa shrugged. 'Old things. Candlesticks and some old books and clothes, stuff like that. Maybe they were her grandma's. She never knew her grandma and grandpa but she talked about them all the time like old people do.'

'And what about her brother? Did she talk about him?'

'No. Only her grandparents and sometimes her mum and dad. There was a picture of her mum and dad in the safe and another picture of flowers. That was her secret, she said, having those pictures. Don't you think that's weird?'

'It depends. Were the pictures paintings? Perhaps they were valuable.'

'These were just old black-and-white photographs. So is it a real secret, or not?'

The marshal considered. He was never dishonest with children if he could help it.

'I'm not quite sure. I promise you that when I find out I'll tell you. In the meantime you keep the secret.'

'Even from my mum and dad?'

'Even from them. You have done up to now, haven't you?'

'Yes . . .'

'You needn't tell a lie. If they ask about it you can tell them I said to ask me. You've been a big help, Lisa, and I'm very grateful to you.'

He could see she was pleased and felt he could rely on her. On his way downstairs he heard the noise of journalists and press.

'Is it true that her throat was slashed?'

'Must have been in there for days judging by the stink.'

'In this heat . . .'

'Just one from outside the door showing the hall?'

'Was the house ransacked?'

'Just one of that cupboard—was there a safe?—'

'Gentlemen, please.' This prosecutor was quiet-spoken, very calm and very much in control. 'We're trying to remove a body here. If you'll let me complete my business in peace I'll give you a statement. Downstairs. Ah, Marshal. Have those carabinieri clear the staircase and the exit, will you? And don't let the TV cameras up. They can film the body being loaded and that's it.'

The story of the safe would get into the papers and no journalist would be so lacking in imagination as to invent contents for it as dull as old clothes and a few photographs.

Within twenty minutes or so the prosecutor emerged into the street and gave them a provisional date and time of death as established by the marshal, who had visited the building next door. Its second-floor occupants had been infuriated by the battering on the wall during the removal of the safe: 'Apart from anything else, we were giving a dinner party that night—and since when do builders work till that hour? What was worse was that we thought they were going to knock right through. It happens with these old houses. Half past eight, anyway, give or take a few minutes. Is it true they slit her throat? I always said there was something funny . . . of course, she was a foreigner, wasn't she? She had no accent but her name . . .'

The pathologist joined the prosecutor and, unwisely in the marshal's opinion, gave the press a statement which, while not giving a cause of death as such, admitted to the throat wound and considerable loss of blood, which had them all scribbling 'Murdered woman's throat slashed!'

Then the questions: Did the safe contain stolen jewellery she had never dared wear? Was it true she paid regular visits to a mysterious stranger who never returned her visits? Could it be the man was in prison, which would explain why she wouldn't have wanted to tell anybody? They received no answers. They would quote their own questions and any more exotic ones they could think of to pad their articles for the next day's paper, ending with the usual 'Investigators are releasing no further information at present.'

'Oh, well,' thought the marshal, in a philosophical mood as he climbed the slope towards his station in the left wing of the Pitti Palace, 'only doing their job, I suppose.' As he walked under the stone arch with its great lantern, which was now lit, he hoped his wife was also in a philosophical mood. He was late again, very late, and he hadn't phoned.

//

'The war on football hooligans: forty-five Fiorentina fans to be excluded from the stadium for the rest of the year—

'The mayor on line: Work is to begin in the Clemente VII room in the Palazzo Vecchio, where the mayor will be in contact with citizens on their personal computers once a month from next October—

'A woman bled to death in her own home after thieves slit her throat. The death is thought to have taken place four days ago—

'Good evening. Those are the main headlines of our third edition of the *Regional News*. Now from the stadium here's—'

'Salva! Hurry up, your case is coming on!'

The marshal appeared after a moment, muffled in a white bathrobe, and stood near the sofa rubbing at his head with a big towel. Supper had already been spoiling when he got in so he'd had to wait for his shower.

'Aren't you going to sit down and watch it?'

'There'll be nothing much to see.'

'Look! You see, now we've got a PC we'll be able to contact the mayor.'

'We haven't got a PC, the boys have, and unless the mayor wants to play computer games with them I don't think he'll be hearing from them.'

'Is that her they're putting in the ambulance?'

'Yes.'

'I've read about these thieves who gas old people and rob them, but slitting her throat . . . Why do they keep saying 'they' anyway? How do they know it wasn't just one person?'

'A safe that size would be too heavy for one man to—'

'There you are! Isn't that you next to the ambulance? No, it's not.'

'Let's go to bed.'

The first forty-eight hours following a murder are crucial. After that, witnesses are already jumbling times and dates, alibis have been set up, and borders crossed. Stories which might conflict are adjusted, phone calls are made, stained clothing destroyed. And anyone who in those first two days of limelight might want to take centre stage giving vital information shouldn't be given time for second thoughts about getting involved. So, surely to God, the captain wouldn't expect him to go trailing up to the Villa L'Uliveto to waste time over a few trinkets?

'I've got the prosecutor on the other line now. Hold on,' Captain Maestrangelo said.

The marshal held. Of course, he didn't have a suspect, not even a shadow of one, but he wanted to go through her papers this morning and find both her brother and her lawyer without delay. He realised that he had as yet told no one about the bag-snatching episode, which would suggest that a stranger might have had her keys, rather than that she had opened the door to her killer.

'Marshal?'

'Yes. There's something I should have mentioned—when the victim came to me, she reported having had her bag—'

'It's your case. Tell the prosecutor. He'll be at the Hirsch flat in fifteen minutes and wants you to check on the two shops below before you join him—but I'd like you to postpone your visit to Sir Christopher rather than give it up. I'll make your excuses myself and get the fingerprinting done this morning. I'd send somebody else but he'd take it very badly, you know, and I wouldn't like there to be any repercussions . . . Guarnaccia?'

'Yes. Yes, I'll do as you say, of course.'

'Is there a problem?'

'No . . . I think. If we move fast on this Hirsch case, we can get to the bottom of it. She led such a confined life that—' He was amazed at himself. He was no detective. What was he thinking of to claim he could solve a case he knew nothing about yet? The captain would wonder what had come over him. It was embarrassment which made him so far forget himself as to say whatever came into his head so long as it changed the subject. 'You haven't told me . . . this business of Sir Christopher. Are we just obliged to put up a good show for an important foreign resident? I'm sorry, I was just wondering, because in that case I only need to make a courtesy visit, as brief as possible. You see what I mean. To tell you the truth, since they haven't a hope of recovering the stuff and have warned us off accusing any of the staff, I don't see why they called us at all. These people must think we've nothing better to do.'

'They do think that, if they think about it at all, which I doubt. I'll be frank with you, Guarnaccia. Of course it began as a matter of courtesy and I've told you why I came along. Pay him the courtesy of the visit he's asked for, however brief, if not out of respect for the uniform we wear then out of respect for his sickness and his age. You have always had more patience with age and loneliness than anyone I know.'

'*And this good man, too . . .*'

'Yes. He's not old, though.'

'No, I suppose by today's standards . . . and they say he's ill but he could go on for years with the best care.'

'No.'

'No? He told you more about his illness? Despite being embarrassed about it?'

'No. He didn't tell me much but he wasn't embarrassed about it at all. No, no . . . he's dying and he knows it.'

'He said that?'

'No.' No, no, no! The marshal wanted to be let off. The Hirsch murder, with its background of Sdrucciolo de' Pitti, with the Rossis and the local shopkeepers as witnesses, he could deal with. He might not solve it—not a scrap of evidence had come to light yet—but he knew where he was, he knew what to do. Why couldn't the captain send some smart young officer to the villa, one of those military academy types from a good family who would drink tea with the Englishman and not fall over his own boots in the flower garden.

'And this good man, too. Will I see you again?' That sad, almost pleading look before Sir Christopher turned away.

What did people want, what did they expect of him?

'You'll really come and see me as you promised?' Signora Hirsch's frightened eyes. He wanted to concentrate on her now but it was a bit late, wasn't it? He had forgotten her for days.

'And this good man, too . . .' Sir Christopher would die. That's a road we all have to travel alone. What help could he possibly be?

'Guarnaccia?'

'I'll go as soon as the prosecutor can spare me.'

He got up, put on jacket and holster, lifted his hat from its hook, checked with Lorenzini, and started down the narrow stairs, already feeling for his sunglasses. The sky was almost colourless, the glare enough to have his eyes streaming in seconds. He went down the side of the palace forecourt in the shade offered by a high wall. It didn't help. The heat was all-suffusing, the air was stagnant. Sometimes, when it was like this, car tyres made the wet sound of a rainy day but it didn't rain, except sometimes for a minute or two, a few fat drops that rose as steam on the instant to increase the Turkish bath effect. The marshal walked slowly. He didn't want his shirt sticking to him. He didn't want to get so distressed by the suffocating heat that he would start forgetting things and lose his patience. If you lose your patience in July you're not likely to get it back again until after your evening shower. And to think that people paid good money to suffer not only all this but the stress of an unknown city and a language they couldn't speak.

'You're holding the map upside down!'

'I've told you I'll go in no more shops!'

'Mum, I'm thirsty!'

'A very important collection of paintings and I don't want to hear another word out of either of you until—'

'Did you *have* to let it melt all down your front?'

Without understanding a word, the marshal recognized these complaints as they drifted around him in a dozen languages. He stood waiting to cross the road, muttering as he did every year, 'I don't know what they come here for, they'd do better to stop at home.'

There was a traffic pileup and the marshal gave up waiting and wandered across the narrow road between the cars and the inevitable chorus of horns.

Sdrucciolo de' Pitti was a haven of peace in comparison. It was cluttered with parked mopeds and bikes and it was occasionally necessary to flatten yourself against the wall to let a white Mercedes taxi by, but otherwise you could walk in the middle of the paved alley and you were away from the worst of the noise. Rinaldi, the antique dealer, was at his door, looking down the street as though expecting someone. He turned and spotted the marshal coming down, though.

'Ah. I heard about the Hirsch woman. Come in if you think I can help you. You'll excuse me if I keep an eye on the street? I'm waiting for a delivery. Very good men, the best there are, but with things of great value, you understand . . .'

'Of course. Why don't you see to that. I'll go in and wait, then we'll talk.' Once inside, the marshal almost regretted having suggested this. He liked looking round places unobserved, not to mention observing people from behind. But 'things of great value' was an understatement in this case, as would be 'bull in a china shop'. So he removed his sunglasses and kept very still. Only his huge all-seeing eyes scanned the long, dark room with its deep red polished floor, gilded frames, and weathered statuary. Rinaldi's broad back excluded most of the spent light from the alley. A fancy lamp with a silk shade made a golden pool on a tiny inlaid desk where Rinaldi must habitually sit. There was no clutter, only an elegant desk set and a silver box of visiting cards. The rasping engine of a three-wheel truck at the door announced the expected delivery. Rinaldi came inside. He looked as anxious as a mother cat, and his hands clenched and unclenched as two huge men struggled with a crate that was almost as tall as a human being and clearly a great deal heavier. The men's faces were red with strain and they gasped for breath.

'Down! Put her down! I can't make it . . .' They stood the crate on its end in the centre of the small room and bent double, heaving, clutching their chests. One of them, whose greasy blond hair was tied back in a ponytail, was sweating so much that big drops rolled down his nose and splattered onto the polished floor. The dark head of the other was shaven but it gleamed with wetness even so. 'I thought we'd never get her on that truck. Next time it's got to be three men . . . Jesus . . .'

'There isn't a third man I can trust like you.' Rinaldi seemed barely able to breathe himself. 'You must get her through to the back for the restorers.'

They did it, too, though the marshal feared they might have heart attacks in the attempt. The crate was broken open and he caught a glimpse of sculpted draperies. These disappeared under sheeting and the men reappeared, shutting the rear door behind them.

They left without being paid, an almost invisible signal passing between them and Rinaldi. The marshal was used to this sort of thing. He was investigating a murder and they were trying to hide a cash payment without receipt from him. Half the trouble in any investigation was caused by people hiding things from you that were self-evident and that you didn't care about anyway. The two most common were tax dodges and adultery.

The marshal decided to distract Rinaldi at once.

'If you don't mind my asking, do you always call the crates of stuff you get delivered "she"?'

'What . . . ? Oh, I see.' Distracted and relieved. 'Inside that crate was a statue of the goddess Athena. Very much a 'she'.

And very much damaged by pollution, I'm sorry to say. I imagine you're looking for information about what happened upstairs but I'm afraid I barely knew the woman.'

'Yes, well, I've heard she was very reserved, didn't chat much with her neighbours.'

'Not at all, as far as I'm concerned.'

'You never visited her?'

'Never. "Good morning, good evening" in the street or on the stairs, nothing more.'

'Really? Probably just gossip, I suppose, but somebody mentioned a bit of a disagreement . . .'

'As you say, people gossip.'

'No disagreement then?'

'No.'

The marshal fell silent and stayed that way. He stood there, immovable, solid, staring, taking his time in examining Rinaldi. White hair, wavy, rather long, resting on his sweatshirt collar. Red face, crinkly eyes that gave him a jovial look. Bit of a tummy on him. You could see from his hands as much as anything that he was nearer seventy than sixty but he was wearing blue jeans. A vain man whose vanity wasn't confined to camouflaging his age. He probably enjoyed risky and lucrative deals, executed with panache. Maybe had a couple of such deals on hand right now, but even if one of them concerned the 'she' in the crate, he would laugh at the idea of the marshal's posing any threat to him. He'd be right, too. But then the marshal didn't want to pose any threat. He just wanted to embarrass the man into saying something, anything, about his neighbour so as to put an end to the marshal's discomforting silence. The length of time this took was always in inverse ratio to the victim's intelligence and education. There were men who would hold out through interrogations, trial, appeal, prison, death. Rinaldi didn't make half a minute. A very cultured man.

'Look, I'm sure you know the saying 'no smoke without fire'. In your job you must be used to hearing gossip and interpreting it.'

'Oh, yes, yes.'

'So there was—not a row—but, shall we say, a coolness, arising from the fact that she tried to sell me something and the offer I made she found insulting. I'm sure if you look around you, you'll understand that the sort of thing she had would hardly . . .'

'Oh, yes, yes. Very high-class stuff this, very.'

'Quite. You must have been in her flat. Need I say more? Perfectly understandable, of course. Sentimental value probably and if she was hard up and needed to sell she may well have felt slighted, which would cause her to speak ill of me.'

'I see. I don't think I've heard anybody say she actually spoke ill of you. You did buy the candlesticks though, in the end?'

'I'm sorry?'

'I'm perhaps mistaken. I heard she had these candlesticks and they're not there now so I was assuming . . . still, if you didn't offer enough maybe she sold them to somebody else. Yes, that'll be it. Were you at home the evening she was killed?'

'I understood you didn't know when she was killed, that she'd been dead for some time.'

'Monday evening. It was in this morning's paper.'

'I see. I don't buy a newspaper every day.'

'Not even when your neighbour's been murdered?'

'Not even then. Since I hardly knew her I don't feel involved. Incidentally, I spoke to the public prosecutor on this case this morning. He arrived shortly before you. Turned out we'd met before. Some dinner party or other.'

'Oh dear. Arrived before me, did he? I'd better join him at once. I expect we'll be seeing each other again. Good morning.' And he walked into the grocer's next door.

In the grocer's, the owner, Paolo, left his cheerful son in charge, gave the marshal a chair in the storeroom behind the shop, and rang the bar in Piazza Pitti for a tray of coffees to be delivered. They had a good talk.

'Did you ever hear about a quarrel—or, as he calls it, a coolness—between Rinaldi the antique dealer and Signora Hirsch?'

'A row or a coolness? I wouldn't call it either. She was in tears, I do remember that. She came in here right after, crying.'

Signora Hirsch, one minute all elegance and dignity, the next crumpled in tears.

'I said to her, I said, "Signora, you go on up and my boy'll bring your shopping up. The water's too heavy for you, anyway." She had angina, you know.'

'She did? You know that for sure?'

'I certainly do. My wife's the same. Hasn't worked for years. She has to be careful and that's what I said to Signora Hirsch. I said, "You want to be careful. No need for carrying heavy stuff up those stairs as long as I'm here. And no good getting upset, either," I said, "it's not worth ruining your health for." Am I right?'

'I—yes. What isn't?'

'That business of the facade. Well, the roof too, of course, and I'm not saying that won't have cost a bob or two.'

'And that's what the trouble with Rinaldi was about? He did say she was hard up—she must have owned her flat then, if she had to pay for repairs like that . . . Funny . . . he said she tried to sell him something and he told her it wasn't worth what she expected.'

'Poor thing. Well, she managed somehow. The work's been done, as you see. And she's dead, anyway. As long as you've got your health there's nothing else worth fretting about.' Paolo leaned forward to speak in confidence, his face pink, his smiling eyes very blue. 'This is nothing you don't know, anyway, but my daughter was at that dinner party Monday evening with her husband. You know, at number 6. Now, he's an architect, my son-in-law, and he knows Rossi who lives on the top floor above Signora Hirsch and he was there, too, so when there was all that racket from next door my son-in-law suggested he and Rossi go round there and intervene. We couldn't help thinking after, would they have been in time to save her?'

'I really don't think so. I think it was probably over for her by then if they were removing the safe.'

'Too late to worry about it now, of course, but you can't help thinking . . . Shall I send for more coffee?'

'No, no . . . but thanks very much for the coffee and your help.'

'Anytime. We're always here.'

Trudging up to the second floor, hat in hand, the marshal considered the phenomenon of the Florentine dinner party. It didn't seem to matter which circuit you were on, the same gossip circulated. The grocer who knew the architect who knew the neighbour . . . The journalist who knew the barman who procured boys for the marquis who married the American whose cleaner also worked for a translator who

knew the journalist . . . And the stories got better as they travelled so that the last version was barely recognisable as being
based on the first.

The seals hung loose, the door was open. The marshal
found the prosecutor sitting on the unused double bed with
a pile of documents in front of him. He looked up, smiling,
and spoke quietly.

'Ah, Marshal. Good morning. And what can you tell me
about our friend Rinaldi downstairs?'

'He says he knows you.'

'Yes, he told me that, too. At some dinner party that must
have slipped my mind. Could be true, of course. I have no
memory for that sort of thing. What else?'

'He says he was never in this flat. He also says her stuff is
worth nothing, not up to his standard as we know, having
been in here. He said he barely spoke to the victim but
admitted he'd had a disagreement with her. He said it was
about something she'd tried to sell him.'

'What was the something?'

'Wouldn't say.'

'But the grocer would, I'll bet.'

'He said the argument was about repairs to the building.'

'Condominium row. Classic. Marshal, sit down.'

The marshal lowered himself carefully onto a round-
backed brocaded chair beside the bed. The sort designed to
hold a carelessly thrown negligee rather than one hundred
ninety-eight pounds of carabiniere. In these frequently
occurring circumstances he tended to sit up very straight and
let his feet bear much of his weight.

'I thought you were the best person to talk to those
two,' continued the prosecutor. 'I had two men from Borgo

Ognissanti do a door-to-door check. After all, they had to carry that safe out of here. Nobody noticed a thing, I'm sorry to say.'

'The shops were shut and it was supper time,' the marshal said, recounting the grocer's story, 'which would practically leave only tourists on the streets.'

'I'm afraid you're right. Now, I've heard this woman came to see you. I want to know why.'

'I'm sorry but I don't exactly know why.'

The prosecutor considered him for a moment, then, popping a tiny unlit cigar in the corner of his mouth, said, 'Sorry about this habit. Trying to give up. I hold out as long as I can. It helps. Now . . . your commanding officer thinks very highly of you, do you know that?'

'Yes. I know he does but I'm afraid he sometimes overestimates me. I'm no great shakes at investigating. Bag snatching and stolen bicycles are what we get at Pitti Station.'

'And the occasional murder.'

'These things happen. Now and again. You've got to expect that in a city.'

'Well, Guarnaccia, I'm inclined to believe your commanding officer. Maestrangelo's a good man. He'll be a general one day. He's also known you a long time—have you ever seen him smile? Oh, never mind, just a thought. I think he's the most serious man I've ever met in my life. I hear that among journalists he's known as The Tomb. Anyway, I intend to follow his advice. You bring me your observations and any information you collect and I shall refrain from asking you questions beginning with Why. All I ask is that you don't keep your observations to yourself, no matter how muddled or inexplicable you may imagine them to be. Is that reasonable?'

'I'll do my best.' That was true enough. He always did his best but his best wasn't much. And as for presenting himself at the public prosecutor's office and saying he had a funny feeling about something or other—well, he could see himself!

'Your best is all I ask for. In turn, I'll do my best to wait until you are ready to talk and not annoy you with my impatience. There's very little press interest in this murder except as a space filler so we need fear no pressure from that quarter. Also, I am a very patient man, which is why we haven't come across each other before now. Until last year I was a children's judge, a job which requires, as you can imagine, a great deal of gentleness and patience.'

The marshal was mortified, remembering the business of the Rossis' child. He tried to remember exactly what he'd said but couldn't.

The prosecutor understood and smiled. 'You were right to be cautious. In the case of perhaps ninety percent of my colleagues you'd have been right. So, Guarnaccia, shall we get to work on reconstructing the life of Sara Hirsch?'

The marshal was waiting. He waited standing, hat in hand, in the dim coolness of a spacious, shuttered room, breathing in a cloying scent of beeswax. The heavy furniture reminded him of long-ago days when he was an altar boy. Starch and incense, the Host sticking to his dry tongue, hot jam oozing from the brioches they were given for breakfast . . . There was a cupboard just like that one where the bottle of Marsala for the mass was kept. Vittorio, whose dad was dead, had dared them to take a sip.

'You'll go to hell.'

'I will not. It's not the blood of Christ until after the consecration.'

'Well? It's still wine for the holy mass, it says on the label.'

'Who cares?'

'You'll go to hell!'

Had he really taken a sip or just pretended? They had all stepped back and turned away from him. He didn't have his breakfast with them. It pained the marshal now to remember that, since the boy was half starved. The other boys said he ran all the way home crying, and one boy said he'd been sick, green sick, which meant he was possessed by the devil. How did they know? They'd all been sitting together stuffing down their warm brioches so how could any of them have seen? Vittorio hadn't come to school on Monday morning but he wasn't ill because they'd seen him afterwards by himself in a vineyard on the way home. He was ripping bunches of grapes from the vine, crushing them against his uplifted face, biting and sucking, chucking the remains and reaching for another. Purple juice dribbled down his chin and arms. The September sky was clear and blue but it must have rained before because he remembered how Vittorio's shoes with no laces were sunk deep in the clay soil and the big yellowing leaves were stuck to his bare legs. He never appeared to serve at mass again and everybody said it was because his mother was a prostitute.

Not much Christian charity in sight there. And yet . . . the quiet coolness of this place, the order and tranquillity . . . he'd have waited, soothed, for an hour, but he soon heard footsteps on the dark red tiles.

'Marshal? I'm sorry but we like her to sleep for a while during the hottest hours. She's still very shocked, as I'm sure you understand. She needs to rest and eat as much as possible before the hearing. Of course, I'll wake her if it's absolutely—'

'No—no.' The marshal, his mind filled with the Hirsch case, at first stared at the nun, as tall as himself and very thin and agile-looking, without understanding her. Then he hastened to reassure her that he wasn't there to talk to the Albanian girl they were sheltering and explain his errand.

'I see. Then we must look through our records. And perhaps Sister John Dolores can help you. She was here in those years, I know. Please sit down. I'll give you a little more light.' She went to open the windows and pushed the slatted brown shutters further apart, lifting their lower flaps to let in light without heat. They were almost the height of the room, and the marshal was struck by her slim, strong hands and the grace and precision of her movements. He was a clumsy man himself and such things always impressed him. How old would she be? He wasn't much of a hand at guessing any woman's age and a nun was impossible. Sister John Dolores, when the two of them joined him after a further pleasant wait, was very old. She was also sick, or had been, and walked very slowly with the aid of two claw-footed sticks because both her feet were turned inwards. Her eyes, behind ugly glasses, were bright, her memory sharp. Once seated at a table, with the help of the entries in the big book placed before her by the other sister and the two baptismal certificates presented by the marshal, she was able to reconstruct what little she knew of Sara Hirsch and of her mother, Ruth.

'Sister Philip Anthony keeps our records on a computer these days. I'm too old to learn . . .'

'I'm the same,' said the marshal, his sympathy for this rather formidable woman increasing at once.

'Here . . . I recognise my handwriting. So long ago. . . . Ruth came to us at the beginning of 1943, though I remember she had been in Florence for some time. She came from Prague, sent by her father, who I believe had business contacts here. They naturally wanted to save their daughter. They themselves died in the camps. They could not have imagined how things would go here at the end. No one could. No one believed that the race laws passed so suddenly at the end of 1938 would be applied. But they were applied. Ruth herself was reluctant to come to us but her foreign passport would have made her noticeable. It was a problem for us, too. Hiding Italians was much easier. We baptised them and nothing more was necessary, at least until the Occupation. It was obviously much more complicated with foreigners who needed Italian documents, too.'

'Was that possible?'

'Sometimes. For Ruth, yes. Many others, of course, remained stateless when their own countries fell to Communism. In Ruth Hirsch's case there was the additional problem of her condition. The safest way to hide her was to dress her as a novice but, as you can imagine . . . However, we succeeded and the little girl was born and baptised here in 1944 as you've seen.'

'How did she contact you?'

'Through the Jewish community. Like many others she came to us through Cardinal Della Costa, who was in contact with the Jewish community through Mayor La Pira. More than twenty convents in Tuscany collaborated and we were able to save many people. We could perhaps have saved more if it weren't for the unwillingness of many Jewish families to consider themselves at risk until it was too late . . .

'Ruth and little Sara stayed here until the deportations began. It became too dangerous since there were searches, checks, all the time and we couldn't have explained the child. We moved them to one of our houses in the country, an orphanage, along with such other children as we were hiding. Here is the record of Ruth's transfer.'

'Sister Perpetua . . . that's what you called her? Did she ever speak of the child's father?'

'She told us they had been separated by the war. She spoke of him as her husband . . .'

'But you didn't believe her.'

'She was eighteen when the child was born and she had already been in Florence, as I said, for some time. She would have had to have arrived here and married almost at once. It is not for us to judge. We must thank our Lord that, however tragic the cause, we were able to baptise them both.'

The marshal, feeling unreasonably defensive about Sara, whose birth and death had been attended by such violence, said, 'I understand from her neighbours that Sara's mother was married—that is, she had a photograph of her mother and father. There was another child, too, I think. She talked of a brother . . .' Judging by the sister's cold eye, he wasn't making a good job of her defence. He gave up. 'Did she leave you immediately after the war?'

Sister John Dolores turned the big pages and sought an entry with a dry white finger.

'January 15th, 1945. She had no money and no home up to that point.'

'And then? Someone provided both? You think the father—'

'I'm sorry, Marshal, I can offer you only the facts recorded here. You will appreciate that we do not allow ourselves to indulge in speculation.'

'I beg your pardon. It was only your opinion that I—she was murdered . . .'

'I will pray for her.'

The marshal turned his hopeful gaze on the younger nun. 'She never visited you in later years? To thank you?'

But the only answer was a glance down to the record book whose pages Sister John Dolores was turning.

'A donation, a substantial donation, was received, as you see—"On the part of Ruth and Sara Hirsch"—in September of 1946. That is the last entry concerning her.' Sister John Dolores had to be helped to her feet, the claw-footed sticks placed at her sides.

The marshal thanked them for their help and said he would see himself out.

When he joined the prosecutor in his office his dissatisfaction must have been evident if unspoken. Quite forgetting his promise, the prosecutor began, 'But why? What reason could they have for hiding anything from you? Oh, dear. Just go on.'

'That's all I was told.'

'Yes. I suppose it's what you weren't told that bothers you.'

'It's difficult not to think that, at least in their minds, the father was Italian, not Czech, and a Catholic, of course.'

The prosecutor tightened his lips over the small cigar in the corner of his mouth and waited. Then he lit it. 'Been holding out since lunchtime.'

'It must be difficult.'

'You've never been a smoker?'

'No. I've tried to diet, though.'

'That must be worse. No way of avoiding the "occasion of sin," as the good sisters you visited today would put it.' He smiled. 'I got used to doing without my cigar because of working with children. These days I'm slipping.'

He was also, the marshal realised, being as patient with him as he had been with the children, only pretending to attend to the wobbling stacks of files that surrounded him, perhaps—no, trying to unearth an ashtray . . .

'There's one on top of the pile of papers, there on the floor.'

'Ah, thanks.'

He made an effort: 'The sister said she'd given me the facts and I believe that. There was the donation, too . . . that money came from somewhere. She gave me the facts. The rest is just . . .'

'Impressions?'

'I think so. You never know, you see, except with hindsight, whether it's a question of impressions or there really was something. I'm sorry, I'm not being clear, I know.'

'You're being perfectly clear, Marshal, though I confess I can't quite see how she would have found that particular occasion of sin, entrusted to her parents' acquaintance in those nonpermissive days. Well, now, let's look at what the hospital gave me. I have Sara Hirsch's clinical file here but I'll try and give you a shortened version: It seems she was admitted to Santa Maria Novella at her own request, when the death of her mother, seven years ago, left her too grief-stricken to cope with daily life. She was afraid she was losing her mind. Her general health was checked out, given that undiagnosed illness often turns out to be the cause of tiredness and depression. She was found to be suffering from angina. A diet was recommended since she was a bit over-weight—incidentally, her mother died in the same hospital, in intensive care, after a heart attack. Sara was seen by a psychologist and there's a separate report here . . . bit long . . . says she didn't seek help for about seven months after the onset of her depression, which in turn began some months after her mother's death. The first delay seemed to puzzle the doctor more than the second—people are often reluctant to seek psychiatric help—but she doesn't seem to have reached any satisfactory conclusion about it. She says the patient, when interviewed, was deeply anxious and became very agitated when questioned about her daily life, expectations, rapport with people around her, and so on. The overall impression was of a very isolated person who probably had no valid relationship other than that with her mother.'

'No mention of a brother?' asked the marshal.

'Oh yes. Apparently he came up in every other sentence but she seemed unable or unwilling to give any precise information about him. This was so marked that the doctor made a note to the effect that she had doubts about his existence. I must say that, though this is a common enough phenomenon with lonely children, I've never heard of it myself in the case of an adult. Have you?'

'No, no. There was no photograph, though, none of a brother, just the mother and father, according to the Rossis' little girl. There could have been one, of course, and she didn't show it.'

'In the same way as she didn't give concrete information about him? I must say, up to now, he sounds mythical to me. By the way, I only found one Hirsch in the phone book, eliminated, so I won't waste your time with that. However, let's go on. Questioned about whether she had ever worked, she answered that her mother had not wished it, that there was no necessity for it, that she herself had thought of it when she was young but had accepted the guidance of her mother, who would tell her, "Remember who you are, that you will one day take your rightful place in the world." Oh dear me . . . that rather lends credence to what you were saying about her putative father, doesn't it?'

'She didn't explain?'

'She never explained, just gave out a series of apparently unrelated facts. The only thing she made clear was that she was desperately in need of help.'

'Hmph. That's exactly how she behaved when she came to see me. It did occur to me that she was inventing the facts.'

'But she was murdered.'

'Yes.'

'I'll read you the psychologist's conclusions: "The patient presents no difficulties in understanding the nature of her own condition and though she feels unable to look after herself at present she has a complete grasp of the realities of her life. Her anxiety is deep-rooted and arises out of real problems which she feels unable to discuss even in absolute confidence. It is evident that such problems are connected with her mother, with whom she nevertheless seems to have had a close and loving relationship. Her sensation of weakness and impotence she reports as having begun with the death of her mother without whom there is no one to 'defend her interests'. The patient has clearly spent her life waiting for the problem she refuses to discuss to work itself out. The death of her mother, aside from the grief it would naturally cause, seems to have triggered a realisation of the passing of her own life, spent in waiting rather than living. No symptoms of paranoia. No history of manic behaviour. Reactive depression."

'That's more or less it, really. Recommends tranquillizers, diet, fresh air, exercise, etcetera, etcetera. After that . . .' The prosecutor sifted through the file, setting aside photocopies of electrocardiograms, blood test results, forms, and handwritten letters.

'Here . . . she was readmitted after two years in pretty much the same condition. Same tests, different psychologist saying much the same things. "Reserved, anxious, reticent about cause of depression." There's even some question-and-answer stuff here:

'*"When you say, 'If things were as they should be,' could you explain that a little better for me?"*

'*"There are problems. One day my life will be as it should be."*'

'*"Have you concrete reasons for thinking that your situation in life is going to change radically?"*

'*"Yes, I have."*

'*"And do you feel able to tell me what those reasons are?"*

'*"Certainly not. They are very private matters and . . . complicated. It wouldn't be easy for you to understand."*

'Do you think she was blackmailing the father?'

'If she was, she wasn't very good at it. She was in tears because she couldn't afford condominium repairs—of course, that's just something the grocer said . . .'

'Did you believe him?'

'I believe he wasn't lying.'

'So you think it's true?'

'Oh no, no . . . it can't be true. No. That's what her visit to me was about, as far as I could tell. She didn't own the flat. The postcard saying "Now we know where you live" is typical of the type of unscrupulous lawyer who wants a quick eviction.'

The prosecutor looked at the papers removed from the Hirsch flat and stacked on his desk. 'I'm not going to find house documents in that pile.'

'No.'

'And probably no rent contract either.'

'Probably not,' agreed the marshal.

'Then we must find the owner through the city Land Registry—always hoping it's not too many years out of date.'

'What you might find among her documents,' the marshal suggested, 'is the name of her lawyer, a letter or something. She mentioned that she had one and that she was going to consult him when I told her I thought somebody was trying to push her out of the flat.'

'That would be useful,' the prosecutor agreed, 'but I'm not counting on it, by any means. These folders came out of a filing cabinet. They were in perfect order. Anyone wishing to remove compromising documents would have had no trouble finding them.'

'That's . . .'

'What is it?'

'I'm trying to remember something she said to me in my office. When I suggested the idea of someone trying to frighten her into moving . . . something like she had a card— or maybe cards—up her sleeve.'

The prosecutor leaned back in his chair, frowning. 'If she showed those cards she presumably signed her death warrant. What impresses me is that whoever she showed them to reacted so quickly and efficiently. Aren't you impressed by that yourself?'

'I . . . no, no . . .'

'But surely, Marshal, between her visit to you and her death—and she saw this lawyer, we assume before showing her hand.'

'She might have just phoned him.'

'But the speed of it! She must have been dead within two days and more likely one. I doubt if even the autopsy report when it comes in is going to be much more precise than that. Have you ever come across a homicide planned and executed that quickly—outside of organised crime, of course?'

'No, I can't say I have.'

'Well then? You surely don't think there's any connection with organised crime?'

'No, no . . .'

The prosecutor looked on the point of losing his much-vaunted patience. He stopped. The marshal was worried, not only because he had nothing helpful to offer but because he ought to find time to check in at his station before making another visit where he had even less to offer, the Villa L'Uliveto. The prosecutor was kind enough to release him when he explained. He didn't seem annoyed as they shook hands but you never knew with prosecutors. They were cleverer men than the marshal, educated men. They could conceal their annoyance and it would make itself felt later. He seemed like a nice man but it didn't do to jump to conclusions, the way the prosecutor himself had done, going on like that about the speed and efficiency. They didn't know for sure what the motive was and, even if they were right about it, the speed wasn't nearly as odd as was the murder itself. If the motive was the contents of that safe and whoever took it had really been in the house before, surely there was no need to kill when a simple robbery would have caused less fuss. An unnecessary killing . . . speed and efficiency? No, no . . .

It was dark and it was sultry. Inside the small, unmarked car the marshal and Lorenzini felt suffocated. They didn't open the car windows. The air in the narrow street was worse, equally hot and heavy with exhaust fumes. The young carabiniere in the backseat, on night rounds for the first time, was too eager for the marshal's tranquillity. He'd seen too many youngsters fail through overenthusiasm and it was a constant source of worry to him. He looked at the dashboard clock. Almost midnight. They were parked in Via dei Serragli. To achieve that, they'd had to drive round the block four times and grab a place as the Goldoni cinema emptied towards eleven. The car was unmarked but they were in uniform. There had been some movement as the cinema filled for the last showing but now there were almost no pedestrians in the long, narrow street. The trattorie were long closed. The lamplight was punctuated here and there by the neon signs of a few bars. Still the cars streamed by.

'You wonder where the devil they're all going at this hour,' grumbled the marshal as he always did.

'Discos, clubs,' replied Lorenzini automatically.

Via dei Serragli was where Ilir's cousin, Lek Pictri, had his 'building firm'. What he really had was a biggish flat on the second floor on the right, almost opposite the cinema. At any given time there might be up to eight Albanian immigrants living there. Lek Pictri's scam was to take these men in and register them with the police as employees in his building firm, which existed only on paper. As fully employed, though illegal, immigrants, their status was legalised and they were given police permits and residence documents. Once they obtained these, they soon moved on—to contacts of the Pictri cousins, usually to a profitable life of crime—leaving space in the flat for new arrivals. Nobody knew yet exactly what price they paid for this service but it was suspected to be part of a countrywide network which controlled the costly and dangerous journey from Albania and this legalisation process, and trade in prostitution and drugs. The marshal himself had uncovered the legalisation scam through a complaint from an old 'business acquaintance' of his, living on the same landing, Giancarlo Renzi. Renzi was a respectable Italian thief who objected strongly to the influx of foreign talent in the criminal world. The marshal and his men were already out on their twice-monthly night rounds when Renzi's call was put through to them on the car radio.

'I heard a commotion on the landing so I watched through the spy hole in my door.'

'And you're sure they were armed? It's important,' the marshal insisted.

'I'm sure one of them was. Don't know about the other two. He was holding a gun to a girl's head, for Christ's sake. There's never been women in there before. If they're going to start running prostitutes from here, that's the limit. I've got two teenaged daughters to think of. It's bad enough foreigners are going in and out at all hours. If you don't do something—'

'We are doing something. We're on our way.' Where arms were involved, the marshal could go in without a warrant. Even so, if the network was as big as they suspected, they needed more time, more information, before making a move. Lek Pictri alone was no use to them. They didn't want to put him on his guard. The regular night patrol car acting as their backup checked in on the radio.

'One one seven here. We're in Piazza Santo Spirito. Drug arrest at the mobile station. Have you decided to go in?'

'I'm not convinced. We'll stay here and observe for now.'

The marshal knew he should make a decision but instinctively he held back.

Lorenzini touched his arm.

'Door's opening.'

It wasn't the Albanians but Renzi, waiting for a gap in the traffic and then shuffling across the dark road wearing a

T-shirt that didn't cover his belly, shorts, and flip-flops. He removed the cigarette from his mouth between thumb and forefinger to complain, 'What are you doing, for God's sake? It sounds like they're killing that girl!'

The marshal and Lorenzini opened their doors. Small fry or not, if Pictri was beating a girl, they couldn't sit still.

'Stay there,' the marshal told the carabiniere in the back.

But they hadn't time to get out of the car before the door across the street opened again and three men and a girl got into a white Mercedes that moved off noisily, winging a parked car on the left and then one on the right farther along before picking up speed as it made for the Porta Romana and the city limit. They slammed their doors shut and followed, leaving Renzi standing in the road, shouting after them.

The marshal called in their backup.

'If they get on the motorway we haven't a hope of keeping up—apart from the size of the car, they're driving like lunatics.' Their own little car was chosen for discretion, small alleyways, and city parking.

As the marshal had feared, the white car swerved onto the Porta Romana roundabout and took the road to Siena. The next roundabout along would take them onto the motorway, where they could really get up speed.

The backup car hit Via dei Serragli just as the cinema was emptying again. In a street like that, one blocked-in car trying to edge into the road could jam the honking traffic right back to the river. Add a bus stuck across the junction with Via Sant'Agostino at the traffic lights and the whole Quarter would clog up. It did. All the drivers were honking in fury except the two carabinieri in the patrol car, one of whom got out to help by trying to shift a huge motorbike. The marshal received this news over the radio, which advised, 'Try and keep them in sight. Once we're clear of this mess, we'll be with you in seconds.'

At least, there would be no problem of the backup car not reaching them before a turnoff. The motorway was black and empty, the white car and its red taillights visible far ahead.

The young carabiniere, a national service boy, leaned forward between them to ask, 'What's happening? Where are they going?'

Lorenzini didn't answer him. 'Come on, come on, One one seven. He's losing me . . .'

The marshal didn't speak. He knew what this all meant. He knew also that if only they were in a marked car that would have been enough to stop it happening. The best they could do was to try and stay in sight but there wasn't much hope of keeping up. The only real hope was their backup.

'Marshal? Where are they—'

'Shine your headlights full on him.'

'What . . . ? Are you sure? What if he just takes off? We'll never—'

'Your headlights. Can't you speed up? One one seven! One one seven! Where are you?'

'Taking the motorway now. We'll be with you—'

'Overtake us. They're in a white Mercedes. Get your sirens going now.' He peered forward.

Lorenzini was baffled. 'I thought we had to be discreet— and where does the girl come in?'

'Lek's running Ilir's girls while he's in prison. If this means what I think it means, the girl's a friend of Dori's, just arrived.

He wouldn't mess with Kobi's big earners—can't you close up on him? Dear God, you've lost him!'

'No, I haven't. It's just the curve. He's no distance away and he can't see us—'

'I want him to see you. We should be in a marked car. Where is One one seven? They're not going to make it in time.'

'You think—I'll flash my lights, lean on the horn—there he is! He's miles away. He's accelerating. D'you reckon he's seen us?'

The red taillights were diminishing. Then, as the white car drew away, they saw the left rear door swing open. Their minds were prepared for just this development, but it was too late. The black bundle hit the motorway and rolled as the white car receded from view. Lorenzini braked. For a moment they could make out nothing but they were able to stop without having hit anything.

'They've thrown something out, like one of those big black rubbish bags . . .' The young carabiniere's voice was shaky. You could hear him trying to swallow. He knew it wasn't a rubbish bag but wanted it to be one.

'Get out and put the triangle in place. Then stay on the verge.' Lorenzini pulled over to the right as far as possible, warning lights flashing.

The dark bundle had stopped rolling. They had it in sight. It shifted and rose up in the road, alive and on all fours.

'Look! There on the left!'

'Triangle! All we need is an accident now!' The lad ran back with the red warning triangle. The marshal and Lorenzini got out and lifted their hands towards the girl.

'Stay where you are!' Lorenzini called. 'It's incredible, she looks like she's not hurt at all. She's on her feet. . . .' He stepped into the road, shouting, 'Stand still!'

Her clothes must have been black or nearly so. They could only see her face, small and white. She swayed and took a step towards them.

'No! Lorenzini, get over there. Get hold of her!' Oh no, no . . .

Lorenzini started across and stopped as headlights came from his right. To the left came others, a spinning blue light, a siren.

Lorenzini was silhouetted against the lights of the car speeding at them from the right, holding up his hand. The marshal's eyes were fixed on the girl's face, willing her to react, knowing that she wouldn't, seeing she was stunned, realising what would happen. It was a child's face that he saw as she tottered towards him. She seemed to be speaking but the siren coming nearer on the left drowned out her voice. In the seconds before the car coming from the right hit her, she met the marshal's gaze, reached out her hand to him, and smiled.

She spun in the air like a dummy in an action film, then flopped into the road. The car, its brakes screaming, ran over her with a loud crunch and stopped.

There is a moment immediately following any disaster which seems interminable, a moment when the world around you holds its breath. A crack has opened up in life's surface which will swallow up some and to which the rest must adjust. But first the shocked pause. Then, if it is a road accident, the unbearable silence is filled with shouts for action, murmurs of distress, or cries of panic. Windows crash open, a crowd collects, the right uniforms are summoned, black ones and white. The right noises are heard—sirens, brakes, the clatter of stretchers lowered from the backs of ambulances—another moment of silence, this one heavy with interest, as the dead or injured are collected, then a slower, duller scene as numbers are recorded and measurements taken. All but the most assiduous spectators start drifting back to their houses, their jobs, their interrupted topics of conversation. The unaffected, the unknowing, press in and want to press on, their horns hooting at the inexplicable, irritating delay. The last scene is dull and brief. Someone tosses sand or soapy water over a blood slick, damaged vehicles are towed away, and traffic resumes its normal route as life absorbs the event and flows on.

But a motorway at night is a desolate place, a no-man's-land, the marshal thought, as they waited out in the hot darkness for the ambulance, with only two sets of car headlights and the blue light on the roof of One one seven circling in the silence to illuminate trees, a pylon, a man vomiting in the grass verge, a barrier being set up down the dark road, trees, the car with a twisted bumper standing crooked across two lanes, trees, a pylon, a man vomiting, a barrier . . .

Under the car with the twisted bumper a torch had revealed a widening pool of blood that issued from a white patch in the girl's skull. Somebody had felt for and found a faint pulse in the neck. Nobody dared risk moving her or the car. She was bleeding to death.

The marshal didn't speak. He breathed more easily once the ambulance and the fire brigade arrived and there was strong light, movement, voices. They said she wasn't trapped and the car was moved. They said she was alive, and a doctor inserted a needle in her arm and held a bottle of colourless liquid above her. They put her on a stretcher, and the marshal glimpsed a small white face. When they were moving her, the body looked too limp and formless to be a live body. Yet they said she was alive. The floppy little limbs conjured up an image of his father dumping the flaccid, still-warm body of a rabbit onto the kitchen table for his mother to skin. A sliver of skull showed as white as the small face. She looked too young to be out alone at night. If, when she had got to her feet, stunned but evidently not much hurt, she had taken two steps in the opposite direction, she would have been on the grass verge when that car came by. But she hadn't. Probably attracted by their car lights, by the figure of the marshal holding out an arm in her direction, she had moved towards him, saying something he couldn't hear, and smiling.

Six

'There's really no point in your waiting about—unless you can identify her for us.' They had found no documents on the girl, as was to be expected.

'I can't identify her now but I've an idea I'll be able to later.' The marshal would have liked to ask the nurse about the limbs, flaccid and out of alignment, like those of a corpse, a little dead rabbit, when they transferred her from the stretcher to a hospital trolley, but he hadn't and he didn't know how to broach the matter now. 'We'll wait to hear what the doctor has to tell us, then we'll go.'

'Well, as long as you're not expecting her to regain consciousness, make a statement about what happened.'

'No, no . . . I'm afraid we know what happened. We were following the car.'

The nurse had no time to comment. Ambulance men were bringing an overdose case in, followed by two policemen. A man had just been pronounced dead on arrival after a heart attack and his wife was sobbing and protesting, beating her fists against a young doctor's chest. Three or four people with minor injuries were sitting on a row of plastic chairs, their faces grey, their energy sapped by waiting as more urgent cases were wheeled past them.

Lorenzini said, 'I'll get us a coffee from the machine,' and they, too, settled on hard red chairs and sipped the boiling coffee, burning their fingers on the tiny plastic cups. 'Will you get in touch with Dori?'

'I'll try. I'm hoping she's married by now but if she's not this should tip the scale whether this girl's her friend or not.'

'D'you think so? She always looks to me like somebody who can take care of herself.'

'They always look tougher than they are. What they are is brutalised, hard-shelled.'

'You may be right. Here. There's a bin at this end.' Lorenzini tossed their cups and yawned. 'God, what a long day. How did your visit to the villa go?'

'It didn't. At least, I went up there but Sir Christopher wasn't well. He's had a bit of a stroke recently and now he can't stand any exertion or excitement. He told me he had rheumatic fever as a child.'

'Ah, like my mother. She had two or three minor strokes before the one she died of. Does for the heart valves, that's what it is, bits floating free, blocking the circulation. Does that mean you'll have to trail up there again? Three visits for a stolen hairbrush or whatever it was? One law for the rich . . .'

'Mmph . . . But not one rheumatic fever for the rich . . .'

As a matter of fact, though he hadn't seen Sir Christopher, the marshal's visit had at least served to satisfy a little of his curiosity about the day-to-day running of a rich man's life, though in some respects it left him more baffled than before, especially as to the lack of an adequate staff for a place of that size. A young foreigner, a gardener, very tall and fair, had met him at the gates, saying he'd had orders to take him to the housekeeper. He spoke into a walkie-talkie before they set out up the drive together on foot at the marshal's suggestion.

'Your driver can go into the lodge, if you like.'

'No, no. He's all right parked in the shade there.' A walk meant time for a few improvised questions. 'Do you work here full-time?'

'In the garden, yes, sort of—that is, at the moment I do but that's because I'm on holiday. I'm a student of horticulture from England.'

'From England? You speak Italian well.'

'For a foreigner, you mean. Of course, I picked up a Florentine accent from the other gardeners, which is better than the horrible English accent you get when you study a language instead of just speaking it. Anyway, it'll look good on my CV having worked here and this is my fourth time. I'd like to be here permanently when I get my degree.' He slowed his walk and turned to the marshal, lowering his voice, though there wasn't a soul in sight. 'What I am, really, is a sort of poor relation.'

'A relation?'

'Distant. Very distant and very poor.' He laughed. His deep blue eyes were merry but his voice remained cautiously lowered. 'My mother's a distant relation, second cousin twice removed or something, of somebody who married into Sir Christopher's mother's family. She wrote to Sir Christopher about me and got a polite reply, so here I am.'

'And how do you get on with him?'

'Oh, he's very gracious. He comes every morning to talk to us, mostly to the head gardener, of course. He was born here and he inherited his cottage, under Sir Christopher's father's will—can you see it? Over there between the two vineyards.'

The marshal was astonished. 'Up on the rise? The gardener lives there?'

'No!' The boy lowered his voice to such a whisper that the marshal had to pause and bend closer to hear him. 'The gardener's cottage is much nearer, low down; you can only see the roof. That house up there is quite a big villa, used to be for guests, Sir Christopher's precious royals and writers and artists and multimillionaires. The housekeeper could tell you a thing or two about that. She says his father's hobby was picking up antiquities and his is dropping names. She disapproves. It seems a harmless enough pastime to me. Got him a knighthood, as well.'

'I thought painting was his hobby.'

'Oh, good Lord, no! He takes that seriously. That's less harmless in my opinion. Entitlement complex, d'you know what I mean?'

'I—no, no, I don't follow you.'

'People born with a silver spoon—or would you say a silk shirt?—think they're entitled to be whatever they fancy, including being a famous painter, without a smidgeon of talent. As far as artistic things go it's kind of pathetic, really, because it allows rich people to waste their entire lives on something they're no good at and they must *know*, however hard they try and kid themselves, don't you think? The trouble is that in some areas it works, like in landscape gardening, which is what I want to do. I haven't a hope unless I'm lucky enough to stay on here but I see plenty of people who do make it, not because of talent but because they either inherit a good house and land or marry it. I wish I could swap ambitions with Sir Christopher—I mean, I could afford a box of paints and a canvas but what I need to work with is all this.'

The marshal looked around him at 'all this' and saw his point.

'It's a shame, from my point of view, that the fancy visitors don't still come. Potential clients, you know. But there's nobody up in the guests' villa now. What's the main villa like? Have you been inside?'

'For a minute. Do you mean you haven't?'

'Never set foot. He acknowledged my arrival through the head gardener but I doubt if he'd know who I was if he came along now and saw me.'

Which brought the marshal to the point that so baffled him.

'How is it that I've seen so few people here? This is only my second visit, I know, but I don't seem to see any staff—apart from a secretary.'

'You're not supposed to see the staff in a place like this, Marshal.'

'I suppose not . . . I hadn't thought.'

'Even so, you have a point. For instance, apart from the head gardener and myself, there are six gardeners who live out and who are mostly on holiday now. This is a dead period in the garden. Even the weeds don't grow in this dry, hot season. The head gardener himself will go on holiday for all of August. As for the house, well, since there are no guests now because of Sir Christopher's health, poor old sod, there's nobody left of the live-in staff except the housekeeper and the cook. The last butler wasn't replaced when he went after the big robbery, and the house and kitchen maids come in from outside. The cook's on her holidays at the moment and there's an English cook filling in for a month. The housekeeper goes away in August and, given the mood she's in, I shouldn't be surprised if she didn't come back. The head gardener says it's because of your fingerprinting. You don't really suspect her, do you?'

'Of course not. I wasn't here but I'm sure everyone working in the house was fingerprinted. That's because they have to be excluded, and only unidentified fingerprints and those found where they shouldn't be need checking.'

'They think here it was poor Giorgio. That's because he's Albanian. The housekeeper keeps going on about letting foreigners in the house. In front of me, of course.'

'If she's that distressed about it perhaps I should have a word with her while I'm here.'

'She's distressed all right. Hers were the only prints in Sir Christopher's father's bedroom and she knows it. She looks after that room herself. It's never used except when Sir Christopher gets sentimental and goes in there and communes with his dead father. She lets him in and she's actually *heard* him. She has the keys, so you see . . .'

'Keys can be copied.'

'I know. And thieves wear gloves, which housekeepers don't. His hairbrushes . . . I ask you . . . what an idea. Well, it'll all be dropped now, I suppose. Of course, if the housekeeper does leave it'll suit some people . . . I suppose you know all about the big robbery a few years ago?'

'Yes. You seem to know a great deal about everything yourself.'

He laughed quietly. 'Oh, yes. Gardeners work in pairs most of the time, you know, and we have to have something to talk about other than the greenfly problem. Well, here you are. I'll be surprised if you get to see him. They say he was very ill yesterday and this morning. Upset, I suppose, poor chap. I think he's a good man. All the workers here like him and I go by that more than anything. In any case, I'd really like to go on working here after . . . I hope you do see him. The head gardener says, and the housekeeper as well, that he's really taken by you. My name's Jim, by the way. We must have a talk one day . . .'

The marshal didn't get to see Sir Christopher, or even the disgruntled housekeeper. He had just started wondering if the young gardener had hopes of the marshal's putting in a good word for him—which was ridiculous, though he liked the lad—when Porteous appeared in a doorway and the youngster melted away as if by magic, without another word.

'I'm sorry but Sir Christopher is unwell, very unwell. I fear you've had a wasted journey.'

'No, no.' The marshal showed Porteous some sheets of paper from a plastic folder. 'If you would give this to Sir Christopher to read and sign—it's the official report of the robbery. The copy is for him to keep for the insurance.'

'Yes, yes. His lawyer will see to all that. He's with Sir Christopher now.' He hesitated and evidently had second thoughts about turning the marshal away quite so brusquely. 'Follow me.'

Not to the kitchen offices this time, at any rate. After the high-domed hall with the mosaic floor and dry fountain they had turned left and walked through dim corridors for some time in silence before the marshal was left waiting outside the door while Porteous slipped into a room. His hand remained visible as he held the door slightly ajar. The marshal, though trying his best, was unable to distinguish a word of what was said until Porteous had come out and walked off in a hurry, telling him to wait. Then the door began to open again and Sir Christopher's voice was audible, high-pitched, weak, and anxious.

'The small bequests particularly—' Was that what he said? 'Maul . . . becess . . . pe-ic-yery.' He kept repeating it. Was he drunk? Was that why the marshal had been sent for and then not admitted?

'Don't worry. I'll have everything drafted for tomorrow.'

'Pe-hicu-yery!—' All those bottles in the garden that day. Perhaps the marshal, influenced by the sleepy beauty of the summer garden, had been romanticising and it wasn't the approach of death that made Sir Christopher close his eyes and forget their presence but an excess of alcohol. The English were said to drink a lot.

An almost inaudible murmur and the lawyer appeared, closing the door softly behind him. The marshal's big eyes bulged at the sight of him. The man had extraordinary deep blue eyes and thick, soft lashes, remarkable enough in themselves, but what surprised the marshal was his youth. Surely the lawyer of a man as important as Sir Christopher should be someone mature, experienced. Of course, he might just be a junior partner from a large firm. A very prosperous-looking one, mind you. Or else it was the marshal showing his age again.

'You have something for me?' He took a gold pen from his inside pocket and, with a plump, manicured hand, put a tiny signature on one copy of the theft report and kept the other without comment. He guided the marshal back for most of the way he had come with the air of someone leading a bear on a chain.

'Straight across the hall . . .'

'Thank you. I can manage from here.' He hadn't hurried, taking the opportunity to peer up into the gloom of the frescoed dome and walk, almost on tiptoe, close to the fountain. He wondered if it was ever turned on and decided not. The marble bowl was dry and dusty.

'*No guests now because of Sir Christopher's health, poor old sod.*'

The whole place, in the marshal's opinion, looked dry and dusty and very sad. A noise from his right attracted his attention. Somebody was crying. A light was burning beyond partly open double doors. A boyish voice protested something the marshal couldn't understand though he made out one or two words. Then the same voice dissolving into tears. The marshal stood still. He saw a hand, Porteous's hand, he was sure of that, making a small repetitive movement. A face turned into the light. The upturned face of a young, tearful boy. Porteous was touching his shoulder, making not so much a patting movement as a tiny, circular massaging one.

At that point the marshal had walked back as quietly as he could to the doorway he had come through, then started across the hall again with heavy steps. When he passed the double doors this time they were shut.

In the hospital at one in the morning, none of this seemed real as he told Lorenzini about it, more to distract himself from the news they were waiting for than anything. It didn't make much impression. Lorenzini just shrugged.

'So they're all homosexuals including this Sir whatever-he-is. And if stolen hairbrushes are all he's got to worry about—'

'And his health,' the marshal reminded him. 'They said he was very bad yesterday and today.'

'So they got a lawyer in?' Lorenzini, a dyed-in-the-wool Tuscan, spoke as he found. 'You'd think they'd call a doctor.'

'Yes, you'd think so . . . Of course I was only there a minute. They probably had the doctor at some point, but I get the impression he's more agitated by who to leave his estate to than by the fact that he's going to die.'

'Wish I had his problems—is that nurse looking for us?'

She was, but only to send them away. 'If she's still alive tomorrow the surgeon will have a scan done and decide if he should operate.'

'Is there much chance that she will be alive?'

'No, but if she is she'll have a grim future in front of her. If you can get us that identification we'd appreciate it.'

'Of course. We'll be in touch.'

They stretched their limbs and left the cool of the big waiting room for the suffocating night outside. The young carabiniere had been left in the driver's seat and it was easy to tell from his voice and slight unsteadiness when he got out to return to the backseat that he must have dozed off and was worrying about it.

Nothing was said to him. Lorenzini drove them back to Pitti and set off home in his own car. The marshal, feeling for his keys, could not remove from his head the images that filled it in turns. That trusting smile as she tottered towards him—what had she been saying? Who did she think he was? Then the floppy little body, poor rabbit ready for skinning. As he let himself in quietly he prayed that the faint click of the door would wake Teresa so that she would talk to him.

'Salva?'

She didn't talk much at first. She listened to him tell her about the girl, looked carefully at his face, then let him get washed and into bed and brought him some camomile tea with honey in it.

Then she got into bed, leaving the bedside lamp on so he could drink his tea while she talked. It didn't matter to him what she said. She'd never understood that, and when they were much younger he had sometimes offended her by saying what a chatterbox she was. He didn't say it unkindly; he wasn't even making fun of her. He was just amazed at the pleasure she took in talking to him since he didn't know how to chatter himself.

'Don't stop. I didn't mean you to stop.'

'I'm wasting my breath if you're not listening to a word I say.'

'That's not true. I am listening, I really am.'

She was right. He wasn't listening to a word she said, he was listening to her—her voice, her presence, her affection. One of those permanent misunderstandings that occur in all lasting marriages, lasting because they lead not to understanding but to acceptance. So she took his cup and went on talking to him, sensing his need, talking first of what had happened and then meandering on quietly, naturally, to their own problems, especially Giovanni's next school, to those of other people, family and friends, winding down with a coda on the minutiae of her day—Totò getting eight in his math test, the plumber who hadn't turned up. He kept hold of her as she talked, needing to feel the vibration of her voice against his chest as well as to soak in its comforting murmur. His heartbeat became calmer and his breathing more relaxed. After a long time he fell asleep. In his sleep he sensed her absence, a cooling, and knew she had gently extricated herself from his bearlike grasp and switched off the bedside light.

The story of the girl thrown out on the motorway, given that she was yet another Albanian prostitute and not even dead, warranted only a small paragraph on the local news page of *La Nazione*. It wasn't the sort of thing that sold newspapers. It had happened too often, and those not working actively against it reacted to it no more than to the dogs who would meet a similar fate at the start of the August holiday. The paragraph had been cut out and put on the marshal's desk for him when he came back from the Land Registry with disappointing results. He was glancing at the cutting when Lorenzini came in.

'This report came for you.'

The marshal took it. 'Did you find Dori or Mario at those numbers I gave you?'

'Mario. I left a message and he called me back about an hour ago. Not married yet but it's definitely on and the girl's who you thought she was. Dori had heard about it. I've found the copy of Dori's letter to her in our files. Name's—wait, I've got it written down but I can't pronounce it—N-D-O-K-E-S— first name's Enkeleda and she's eighteenish. Problem is, this address is no use to us. It's care of the contact for shipping the girls over here. It seems she'd already run away from her family in some mountain village in the north, to escape an arranged marriage, when Dori met her.'

'Nobody's going to be looking for her then, are they? She's already dead for them. Give Captain Maestrangelo the address for the Lek Pictri file. Bring me the name and I'll call the hospital and see if there's any change.'

There was no change. The girl had not regained consciousness. The surgeon was to operate next day. After he put the phone down, the marshal couldn't avoid the image of

that limp little body or the thought that, quite apart from
the Albanian question, youngsters travelled all over the world
these days and if one of his children should get run over in
some foreign country—well, he wouldn't have it. They were
going nowhere alone until they were mature adults . . . only,
when did you stop thinking about your children as children,
when did the fear go away? Did it go from one day to the
next? Did it ever go when you saw the things he saw all the
time? He knew that some of his colleagues went so far as to
have their teenaged children followed, afraid of drugs, bad
company. That was wrong but, if he got really frightened,
wouldn't he do it himself?

Before him on the desk lay the autopsy report on Sara
Hirsch. Hardly a change of subject to cheer him, but at least
one which must concentrate his attention.

It did more than that.

To the Public Prosecutor for the Republic, Florence.

**On the 15th inst, the undersigned pathologist, Dr. Federico
Forli of the Medico-Legal Institute of Florence, was called to
Sdrucciolo de' Pitti 4 to make an external examination of the
cadaver of HIRSCH SARA, and following that was asked to pro-
ceed to a dissection of the said cadaver. In response to the
specific requests of the magistrate, my findings are as follows:**

**1) Death occurred approximately seventy-two hours previous
to discovery.**

2) Cause of death: cardiac infarction of the left ventricle . . .

//

The marshal sat back in his chair, relieved. Sara Hirsch had been to see him on Monday, had gone home and called her lawyer as she'd said she would. She had shown the cards she had up her sleeve, and that same evening, as the autopsy and the neighbours agreed, someone had entered her flat and threatened her to try and obtain those cards. She had heart trouble as the grocer had said. She had died of fright. She had died by mistake. If she'd coughed up the combination to the safe when they held the knife to her throat she would still be alive and trying to get the marshal or some psychiatrist to believe her story without really telling it.

The autopsy went on to give an account of the wounds Sara Hirsch did not die of: a superficial knife wound on the left side of the throat, lifting a flap of skin upwards; a scalp wound and contusion of the skull where her head had hit the marble floor. Most of the blood loss was from there, as the photo file showed. Scalp wounds bleed profusely but this one had not bled for long. The heart attack had been a big one. The prosecutor would now order further detailed reports on those superficial wounds through which the dynamics of the victim's death could be reconstructed.

The marshal was more concerned with what followed. Had they hesitated? A dead body had been no part of their plan. Their plan had included a threatening postcard, warning visits to the flat, the knife in the entrance hall, things—except perhaps the knife—that spoke of an unscrupulous landlord . . .

'*We know where you live* . . .'

It *still* spoke of an unscrupulous landlord. Whatever must be added to the equation had to be added on her side. She had to be the threat. Somebody had been defending themselves from her in the end. If only the Land Registry were up to date. The whole of the building where the victim had her flat was registered as the property of Jacob Roth. An unhelpful and defensive clerk had insisted that the records were never more than two years out of date, which the marshal knew was nonsense. The Rossi couple had deposited their contract of purchase two years before, and Rinaldi supposedly owned both his shop and the first-floor apartment. There was still hope since changes of ownership were deposited in the first instance at the Real Estate Registry in Via Laura by the purchaser and the delay was caused by the bureaucratic backlog between there and the Land Registry map update. There were, of course, people who failed to register and so avoided taxes for years. At first, the name Jacob Roth had given him hope. The name was surely Jewish and could mean a personal connection, perhaps a friendly arrangement without a rent contract. That happened, and there could also be a low rent or rent-free arrangement where the tenant paid, instead, restoration and maintenance; hence Sara's facade and roof repairs problem.

The marshal interrupted his speculations to have lunch. He then visited the Registry of Births, Deaths, and Marriages in the Palazzo Vecchio. He found no Jacob Roth living. Hardly surprising, since the Land Registry printout had given Roth's date of birth as 13.6.1913 in London, G.B. He found no Jacob Roth dead.

'He doesn't have to be living here,' pointed out the prosecutor, when the marshal arrived at his office with this news, 'to own a building here. If he was born in London, perhaps he returned there.'

'Yes . . . it's just . . .'

The prosecutor remained silent and the marshal, to his own surprise, said quite firmly, 'It's just a feeling I have that whatever's going on is going on in this city. Sara Hirsch only gave me bits of a jigsaw puzzle but the other pieces are here in Florence. Maybe it's what she said or maybe it's how she said it. I wish I could remember her exact words but—don't you think if the problem had its roots somewhere else she'd have gone there? She wasn't one of the ones left stateless after the war. She had a passport. And . . . she was nervous, she was tearful, but she was very sure of her ground. Really convinced.'

The prosecutor continued silent, examining a cigar, waiting.

'And then there's the war . . . She was Jewish but they baptised her . . .' The marshal frowned, unable to connect the facts in a logical way.

The prosecutor, very quietly, offered, ' "If things were as they should be . . ." It was in the psychiatric report. Marshal, we must find out who her father was. I don't think we should give up looking for this Jacob Roth who owns or owned the building. And what if he's her father? Mind you, if he was, I can't imagine Sister John Dolores's being concerned to hide the fact.'

'The money. We don't know how much it was. Perhaps it was a lot and she doesn't like the convent's having large deposits of Jewish money in its bank account.'

'If that's the case,' said the prosecutor, 'we've more chance of getting it out of her. If it's false pride we're dealing with rather than a secrets-of-the-confessional type scenario, then another little visit to the good sisters might be indicated. I'll deal with that. What's your next move?'

The marshal failed to notice this extraordinary question. The usual way of things was that he regarded the prosecutor's running a case with respect and wariness up to the point where he became as absorbed as a bulldog locked on to a bone and forgot about him. He was entering into this phase now. So he hardly noticed either that he was doing something he had never done in his life before—explaining quite easily what he wanted to do. He wanted to spend some time alone in Sara Hirsch's flat now that evidence of the crime had been cleared away and he was free to wander at will through her rooms, sit on her sofa, look at her bookshelves, interrogate those things that bore witness to her daily life. He avoided admitting as much, even to himself, but he was about to pay Sara Hirsch the visit he'd promised to make before her death. Armed with a written permit and a bunch of keys he returned to 4, Sdrucciolo de' Pitti.

'Now then . . . ,' he said to the silent drawing room. Now then, what? Nothing except for that feeling a child gets when left alone in the house. It is a bit frightening but mostly exciting. There is no one to say 'Don't touch', no one to dissipate the terror of the shadowy places. The atmosphere tingles with possibilities, with adult secrets to be discovered, locked drawers to be opened, letters to be peeped at. No foreign land, no faraway planet, has so many secrets as a house left unattended, let alone a house where a violent death has occurred. But a crime scene full of investigators and technicians holds none of that magic. You have to be alone and quiet to hear a house speak.

The shutters in the drawing room were closed. The marshal switched on the light, looked carefully at a leather sofa, identified Sara Hirsch's habitual position, and sat down in it to look about him. It was true, as Rinaldi had said, that there was nothing here up to his standard. It was all good-quality stuff, even so. There was no reproduction furniture but no remarkably fine craftsmanship either. None of those pieces that stand alone against a background of rich brocades in the Via Maggio antique shops. There was nothing that the marshal could imagine had been chosen by Sara rather than her mother. There was something not right about the way the furniture was arranged, too. He was certainly sitting in Sara's place. There was a table to his right with a little silver tray on it where he could place his glass or coffee cup while . . . while what? While he read? The overhead light, a chandelier affair with glass drops and half a dozen candle-shaped lamps, didn't give light you could read by and there was no other. So . . . while what? While he stared straight ahead at the doors of a tall oak cupboard? Furniture used to be arranged around the fire. These days it was more often arranged around the TV. He got up and opened the cupboard doors. The television was a large one and there was a videocassette player, too. On a lower shelf he found a bottle of cognac and a balloon glass. He was more interested in what he didn't find on the empty shelf directly above the television. He closed the cupboard and decided on another chat with Lisa Rossi, the little girl upstairs.

'A whole shelf full—well, nearly a whole shelf. Sometimes we used to watch one if I finished my homework before my mum got back. I didn't like them so much, though. A lot of them were black and white and they always look sad, don't they? Because they're about people in the old days. Are they to do with the secret?'

'I don't really know. Perhaps.'

'Is it important, my secret? I haven't told anybody.'

'It's very important. Can you draw?'

'Draw? Not really. I'm never any good at it at school.'

'But could you draw the things in Signora Hirsch's safe—the candlesticks, for instance? Just try . . . here, in my notebook.'

'They were like this . . . kind of flat with a lot of candles but I can't remember how many. It's come out all crooked; I told you I couldn't draw.'

'It doesn't matter. And the other things?'

'I can't draw those. There was a cloth thing with a fringe—I thought it was a long skirt but she never unfolded it—and a little hat. The rest was just books, I think. It was only the photographs she used to show me. She never said anything about those other things but I saw them.'

The marshal hesitated. It was essential not to suggest the answer to a question with any witness but he had to insist. If all the videos had gone, there had to be a reason. They must have known there was one that mattered, one that was something other than a favourite film classic. With an unexpected dead body on their hands they wouldn't have hung around searching but would have taken the lot, just in case the one they wanted wasn't in the safe. He mustn't suggest . . . Lisa gazed at him with calm grey eyes, waiting.

'And she kept all the films in that cupboard, on the shelf above the TV? You never saw a video anywhere else?' Don't suggest, mention any place but the safe. 'What about the drawers, Lisa? People sometimes keep things tucked away in drawers if they're important. Did you ever—'

'No! I never, I never meant . . . I want my mum!'

Tears spilled from her eyes and her pale face was suddenly red. What had he done? The door at his back was open and he called out, 'Signora!'

'What's happened? Whatever have you said to her?' The child flung herself forward and hid her face against her mother's breast, sobbing loudly.

'You shouldn't have done it, you know that?' The prosecutor, surprised, with his little cigar lit, went on smoking and regarded the marshal without a trace of annoyance. 'Always with a parent, or at least a witness, in the room. We live in difficult times, Marshal, times when it's no longer possible to give a child a kindly stroke on the head. This girl, now, could invent anything. She couldn't prove anything but she wouldn't need to.'

'But why on earth . . .'

'She obviously has something to hide, something ridiculously trivial that you've accidentally put your finger on. And you've put yourself in a position that could suggest to her that she could blame you for her tears instead of confessing the truth. It remains to be seen whether she does that. She didn't say anything specific while you were there?'

'Not a word. She just cried and cried. She was pretty well hysterical. I should never have gone up there. Whatever was I thinking of? You were the person . . . when I spotted that the tapes were missing I should have called you right away. I'd no business . . . I'm no investigator—'

'You are the investigator on this case, Marshal, and it's perfectly natural that you should have gone up there. The only thing you did wrong was to speak to the child alone.'

'Yes. What she was telling me, though . . . this secret of Sara Hirsch's . . . it was something she hadn't told her mother about so she wouldn't have talked to me about it.'

'A carabiniere, then, one of the men from your station—too late now. If two of you show up now, the poor little thing will think she's about to be arrested for whatever crime she thinks she's committed. After all, we're dealing with a homicide here and, however unconnected the child's little bit of naughtiness might be, her nervousness must be exaggerated by that. Now go on with your investigation. I'll talk to Signora Rossi and defuse the situation. Trust me.'

The marshal went back to his station. He trusted the prosecutor but he was very distressed. The prosecutor was a good man, a man with years of experience as a children's judge. If anyone could undo the damage, he could. What the marshal was distressed about was that he could no longer trust himself. He, too, after all, had his years of experience, years of caring for the people of his Quarter, of building up a relationship with them, of being someone they could turn to with their biggest and their smallest problems. He'd never stopped to think about it before. If it crossed his mind at all it was only to start him grumbling about the number of people in the waiting room who would talk to nobody but him. The only man they trusted. And was he now to be accused of molesting a child? If that could happen then these really were dangerous times and he had been oblivious, had patted little boys' heads and comforted lost little girls. With horror he remembered, as he walked through his waiting room, that once a tiny lost and hysterical girl had stripped off every stitch of her clothing in that very room and he had quieted her and dressed her as best he could, no witness in sight. This thought made him break out into a sweat. He shut himself in his office without his habitual glance into the duty room. There he sat and contemplated his situation. Lisa had still been sobbing loudly when he left. If he hadn't touched her, had called for her mother without so much as stroking her fair hair, it was only because her outburst had been so surprising, so utterly unexpected that he had failed to react. Well, thank God for that.

But the truth was that he didn't really thank God for it at all. It was all wrong. This business might all come to nothing but things would never be the same again. If that's the way the world was now then there was no place in it for him. If he couldn't do things his way—and what was his way? Forgetting his promise to Sara Hirsch until it was too late? Was that how he cared for the people of his Quarter? If he was now to be accused of something he hadn't done, didn't it serve him right since no one had accused him of what he had done? Of doubly failing Sara Hirsch, failing to save her life and failing to find her killers.

He sat for a while, shifting files from one side of his desk to another, opening and shutting them, pretending to read them. He wasn't breathing properly. He was too hot . . . he'd forgotten to take his jacket off. He got up to do it and stood there forgetting what he'd got up to do. Hot though he was, there was a heavy, cold weight in his stomach. He felt like he'd swallowed a toad. Failure after failure came flooding back. What about that Albanian girl in the hospital? The decision not to go into the flat had been his and only his. And Sir Christopher Wrothesly? '*I'm under your care, too. I'm pleased to hear it.*' He had little reason. Too much trouble to pay a sick man a visit; the great investigator was busy solving the Hirsch case. And then it was too late. The man had become too ill to receive him.

'No, no, no . . .' The world had little use for him and no wonder.

Lorenzini opened the door. 'Is there somebody with you?'

'No.'

'I thought I heard you—'

'No.'

'Are you going out?'

'No.'

'Oh . . . there's a couple of things here need your signature.'

'Leave them on the desk.'

Lorenzini put the stuff down and withdrew.

The toad squatting in the marshal's stomach swelled, colder and larger. He had to move, do something. He opened the door and called a carabiniere from the duty room. He had decided to visit the hospital, check on the girl, give them her name, something useful . . .

At his back he heard Lorenzini's voice: 'I've no idea. He said he wasn't going out.'

On the journey out to the hospital they met a lot of traffic. The marshal gazed out at it without really seeing it. He heard the carabiniere driver make some comment every so often and roused himself sufficiently to say, 'Hmph . . .' Only when he realised that the young man was insisting and that they were in the car park did he say, 'What?'

'Have I to wait here or do you want me to come in with you?'

'Come in with me.'

He sent him to the nurses' station with the girl's name and address.

'Then wait for me in the car.'

As he went on down the corridor, looking in at each ward, a young nurse came at him, trying to head him off, saying something about visiting hours.

'Yes . . . thank you . . .' He was past her and standing still in a doorway. The girl's head was all bandaged but he knew it was her. She looked even more childish in bed. Tubes ran in and out of her small body. Her eyes were closed. He took a step into the room. There was another patient there, sitting on the opposite bed looking intently into a hand mirror. She was wearing a shiny dressing gown with Chinese dragons embroidered on it. The marshal stared at her, alarmed. Not that the dragons alarmed him. He fixed his eyes on them so as to avoid seeing the woman's head.

'I thought it might be my husband when I heard your step. He sometimes sneaks in out of hours. You know how it is—he has a restaurant and visiting hours are just when he's busiest.'

'Yes . . .' He stared harder at the dragons until the thought occurred to him that she might think he was looking at her figure. She was young and slim. He dragged his gaze up as far as her face. She was pretty. A lot of makeup, lips as red as the shiny dressing gown. He turned quickly and stood looking down at the Albanian girl. Enkeleda. The woman behind him kept up her stream of chatter. She seemed oblivious to the fact that, for whatever reason, somebody had recently sawn off the top of her shaved skull—like the top off a boiled egg—and sewn it back on again with big ugly black stitches. You couldn't help being reminded of Frankenstein. Added to this, on the very top of her head was a hole from which sprouted a transparent tube oozing yellow liquid into a plastic bag that was stuck to her head with plasters. It was this arrangement rather than the stitches in the red wound which caused the marshal to keep his head turned away. She seemed to accept this without being offended. It was clear enough that he was there for Enkeleda and equally clear that he would get no response from the girl. So she chattered on.

'I hope you don't mind but I was plucking my eyebrows when you came in and I can't leave them half done, can I?'

How could she do that? The marshal's stomach tightened at the thought of such a painful operation so near that slice through her head.

'My consultant says it's a good sign when a woman patient starts caring for her appearance. That was this morning because I was painting my nails when he came round. Well, that's as may be but I have to care about my appearance becase I have my own business: hairdresser—I ask you! That's about as unlucky as you can get, isn't it? Oh, I know it'll grow again but how long is it going to take? That's what I want to know. I mean, I can hardly show myself in the salon with no hair now, can I?'

'No . . .'

'D'you think I should buy a wig?'

'I don't—'

'They cost a fortune if you want anything halfway decent, you know.'

'I suppose so.'

'But I could go back to work sooner so maybe it's worth it. What would you do if you were me?'

He couldn't tell her what he was thinking—that he'd be screaming in panic if there was a hole in the top of his head with a tube full of yellow liquid poking out of it—and what was that yellow stuff, anyway?

'Of course, they say the more you cut your hair the faster it grows and I do think it has grown a fair bit. I reckon it's about half a centimetre long today, would you say?'

'Oh, yes, I'm sure it must be, yes.'

'You're not looking. Go on, tell me honestly.'

He turned his head, trying not to see. 'Half a centimetre, yes, easily.' He turned back to the silent figure in bandages. A catheter bag was hooked to the side rung of the bed.

'No sign of life from the poor kid yet. I talk to her a lot and keep my radio on. They say it helps.'

'Yes.' It would have helped a damn sight more if he'd got her away from those men while they were still in the flat.

'You should say something, squeeze her arm, let her know you're there. They say she has nobody—Albanian, isn't she?'

'Yes.'

'She hasn't much to look forward to if she does come round then. I heard all about it from the nurses. Thrown out of a car, wasn't she? There's been a few like that. Seen them on the news. Are you all right? You're looking a bit green at the gills. I should have thought you'd be used to this sort of thing in your job. Road accidents, murders, and whatnot.'

'Is—did you have a road accident?'

'Me? No. Brain tumour.'

'A brain tumour? But you look so well, so lively . . .'

'Well, I've had it out now, haven't I? It's my hair I'm bothered about. The thoughts of being a hairdresser with a bald head. I mean, look at me!' She pointed at her skull and the marshal pretended to look. A low delighted chuckle came from the bed beside him. The two of them stared at Enkeleda. Her eyes were wide open. They were dark brown and full of merriment as she stared at the arrangement on top of the bald patient's head.

'That's right, love, you have a good laugh. I look daft, don't I? Daft!' She repeated it, pointing and smiling.

'Daft!' The response was slurred but unmistakable and followed by a fit of giggles.

The marshal got to his feet and pressed the bell hanging by the head of the bed.

'A doctor should see her right away.'

'The nurses will see to that. Let's hear what she has to say first, before they start messing with her.' She came closer and leaned over the bed. 'What's your name, love? Tell us your name. I'm Marilena.' She pointed to herself. 'Marilena. Who are you? You?'

'En-ke-le-da.'

'Enkeleda. That's nice. Look, she can move her arm.'

The arm trembled and the hand was limp but there was no mistaking what she was pointing at. 'Daft.' She chuckled again, her dark eyes twinkling. Then the arm dropped and her expression changed as her eyes scanned the room, searching. 'Ma-ma? Ma-ma!'

'She wants her mum, that's what it is. She must be younger than they thought by the sound of her. Don't you worry, love. The nurses will look after you and the marshal here will find your mum and tell her to come for you. No, no, don't cry. No!'

But tears had welled up in the dark eyes and spilled down her cheeks. Her cry was weaker but desperate now. 'Ma-ma! Ma-ma!' The trembling hand moved across her body and she frowned, protesting like a starving kitten, seeking something.

'Does it hurt? It's only a needle—don't touch the tube, love. Poor little thing. Does it hurt?'

'Does-it-hurt!' She aimed the limp and shaking hand at the intubation. 'No does-it-hurt! No does-it-hurt! Ma-ma!' She was crying in earnest now; weak, frustrated sobs that shook her whole body.

The marshal pushed his way out past a nurse who called something after him but he didn't hear.

'Where are the boys?'

'They've eaten, they're in their room.'

'Playing with their wretched computer, I suppose.' A statement, not a question, since there was no mistaking that irritating noise.

'Salva, for goodness' sake. They are on holiday. And the novelty will have worn off by the time they go back to school.'

'All I'm asking is that we eat our meals together like a family instead of us sitting here on our own listening to that racket while we eat.'

'Have you any idea what time it is?'

'No, I haven't.'

'Well, it's twenty to ten.'

'Is it?'

'Oh, for goodness' sake. I might as well talk to the wall. Your mother was right. There's no point in bothering with you when you're like this. Do you want some more bread? I really do think you could . . .'

He ate mechanically, drinking in the sound of her voice, which kept the toad squatting inside him from moving. He had returned from the hospital to sit alone in his office until now. He vaguely remembered having signed some stuff that Lorenzini had left on his desk and pushed aside a note asking him to telephone someone, but he could hardly account for the rest of the time. It could well be that he had spent it opening and shutting files, shifting them from this place to that, sifting through them as if searching for something. He really was searching for something. It wasn't anything contained in the papers, which he looked through without seeing them, but the sifting, though its practical uselessness irritated him, was necessary, a sort of mime. So the time passed and the meaningless papers, the crying Rossi child, the trembling hand trying to tear out an intravenous drip, all flashed through his mind repeatedly. He had no defence against them. You can't close your eyes to avoid an image in your head. Doggedly, he shifted paper about. Rossi . . . Lorenzini's note. He pushed it aside again to avoid the twinge of anguish it provoked but kept his hand on it. What had she said? No, no . . . not her, the grocer: *'No need for carrying heavy weights'*—was that it? Or Rinaldi had said it. Said what? *'You must have been in her flat . . .'* No, no, it was Rossi . . . He pulled the note nearer, oblivious of its contents. She said it, something about furniture. Linda Rossi's voice spoke clearly in his head: *'Very little movement in this building except for Rinaldi's furniture being shifted between the shop and his first-floor flat.'* Then he pushed everything into a drawer, banged it shut, and sat back to stare at the map of Florence on the opposite wall. He heaved a deep breath, almost a sigh, got up to go closer, and glowered at Sdrucciolo de' Pitti, tapping an index finger on it repeatedly.

'No need for carrying heavy stuff . . . ,' he said aloud, quoting the grocer. No need to take any risks at all.

Then he had come into his own quarters. At twenty to ten. Later, Teresa watched the late news and he sat beside her staring at it. When they went to bed he fell asleep on the instant and at breakfast was as uncommunicative as he had been at dinner. He looked in at the duty room to announce, 'I'm going out.'

'Did you see my note about ringing—'

'Later. When I get back.'

Lorenzini looked hard at him and asked, 'Do you need a car?'

'No. I'll walk. I'm only going across the road but I might be a while.'

It was hotter than ever but the sun was invisible, a glaring leaden light.

'Morning, Marshal.'

'Oh, Marshal! Coming in for a coffee?'

The sort of glare that hurt even through dark glasses. He dabbed a folded handkerchief on his eyes, slid the glasses into his top pocket, and pushed the door of the antique shop. It didn't open. He peered into the gloom. The lamp on the small desk was on but there was no one there. Could be someone in the back, of course.

He knocked on the glass, waited, tried the doorbell. There was probably a yard with a washroom outside the restoration studio in the back but if Rinaldi was there, why the locked door? Besides, some instinct tells us when bells and telephones are ringing in an empty room. The marshal looked at the three-wheeled truck parked half on the pavement and made a note of its number. Then he turned again to the names on the doorbells. His finger hovered over the first-floor 'Rinaldi' and then over 'Rossi'. Other things being equal, he would have asked Linda Rossi to open the street door for him so as to give Rinaldi less warning of his arrival. Sure that Rinaldi was not in the back of his shop, he was equally sure that he would find him up in his flat. But other things were not equal. The door opened and Linda Rossi came outside, carrying a plastic rubbish sack.

'Oh, Marshal, I'm so glad you came. When you didn't call me back last night I thought—I just tried again and they said you'd gone out. I do hope you're not angry with her. She's only a child, after all, and she was frightened after Signora Hirsch's death.'

'Yes. Yes, she was bound to be.'

'And of course it was something and nothing.'

'Something and nothing . . .'

'A child's silliness—I'm sorry, do you want to come up?'

'I need to talk to Rinaldi . . .' He was inside.

Linda Rossi was chattering on, embarrassed. 'I don't want to waste any more of your time. Just a child's silliness, as I said. Signora Hirsch went down to buy some groceries and Lisa looked in her drawers, tried some jewellery on, peeped around looking for secrets. I think it was because of the safe that she imagined antitheft devices, hidden cameras, goodness knows what. Anyway, she thought you'd found out and that frightened her and with the death . . . you see, when you asked her if she'd looked in the drawers she thought she'd committed a crime. Nothing I could say would convince her. She's not going to feel easy until you—'

'I'll talk to her when I've seen Rinaldi.'

'I have to get a few things from the market at Santo Spirito. I'll not be more than half an hour but, in any case, just ring the bell. She's in. I'd be so grateful.'

'Don't worry.' He was moving forward, his gaze turned upwards to the first floor. 'I'll talk to her.' He was climbing the stairs. On the landing he heard voices raised behind the closed door. He waited, in no hurry to interrupt. But there was no real need to strain his ears, either. Not so much because the furious voices were so loud but because he understood the cause of their quarrel without bothering himself with the details of the resulting vituperation, which was not usable evidence. The voices approached the door.

'Not a penny more!'

'You're in no position to dictate terms!'

'Oh, but I am! Oh, indeed I am. '

'We did what you told us to do. Now you pay.'

'For what? For what?'

'It's not our fault! We did as you told us.'

'Did I tell you I wanted her dead?'

'Maybe not but it suits your book anyway, doesn't it?'

'Are you a complete fool? Suits my book to have a murder investigation on my doorstep? You should be paying me for the damned mess you've made and all for nothing.'

'And all that stuff we moved? What about that?'

'What stuff would that be? And where would it be? Where's your proof? If you want my advice, take that envelope and disappear before somebody starts looking for you!'

A third voice now, not so loud nor half so confident: 'If they do we'll take you down with us.'

'No, you won't. And I'm so sure about that I'm quite happy to point my friend the prosecutor in your direction.'

Had he picked up the phone when he said that? It seemed likely. There was a scuffle, a shout of 'You arsehole!' The door opened.

'Good morning,' the marshal said. 'I was just about to ring. Do you mind if I come in?'

A brief flash of fear lit Rinaldi's eyes but the marshal showed him such a dull and expressionless face that he was back in control in an instant.

'Ah, Marshal. What can I do for you? If you'll excuse my porters, they were just about to leave.'

The two enormous men, both as red in the face as when they'd been lifting a crated marble statue, made to move forward, then stopped. The marshal stood still in the doorway, filling it with his presence, fixing them in turn with his big eyes. He waited. Their eyes shifted but they made no further attempt to get past him. They were watching him as though afraid that he would sink his teeth into them at the least provocation. They needn't have worried. It was Rinaldi he wanted. 'Don't leave on my account,' he said peaceably. 'On the contrary, I'd rather you stayed—oh, only for a minute. I'm making a few inquiries that concern Signor Rinaldi here and as . . . collaborators of his, as it were, you might be able to help me at some point. Nothing urgent, you understand. Just leave me your names and addresses.'

Afterwards, when he told them they were free to go they hovered, disorientated, needing an exit line. A bland, empty stare was all they got. They looked to Rinaldi, who practically pushed them out and shut the door behind them before turning to face the marshal.

'So? What can I do for you?' All pretence at geniality was gone. Nor did he try the 'my friend the prosecutor' line. He was confident still but he was no fool.

'A small favour,' the marshal answered. 'I'd like to use your phone.'

'Certainly. There's one right here. I'll leave you to speak privately.'

'No, no. Stay where you are.' The marshal dialled, his eyes on the cigar end stubbed out in a silver ashtray beside the telephone. He gave instructions to Lorenzini, including the licence plate of the three-wheeled truck.

'No, just follow them. There are two men in it, yes. I'll tell you the rest when you're on your way.' He rang off.

Rinaldi was still keeping control of himself. 'I don't know what those two have done but I must point out that they are not my employees so that—'

'No. I don't suppose we'll find so much as a receipt for any transportation they've ever done for you, but that's all right.

I've no doubt they'll tell us all about it. Besides, as I said, it's you I'm interested in.'

'I fail to see why.'

'I'm sorry to say,' admitted the marshal, 'that I'm not so sure myself. I know what you've done but I don't know why. But, after all, it's what you've done that I'm going to arrest you for, not why you did it.'

'You can't arrest me.' Rinaldi was genuinely incredulous. 'I don't believe you've got a warrant.'

'No,' admitted the marshal, 'I haven't. I'll have to ask you to let me use your phone again so I can call your friend the prosecutor and ask him for one. He might refuse, I suppose, but just in case he doesn't, perhaps you should make a call to your lawyer first. Even then we might have to wait and see what happens with your two porters and I don't know where they're going.' He looked at their addresses, frowning. 'I suppose it'll be to this place. Nice bit of country and not too far . . .'

'This is ridiculous!'

The marshal stared at him. Rinaldi was doing his best to be aggressive but he looked a bit green at the gills. 'I wonder if you shouldn't sit down. Even better, make that call to your lawyer and we'll both sit down. What with one thing and another this might well take a bit of time.'

It took most of the day. Rinaldi was removed to Borgo Ognissanti Headquarters, leaving the marshal free to catch up with his own men, who were following the porters' truck in an unmarked car. By the time he reached them they were parked on a country road near the point where a stony track led down into a valley on the right.

'It's a dead end,' said Lorenzini, indicating the sign nailed to a tree, 'and I don't think they've gone much farther than the bend down there where this vineyard ends. We heard them stop from here. There's a backup car on the way.'

'We might need a full-scale search—unless we're lucky.' The marshal sent the young carabiniere who had driven Lorenzini to a villa on the opposite side of the road. 'Ask if there's a tip, or a place where people do dump stuff illegally. It could save us some time further on.' He asked Lorenzini, 'You've told your backup to arrive quietly?'

'Yes.'

'Good.' There was a time to arrive with lights spinning and sirens wailing and gravel spraying in all directions. There was also a time not to. Once the backup car was in place, next to his own, blocking the entrance to the lane, the marshal got into the unmarked car with Lorenzini and drove quietly down to the bottom of the vineyard. It was beginning to rain. On either side of them the big vine leaves bounced as the drops hit them. By the time they rounded the curve and drew up in front of a farmhouse it had stopped again. When they got out they could smell the rain, and the dust had settled in the lane. Thunder was grumbling nearby.

They stood looking at one of the few farmhouses in the area not to have been renovated by city people so as to look like fake farmhouses complete with mini iron lampposts and imitation terra cotta tiles. This one hadn't changed in centuries. It was built of stone and had a central tower with a dovecote. Under the archway fronting the house hung plaits of garlic, bunches of drying herbs, and orange corncobs for the hens, who were picking around in the shade below. An old woman looked up from scooping hen food out of an oil drum. She wore a thin flowered frock fastened at her breast with a big safety pin and flimsy plastic shoes. As they walked towards her, a dog shot out from their right, barking, to pull up short with a yelp of frustration as it reached the limit of its chain and leapt back.

'What's to do?' The old woman looked up but she didn't straighten up. She was permanently bent double.

'We're looking for'—the marshal read the porters' names from his notebook—'Giusti, Gianfranco and Falaschi, Piero.'

She indicated the front door with a twist of her head. 'They're inside.'

She showed neither surprise nor curiosity, which told its own story.

They went inside. The marshal removed his sunglasses and peered into the dim room. There was no one there. They heard the noisy little truck start up out back and rattle away.

'Good,' murmured the marshal. 'A little look round, I think.' He turned back to call to the old woman, 'Signora? Do you mind if we take a quick look around? We won't touch anything.'

She shrugged and scattered the last of the hen food before picking up a basket and going off to collect her eggs.

They looked at the big kitchen.

Lorenzini said, 'I reckon they were sitting here trying to decide what to do rather than trying to hide anything.'

'Yes.' The room was clean and spartan. On the big marble-topped table stood a straw-covered wine flask and two kitchen glasses with a drop of red still in them. Two facing chairs had been pushed back. Such houses have usually only one entrance but the marshal soon found a room containing feed sacks and fertilizer that had an exit to an outside staircase. At the bottom was a jumble of sheds on the lower ground behind the house. They went down to look. One of the sheds was empty and presumably housed the truck which had just left. In another stood a battered tractor, a moped, and various farm implements. The next was dark and smelly and filled with rabbits crammed into cages.

'Are we looking for anything special?' asked Lorenzini.

'No . . . yes. Not the safe but whatever they opened it with. I don't know these two characters. Perhaps you should . . . ' He fished out his notebook and passed it over.

Lorenzini, accustomed to interpreting the marshal's thought processes without the aid of the spoken word, took it and went off. 'I'll not be a minute.'

The marshal continued to look, not touching. Lorenzini would run a check on their previous convictions from the car. By the time he came back, the marshal had found an oxy-acetylene cutter and a protective mask in a three-legged kitchen cupboard with no doors. He had touched something, twitching back an old flowered sheet that had covered it. Lorenzini returned to confirm his suspicions.

'Grand theft auto, three convictions. I suppose they changed the licence plates here. What now? A warrant to pull this place apart?'

'No, no. They were sitting in the kitchen drinking wine. We'd better go. They're still waiting at the top of the lane?'

'Still there.'

The old woman appeared with food for her rabbits. The marshal asked her, 'One of them is your son?'

She made a grimace. 'Piero. As spineless as his father but he's all I've got now. That crook Giusti's got him in bother again, hasn't he?'

'I'm afraid so.'

134   •   MAGDALEN NABB

'And how am I supposed to manage if you put him away? Can you tell me that? I know what goes on in prison. They sit around playing cards, smoking, taking drugs, planning more trouble for as soon as they get out while I'm struggling here by myself.'

'No, Signora, you can't possibly manage. You need some help.'

'I do need some help. I do! I've a son, haven't I? He's supposed to help me! Him!'

She peered up at them, her wrinkled face tearstained, a huge bundle of cut grass on her bent back. They didn't know what to say to her and she knew it. Her lament was an automatic response like the charge of the chained-up dog. No answer was expected, no effect. Hope had long since evolved into habit.

The two men left. The thunder rolled nearer.

It had been decided that Lorenzini and the young carabiniere driver should take Giusti and Falaschi in. Falaschi, the one with the greasy blond ponytail, was the old woman's son. If it occurred to him to be concerned about his mother's struggling to keep a farm going in his absence, he didn't mention it. No doubt his lawyer would make good use of the idea later on. Giusti, the heftier of the two with the dark shaved head, had a wife and two small children at home. Lorenzini would be giving them the bad news.

The marshal was standing at the edge of a path through a little wood which sloped steeply down on the right. A notice was nailed to a tree beside his head saying 'No tipping'. Somewhere down there out of sight, his driver and the two men from the squad car were searching. He was glad enough of the shade this pretty wood provided but the air was nevertheless still and heavy. Lightning flashed every so often, followed very quickly by thunder near enough now to crack and roar.

'Marshal!' They were waving at him. They were climbing back up.

'It's down there, all right. A safe, not very big, been opened with a cutter, axe, bludgeon, everything, just about unrecognisable.' There's some stuff in it but we need to get a move on, get forensic people out sharpish. It's going to pour down.'

'I doubt there'll be prints,' the marshal said. 'What else—'

'Blood. A lot of it on some men's clothing and on the safe itself. There's all sorts of junk down there so we've rigged up a makeshift shelter with bits of furniture and mattresses but we've got to move!'

They moved. The marshal called in for a forensic team. It was useless. With a deafening crash of thunder the summer deluge began.

'I can't arrest this man.' The prosecutor looked at the marshal and then at Captain Maestrangelo, who was receiving them in his office. He and the prosecutor were seated on a long leather sofa. The marshal hovered, hat in hand, staring at the oil painting in a gilded frame above their heads.

'If you'll give me a minute with those two . . .'

'You seriously think they'll talk?' Maestrangelo looked doubtful. 'It doesn't need much imagination on their part to know that Rinaldi will cough up for a decent lawyer who'll keep his name out of it. You could sit down, Guarnaccia.'

'I'm all right as I am, thank you. Not everybody has imagination, do they? I don't think I have any myself. They've been separated all the time, that's what matters. Rinaldi, now, he's arrogant. He wasn't expecting this.'

What was that look that passed between the other two? It was a split second but he saw it. Was it that they didn't believe him?

'The trouble is,' pointed out the prosecutor—was he smiling? 'I wasn't quite expecting this either. I don't know . . . and you have a reputation—well—for being a bit slow, so it's all the more—'

'Yes. I'm sorry.' He did his best but it was always the same, he was always too late. 'That downpour. It was just that I couldn't call Forensics until I was sure where the stuff was.'

'The stuff' was still in evidence bags, spread on the Captain's desk on the other side of the room: the seven-branched candelabra, the Talmud, the prayer shawl, and the skullcap the prosecutor called a *kiphah*, the sepia photographs.

The captain got to his feet and went over to look at it all again. He shook his head. 'It's not going to help us because we don't want what they left, we want what they took, whatever it was that caused her death, intentional or not.'

Behind him, the marshal coughed. 'I don't think . . .'

'What?' the two of them asked together. He was embarrassed and didn't meet either gaze, saying to another oil painting, a shepherdess in a silk frock and pointed shoes— what would she be dressed like that for?—'I doubt if they found what they were looking for.'

Even with his gaze averted he sensed that look pass between them again. They shouldn't be wasting time like this. Rinaldi was sitting there waiting in the next room for what had been called 'an informal talk'. It was a way of defying him to be the one to recognise that he needed a lawyer. Up to now he had brazened it out, pretending that he didn't. Something had to give. Once there was a lawyer involved, he would surely defend the two porters as well and information could go back and forth. Didn't they see the danger?

'Of course you're right,' the prosecutor said. He interrupted himself to take out one of his small cigars, caught the captain's eye, and put it away again, conscious of the polished floor, the elegant rugs, the gleaming rubber plant, the mote-free air, so unlike his own habitat. 'Keeping them separate is of the essence. But I can only do it by keeping them inside—there's evidence enough for that—and letting him go.'

'He'll send them a lawyer.'

'Yes. Yes, all right. He'll send them a lawyer. Give me evidence for an arrest warrant, otherwise all I can give you is a search warrant. How do you *know* they didn't find what they were after? That it's not in his apartment?'

Why did people spend so much time talking? Where was the use in finding words to explain why and how? There'd be time for all that in court. Words were lawyers' business. He gazed hopefully at Captain Maestrangelo, needing to be let off, needing to be let loose. The deluge had washed away every trace of blood, yes, but downstairs there were two men in the cells, sweating with fear. It wasn't their first time inside, but even so, they were car thieves and though probably up for any scam going, they were not hired killers. That was what they were thinking about now, down there in the claustrophobic heat, one to a cell so they couldn't even talk. He'd been too late for the blood; he couldn't lose more time now.

He edged nearer to the door and mumbled some excuse or other, watching their faces. They were letting him go.

'I've a feeling I should prepare that warrant. What do you think?'

That was the prosecutor's voice behind him. Did he mean a search warrant? No, no . . . that wouldn't do at all, no. The two men downstairs would tell him. A couple of hours with the shaved chap. A couple of hours of near silence, most likely. Then the weaker one. Falaschi, with the greasy tail of hair. His had been the voice that made that weak threat, heard from outside Rinaldi's door, 'We'll take you down with us.'

His mother, that was the key. 'He's all I've got now. How am I going to manage?' Falaschi had to be saved from a prison sentence and the marshal was going to save him. It took little more than an hour and a half. If Giusti, his shaven head gleaming even in the poor artificial light of the windowless cell, could be used against the weaker Falaschi, Rinaldi's not being arrested was the best possible weapon against Giusti. The marshal got everything they knew and arrived home in good time for lunch. He had an appetite, too.

Teresa said, 'You look pleased with yourself.'

'Yes.'

'Well? Is it a secret?'

'No, no . . . Just something I was a bit worried about that turned out all right. Do we have to have *pasta corta*? I don't fancy it today. '

Teresa spun the lid back on the jar and took a fresh packet of spaghetti out of the cupboard. 'I suppose you'll tell me all about it sometime.'

'What?'

'Probably halfway through some film on the television.'

'What film?'

'Salva, you're standing in the middle of the kitchen again.'

He stopped her in her tracks and hugged her. Then he went over, reminded by something she'd just said, and switched the little TV on for the two o'clock local news on channel three.

'Boys! Come to the table!' She tossed the spaghetti into the boiling water.

'And switch that infernal machine off!' added the marshal, adjusting the volume of the television. The Rossis had been eating spaghetti and watching the news on channel two when he'd called there on his way home. The chair between them had been pushed back, the pasta half eaten.

'She's so embarrassed. We tried to explain to her that what she did was just childish and that it had nothing to do with . . . what happened. That is true, isn't it?'

'Yes, it's true.'

'She wants to apologise to you for causing a fuss. She's mortified about it because she likes you. Would you mind? She'd be too shy in front of us.'

Lisa was sitting on her bed. Her face was flushed and a little tearful even now.

'You won't need to tell anybody else what I did, will you?'

'Nobody at all. You kept our secret, didn't you? We'll keep this one, too. Just forget about it. It's not important. Now, your pasta's getting cold. Come on.' As they went he had given her a kindly stroke on the head.

'Dad? *Dad!* I'm talking to you! Mum, he never listens.'

'He is listening.'

'I am listening.'

'Well, if we shouldn't have the computer on at mealtimes, why can you have the telly on?'

'Because . . .'

'Because what?'

'Because until you're an adult you do what you're told.'

'Oh, Dad!'

'Totò, behave yourself,' intervened Teresa, but she gave her husband a look that brought him to his senses.

'Eat up and we'll have a game together before I go back to work.'

'Good,' said Totò, wriggling his wiry little body in the chair and stabbing at an imaginary keyboard with his fork. 'I'll win.'

'Sit still,' said his mother sharply.

Afterwards, as they went to the boys' bedroom, Giovanni murmured, 'Dad?'

'What, son?'

'Can we have a game by ourselves one day so that I can win?'

'Yes, we can, right now. The first game's between us two and the winner plays Totò.'

After five minutes, four of which were spent in useless explanations, he was free to have his coffee with Teresa.

Eight

The 'informal chat' which Rinaldi agreed to return for in the afternoon—no point in disturbing his lunch hour, as the prosecutor said, performing in the role of dinner-party acquaintance—was almost as brief as the computer game. It couldn't be brief enough for Rinaldi, that was clear, and the reason was the marshal. It was his custom on these occasions to park himself somewhere in the background, leaving those better qualified than he was to do the talking. The effect of this was usually that the suspect or witness soon forgot his existence and he was better able to observe and read the signs. It wasn't so this time. With only the captain and the prosecutor, Rinaldi would have done well. The 'we men of the world', 'we men of sophistication and culture' stuff. He didn't know what they'd found on the tip and was still fairly confident. But as he talked, too much and just a little too fast, his eyes flickered towards the marshal, who today felt he was about as invisible as a large black ticking bomb.

Rinaldi said the things they expected him to say, that the porters were strong and reliable with statuary and other antiquities, that he knew nothing else about them and had no other dealings with them. He admitted, with exaggerated emphasis, to employing them on the black market and then relaxed, with even more exaggerated sighs and chuckles of relief after having 'confessed' the only thing he had on his conscience.

Then the prosecutor stood up and begged his pardon for the interruption of his busy day and the captain stood up, too, and thanked him. The marshal, by the door, was silent. Rinaldi had to walk towards him to leave and he was afraid to. Over his head, the marshal sensed rather than saw the other two raise their eyebrows and smile almost in unison. Was he doing something ridiculous? He was, he was watching Rinaldi's dishonest face with such concentration that he was absentmindedly blocking his way and the little talk must be over without his having listened to a word of it. He excused himself and opened the door. 'Please . . .' He stood back, aware of Rinaldi's fear of passing him, knowing the man was hard put not to walk on tiptoe. Just as Rinaldi set foot in the corridor, the marshal shook himself out of his stupor of concentration and remembered to ask, 'Would you mind telling me—we're having a bit of trouble finding out who owned the victim's flat—who owns yours? And the shop. I think somebody mentioned you owned the place yourself, is that right?'

Rinaldi turned. 'I have the usufruct of my flat and the shop.'

'But not of the rest of the building?'

'No.'

The marshal thought for a bit. He saw beads of sweat appear on Rinaldi's temples and roll down the side of his face.

'It's very hot, isn't it? Even after the rain. Like a Turkish bath. How long have you had the usufruct?'

'Two years or so. I'd rented the place since the fifties. When the owner died he provided for me . . .'

'Oh, good, good . . .'

'What's good about it?' The other two men came up to the door and Rinaldi looked past the marshal at them as if he hoped they might save him. They were silent.

'It's good,' the marshal said, 'because you can tell us who this owner was and if he owned the rest of the building. Was it this . . . now what was his name?' If only he had a memory for names and facts instead of just pictures and smells. He shouldn't have opened his mouth if all he could do was to make a fool of himself. His superiors had been so cool and intelligent, given nothing away, and here he was annoying the fellow, keeping him standing there, sweat rolling off him.

'Roth,' said the prosecutor. 'Jacob Roth. That was the name the building was last registered under.'

'Ah yes.' The marshal was relieved. 'Jacob Roth.'

The name hung in the air. Rinaldi was red in the face. His eyes glazed over with fear and he looked as though he were holding himself to the spot by willpower.

'If he provided for you in his will, I suppose he was a relation or at least a friend.'

'Do spare us a few more minutes, Rinaldi,' said the prosecutor, maintaining their fake familiarity. 'This could be such a help. We'd be grateful.'

Again Rinaldi had to negotiate the space around the marshal, whose gaze followed him and remained fixed on him, making the back of his neck redden as he talked. He talked because he had no choice but, in the marshal's opinion, there were moments in his narrative when he turned back from one path to venture onto another, sometimes even rejecting two before choosing a third. The captain sent for a carabiniere to make notes and they all settled down in silence to listen to the unwilling storyteller. Despite what the marshal afterwards called his 'twisting and wriggling', Rinaldi couldn't avoid giving them some solid facts.

Jacob Roth was the son of Samuel Roth, a Jew from the East End of London who dealt in paintings and antiquities and whose business travels brought him, among other places, to Florence, where he dealt with the owners of the little shop in Sdrucciolo de' Pitti. He married the daughter of these people, Naomi, and took her back to London with him. There, their only son, Jacob, was born. Business and family contacts were interrupted by the First World War and Naomi's parents died in the flu epidemic immediately afterwards. The young couple moved to Florence and took over the shop. Young Jacob grew up in Florence among the world's finest paintings. He was a talented painter himself and would have liked to study at the Liceo Artistico but shopkeepers' sons didn't get further than elementary school in those days. Jacob started working for his father at the age of twelve. For a while he used his painting skills to touch up the pictures in the shop but at fifteen he threw away his paintbrushes. He refused to be an amateur but dedicated himself to the business. He and his father developed a European network which flourished in the late twenties. Young and inexperienced though he was, Jacob's aesthetic sense and flair for business turned what had been little more than a bric-a-brac shop that occasionally turned up a decent painting into the fine art and antiquities business still successful today. Samuel and Naomi gradually bought up the rest of the building. Jacob travelled from Florence to London as his father had done before him, where their best clients were, whilst Samuel dealt from home with other European capitals. Then came the Second World War. In 1943 Samuel and Naomi were deported and they died in Auschwitz. After the war, Jacob returned to Florence but he decided to leave the business and eventually Rinaldi took over. Jacob set up a trust before he died, under the terms of which Rinaldi had the usufruct of his shop and first-floor apartment.

Every so often, during this account, Rinaldi's glance moved from the captain's face to the prosecutor's, gauging their reaction, trying, by adopting a confidential tone and putting in unnecessary details, to maintain the fiction that his only thought was to be useful to them. He was careful to avoid the marshal's stare.

When he stopped, there was a moment's silence. The prosecutor thanked him.

'You've been a great help. Quite cleared up the mystery. There are just two things . . .'

A lot more than two, the marshal thought, watching the flush of fear return to Rinaldi's face.

'Two things . . . these European contacts you mentioned, would they include Prague?'

'Well, of course, I'm only going on what I was told. Bit before my time but I think so, yes.'

'So the contacts could have included Sara Hirsch's mother, for example. Jacob perhaps gave her, too, the usufruct of her flat under the terms of the trust.'

'I suppose it's possible but I really don't know. I wasn't in his confidence to that extent. I can only tell you with certainty about things which concern me personally.'

'Of course. It was just a thought since we found no rent book. And the other thing was—now, what was the other thing I wanted to ask?—ah, yes. The mystery of mysteries. Where is Jacob Roth now?'

'He's dead of course! I've already said so!'

'Yes, yes, quite. But even when we are dead our earthly remains must be somewhere, mustn't they? Did he die in Florence?'

'He might have done.'

'Lost contact, over the years, had you? With his having retired from the business, I suppose you saw less of each other.'

'That's right. It's only natural.'

'Perfectly natural. But he didn't forget you at the end. You must have appreciated that. Did you go to his funeral?'

It seemed an innocuous enough question but the man was struck dumb and you could see by his eye movements how he was sifting through possible truths and lies for an answer.

'Was it so long ago that you don't remember? After a certain age one has to go to so many funerals—a colleague of mine died only last week, fifty-three, heart attack—reminds us of our own mortality. Perhaps if you give yourself a moment . . . cast your mind back . . . you might remember.'

'Of course I remember! It's just not something I care to talk about.'

'I understand. However, I'm sure that you in turn understand that in the circumstances, a woman having died—'

Rinaldi cut him short, saying slowly, deliberately, 'I did not go to Jacob Roth's funeral.'

'I see. Fine. Well, then I don't think we need trouble you further—unless there's something you would like to ask, Captain?'

The captain, immobile, solemn, silent, indicated with the tiniest movement of one finger that he would not.

Rinaldi began to breathe easily again.

'Marshal? Anything you would like to ask Signor Rinaldi?'

Somewhat taken aback, the marshal said, 'No, no . . . I'm not—'

'This is your case, after all, so please . . .'

The marshal cleared his throat and took the plunge: 'I would like to ask Signor Rinaldi a question.' He couldn't do any fancy steps around it either. Besides, he didn't want the man to feel at ease; he wanted to arrest him.

'Who told you?'

'Told me what?'

'That he was dead? About the trust?'

'His lawyer, naturally.'

'What's this lawyer's name?'

Rinaldi was really alarmed now, and undecided. The marshal gave him no time for inventing names. 'Only, Sara Hirsch left a name with me when she came to see me and I just wondered if, with there perhaps being a connection, it might be the same. We could check ourselves, of course, now we know about Jacob Roth, but you could save us the time . . . . I can see it's coming to you.'

'Yes,' snapped Rinaldi, 'I can save you the time. The name is D'Ancona, Umberto D'Ancona. And I can save you even more time. He's dead. He and Jacob were practically the same age.'

They had to let him go. The marshal would have liked to go with him, stay glued to him until the man couldn't bear it any longer and told him. Told him what? It made no difference. He was gone. They all talked so much, so many words . . .

'Marshal?'

'I'm sorry. didn't quite hear you.'

'You said there was no point in my giving you a search warrant for Rinaldi's place, that you thought they didn't find what they were looking for. How do you know?'

'Something he said. Captain, you'll have him followed?'

'He's being followed now and by the time he gets home his telephone will be tapped.'

'Good, good . . . I can't remember his exact words, I'm sorry. He was paying off those two porters and I was outside listening. Said he was paying them for nothing . . . something like that. I can get it out of one of the porters . . .' All this talking. The marshal, on the edge of his chair, feet planted firmly on the ground, ready to stand, gazed hopefully at Captain Maestrangelo, who was used to him and knew he was no good at words. The prosecutor, who wasn't used to him, was trying to understand. You could see that. You could see he wanted a smoke, too.

'There was a cigar stubbed out. Everything Sara Hirsch said was true and I left it too late . . .'

The captain said, 'Listen, Guarnaccia, you remember you said at first you felt this was some sort of eviction problem?'

'It is. That's why there's no time to lose.'

'But if the woman's dead?'

'Exactly. They may not have meant to kill her but when she showed that card she had up her sleeve they attacked. Well, they must have wanted her out of the flat for a reason and maybe that reason is . . . They killed her by accident. She was in the way and what she was in the way of is what . . . Maybe the crime we should be investigating hasn't been committed yet.' He was getting to his feet. He had to get on.

'I'll walk down with you,' the prosecutor said. He slung a crumpled linen jacket round his shoulders, shook hands with Maestrangelo, and picked up his battered briefcase. As soon as they were on the staircase he lit a cigar. When they reached their cars down in the cloister, the prosecutor delayed Guarnaccia again but only to say, 'I did follow up your eviction idea and got in touch with the archives in Via Laura where documentation of any change of ownership is stored until such a time as the Land Registry is updated. It seems as if Rinaldi's story is true. The building is the property of the RAE—Roth Art Education—Trust, registered in Panama. The Rossis bought the top floor from that trust two years ago. The reason for that sale could have been the extensive repairs that you mention as causing difficulties between Sara Hirsch and Rinaldi. What do you think? Unless we can trace private contracts stipulating the terms of Sara's rental or usufruct, as the case may be, it's not much help. Presumably, it was the usual avoidance of death duties trick, though I wouldn't have thought a piece of property that size would warrant it.'

'No. And . . .'

'And?'

'Death duties payable by whom? Who was the heir? I'm sure Sara Hirsch must have expected to inherit something and didn't. She ended up in a psychiatric ward twice, once after her mother's death and again about two years later. If I can find out what happened to Jacob Roth and when . . . and he must be buried somewhere, for goodness' sake.'

'If he's really dead. Documents of the property have his date of birth as 1913. He could be still alive, you know. I'll have that checked out in England, too,' decided the prosecutor.

'Rinaldi, though . . .'

'You want to arrest him, I know, but we don't know what he's up to. Let's give him enough rope to hang himself. An incriminating phone call—'

'He's too clever for that. He won't make a move.'

'I'm afraid you're probably right, that Falaschi and Giusti in their separate cells are our only hope. I'll interrogate them tomorrow morning in the presence of a legal aid lawyer and let's hope they stick to the story they told you.'

'And if you find they already have a lawyer? Rinaldi will see to that and do it using a mobile phone.'

'Then there's nothing I can do. What about you? What's your next move?'

'There's nothing I can do either except try and understand . . . Would you mind if I sent to your office for the photograph album that was in the safe—and the few photos we took from the flat as well?'

'You needn't send anyone. I'll see they get to you the minute I get back. By the way, there hasn't been time to mention it until now but I did telephone the Rossi parents and they had nothing but praise for you. I'm sorry if I caused you to worry needlessly.'

'You did right to warn me. Given your experience.'

'You have your own experience, you don't need mine.' He pressed the marshal's arm. 'Follow your instinct. You have no better friend. By the way, did you really have Umberto D'Ancona's name?'

'No, no . . .'

'Ha!'

The marshal watched him get in his car and drive off. He stood still a moment, staring towards the exit, feeling for his car keys and his dark glasses. 'I'll find them,' he muttered, 'I'll find both of them. Sara's brother, if he's real, and Jacob Roth.' Glasses first. It was fairly shady in the cloister, where a fountain trickled, and the vaulted, stone-flagged passage leading out of it was dark. Beyond that, framed by the arched entrance, the rainwashed air in Via Borgo Ognissanti was dazzling under a clean, burning sun.

'Don't interrupt me unless you have to.' As if Lorenzini ever did. He was the sort we all take for granted until they are sick or on holiday and life erupts into a thousand pimples of irritation. He closed the door quietly as he left the office and the marshal settled down to open the big photograph album. It wasn't dusty. It had been preserved with great care inside a brown velvet bag with a drawstring. The earliest photographs dated from the end of the last century, formal groups of ladies in high lace collars and piles of hair. The album probably wasn't as old as those first pictures, which were mounted on thick board not at all adapted to the diagonal slits meant to hold them in place so that they were loose under their protective page of tissue. On the base of the mounting board was the name of the photographer, written diagonally in elaborate script difficult to make out, perhaps because the name was foreign. *Praha* was printed clearly. Prague, he supposed. Some pictures of individual ladies and of married couples had props, perhaps a marble column or archway, or a backcloth of a garden or country scene. Portraits of soldiers, seated rigidly holding one glove or standing in dress uniforms holding swords. What looked like an engagement photograph. The young man in uniform, staring straight at the camera, she looking up at him, leaning on his arm. The same couple in wedding clothes, this one mounted, loose in the page, the same Prague photographer, 1919. Then there was another wedding scene, this one with bridesmaids seated cross-legged at the front holding enormous bunches of flowers. There was no date but this was later, the marshal thought, probably the twenties, judging by the shining headbands low on the women's foreheads, the narrow frock and pointed shoes of the bride. The pictures fitted into the slots now and were a little less formal. No more marble columns or painted trees. Barefooted children sat on fur-draped stools, girls and boys alike in dresses and loose curls, their names and ages added in sepia copperplate below.

'Ruth, aged five. 1931.'

There she was, Sara Hirsch's mother in a white sailor suit, a loose satin bow in her long dark hair. Another with a man and a woman in a park—real, not studio scenery. He turned back a page or two and found the same couple, the woman holding a baby wrapped in a long shawl. He looked more closely. They were in a doorway and the narrow strip of window to their right had the beginning of a name on it of which only the *H* was visible.

Further on, he identified the same couple, a little more mature now, no doubt photographed in honour of some anniversary, she in a big carved chair, he standing behind her in a tight suit and stiff rounded collar. Sara's grandparents. The last part of the big album was empty. The world had stopped in 1939 for them. Sara's mother, Ruth, had brought this—the seven-branched candelabra, the prayer shawl, the

Talmud, and the rest, her history, her inheritance—to Florence, where her parents had contacts, where they thought she would be safe. A little girl carrying a great burden. The marshal had no doubt that Samuel Roth in Sdrucciolo de' Pitti was the contact. And Jacob Roth, the son who was so clever . . .

'I'm willing to bet that he was Sara's father!' said the marshal. 'So now, where's *that* photograph? I'd swear young Lisa Rossi said—' He was lifting the receiver when Lorenzini knocked and came in. 'What is it?'

'Someone to see you. It won't take a minute. It's not that—'

'No, no. It's all right. Send him in.' Because he was sure of his ground, could hold the entire picture in his head. No amount of talking could disturb him now.

'It's a she.'

'What?' But Lorenzini had withdrawn.

Dori appeared.

'No . . . !'

'Yes! I've done it and here's the ring to prove it. Registry office, of course.' She looked wonderful. She had always been beautiful but now there was a difference. Perhaps it was because she was dressed more discreetly, perhaps because she was living a more regular life. The pregnancy still didn't show but then she was so very tall and slender. 'I can see you're busy.'

'That's all right. Sit down for a minute.'

'Okay.' She sat. 'What's that? Your family album?'

'No, somebody else's.'

'Hm. That reminds me: You lied to me about Mario's mother. She's dead.'

'I know. Sorry . . .'

'It's all right. You're a good man. You've been to see Enkeleda in the hospital a couple of times, haven't you?'

'She told you? She's herself again?'

'You're kidding. They say she has a mental age of about five and is likely to stay that way. That woman in the other bed told me you'd been, the one with her skull all stitched up—Christ!'

'I know . . .'

'Anyway, they're trying to get her moved to some place where they'll teach her to walk. She seems happy enough. That bastard Lek . . .'

'Yes, well, don't forget your friend, his cousin Ilir, who wasn't averse to that sort of work himself with girls who didn't play ball.'

'Ilir's all right. I'd best be going, leave you to your family album. Thanks again, Marshal.'

'Your testimony's all the thanks I need.'

'And thanks for going to see Enkeleda, as well. Poor little bugger.'

'She's had bad luck.'

'Yeah, right. She was born female.'

Enkeleda . . . When Dori had gone, the marshal thought about that broken little body as he dialled the Rossis' number. Even if she learned to walk, what then? Where would she walk to?

'Signora Rossi? Marshal Guarnaccia here, good evening, good evening. I wonder if I could have a quick word with your little girl—no, no, just something she told me that I'd like to check on—and, Signora—if you wouldn't mind leaving her alone while she's talking. She feels she was in Signora

Hirsch's confidence and I'm trying to respect that—no, I don't think she knows anything dangerous, besides which she's very discreet . . . thank you. Lisa? Lisa, do you remember telling me about the secret photographs in the safe? No, I'm sure you haven't and neither have I. Just tell me again: There was a photo that Signora Hirsch said was of her mum and dad. Can you tell me any more about it? For instance, did it look like it was taken in a photographer's studio or a house or outdoors? What? It was? You're sure of that—she told you so? I can imagine, yes, a very long time ago. And was anybody else in the picture? Just the two of them—how old did you think they were? Try and tell me what they looked like. I see. All right, Lisa. Now, try and remember: Did she ever show you a photo of her brother, or even say she had one of him? No. And the secret picture was the one of her mum and dad? And the flowers, the picture of the flowers. Thank you, Lisa, you've been a big help. Yes, it's very important . . . and still a secret for the moment, yes. You mustn't worry about that because I've asked your mum not to ask you. When it's all over we'll both tell her. Put her back on the line . . . Signora, thank you for your help—oh, you did. Yes, it's true. Two men have been arrested. You've heard already . . . the seven-thirty news? Is it as late as that?'

He mustn't be late for supper again. Nevertheless, he sat a moment, taking in what Lisa had told him.

'He looked old—I mean grown-up. All the grown-ups look kind of old and sad in those brown pictures, and he had sad clothes on, a really gloomy suit and a hat. He was long and thin and dark but she was only a little girl. She was only up to his shoulder and she had plaits.'

A little girl. Sent alone with her past in a suitcase to the place that they thought was safe. Where the photograph was taken.

'*She told me. You could even see the stuff in the window behind them. It was right here in Sdrucciolo de' Pitti.*'

Yes, of course. He had said it before and he was still convinced of it. Despite Prague, despite London, he knew that this was a Florentine story and the important elements were all right here. '*Right here in Sdrucciolo de' Pitti*' . . .

Rinaldi, now, he was as guilty as hell, but guilty of what exactly? He said he'd paid the porters for nothing, that instead of what he wanted he got a dead body, a murder investigation on his doorstep.

The marshal scribbled a list on the left-hand side of a sheet of paper from his drawer.

Photo of mum and dad in Sdrucciolo de' Pitti.

Photo of flowers

Video?

Little Lisa hadn't seen a video in the safe but if all the videos were gone, then . . .

He hadn't paid them for nothing. These things were gone.

'No, no,' said the marshal aloud. Sara Hirsch was frightened but she wasn't stupid and whatever this business was about, it had occupied her whole life. They had already been in her house. She wouldn't have taken risks after such a warning.

'*Talk with your lawyer and tell him what I've told you.*'

'*I will. . . I intend to defend my rights.*'

Her lawyer. He had to find her lawyer. Any trace of him was gone from the flat so Rinaldi had achieved that, at least. If Jacob Roth was her father, then she would have gone to the same lawyer, this Umberto D'Ancona. If he was her father . . .

On the right-hand side of his sheet of paper he scribbled a few more things, copying them from the few documents in the Hirsch file. Jacob Roth's date of birth taken from the Land Registry. Sara's date of birth and her mother's from their baptismal certificates. The purchase of the building in Sdrucciolo de' Pitti. These few facts, and they were very few, had to fit together. If they did, then they would show a gap. An empty space which, if he could define its edges, would tell him what he should be looking for.

Jacob Roth was born in 1913 in Great Britain.

Ruth Hirsch was born in 1926 in Czechoslovakia

In the photograph Lisa had seen, Ruth was a child in plaits, Jacob, would have been thirteen years older, a man in suit and hat. But Ruth grew. Those apartments, he knew, had only two bedrooms. But there was a war on, people had to manage. In 1943 Ruth was pregnant. Was it love, proximity, marriage? Not marriage or why the convent? Jacob had a foreign passport and could have taken her away before the Occupation. Did he himself leave? Where was he that he survived the war when Ruth was hidden in a convent and his parents were deported and killed?

It always came back to the same question. Where was Jacob Roth? Where was he then, where did he die, where was he buried? Rinaldi hadn't much liked telling them anything at all about the man and must have known a great deal more than he told. No knowing, of course, if what he did tell was true.

'Just a minute! Rinaldi . . .' He scribbled a note about Rinaldi's taking over the business.

The door opened and Lorenzini looked in. 'Did you call?'

'No, no . . . I mean—nothing. I was just thinking aloud. Sorry.'

'That's okay. I was coming in anyway. Prosecutor sent this over. Further autopsy report on Sara Hirsch. And there was a phone call from the hospital about the Albanian girl. They said you'd asked to be kept informed.'

'How is she?'

'They've operated again. Condition's stable. I suppose that's not saying much in her case, is it?'

'No. No, it's not.'

'You could almost wish . . . anyway, and there's a young man waiting out here to see you.'

'I suppose . . .?'

'Has to be you.' By this time, Lorenzini had accumulated quite a little 'clientele' for himself but people didn't accept substitutes in every case. The marshal frowned and looked at the sheet of paper in front of him. Two or three scribbled lines, a few dates. The great investigator. He'd have been ashamed to let the prosecutor, or even Lorenzini, see them. Lorenzini was brighter, more on the ball, younger. Well . . . pride never solved a case.

'All right, you can send him in—come here a minute first. Just be taking a look at these dates, will you? Those two men we arrested this morning . . .'

'Falaschi and Giusti?'

'Right. This antique dealer, Rinaldi, the man they work for, do you know much about him?'

'I know him. See him occasionally about the monthly list of stolen goods.'

'What do you think of him? Slippery?'

'I wouldn't say that, no. Not honest, either. The complete opposite of the chap on the corner of Piazza San Felice who does his own restoration work, has a passion for it. Rinaldi's

passion, I'd say, was for clever dealing. And I don't think he
needs to be slippery, as you put it. I've had my suspicions of
him over the years but never been in a position to move
against him and he knows it. He'd laugh in our faces.'

'I'm sure he would. The point is . . . just look through these
dates from the Hirsch case, will you? Rinaldi says he took over
the shop after the war and I'm trying to make sense of it and
I can't. I don't know what it is but . . . everybody's Jewish in
this story except for him, that's one thing. Take the whole
file and come back to me when I've seen this man.'

'I'll send him in.'

Proximity, love, marriage . . . whichever it was, the picture
he'd never seen was the one most present in the marshal's head.
The girl with pigtails standing next to the young man in a suit.
Proximity, love, marriage . . . pregnant at eighteen in a foreign
country, running from a war, prejudice, and persecution.

'Mama!'

That was Enkeleda's voice. They had operated again.
Another child . . .

A young man had come in quietly and was standing in
front of the desk. The face was familiar, blue eyes . . . the
recollection pleasant, but he couldn't quite place . . .

'I don't suppose you remember me. We met at L'Uliveto
recently. I work in the garden there.' He ran a hand through
floppy blond hair, hesitating, a bit shy. He looked excep-
tionally tall in this small room. The marshal had seen him
before but outdoors—

'Of course. The poor relation—I beg your pardon. I didn't
mean—'

'Oh, don't worry. After all, I was the one to tell you that's
what I was. I'm the same myself. Never forget a face but then

when I see somebody in a different setting I have trouble remembering who they are. Jim's the name. And I suppose even now you know who I am you're surprised to see me. Well, do you mind if I sit down? I think it's time we had that little talk.'

Oh, Lord . . . he'd better straighten this out right away. With the best will in the world, he couldn't afford to waste time today.

'Look, it's very kind of you to say that Sir Christopher thinks well of me—and I'm not disbelieving you either because it does seem that way. You're not the first to say it, though I can't imagine why it should be. He hardly knows me. And I understand that these are hard times for young people trying to get work. But I'm in no position to help you. I'm sorry . . .'

'Help me? I think you must have misunderstood me. What I'm worried about is our little robbery. You see'—Jim leaned forward and looked earnestly at the marshal in a way that held him almost hypnotised—'*I* think, and the *head gardener* thinks, that it was faked. You know, an inside job, so when there's a more serious robbery, it will point suspicion at somebody who could have let them in, like at the housekeeper.'

'But I've already told you that no one ever suspected her.'

'I passed that on to her but you know what happened last time: The current "Giorgio" *and* the butler went, pushed out by the powers that be, even though you people didn't suspect them either. Not a scrap of evidence. But the housekeeper says there's more to it this time. She says that with the DNA testing they can do nowadays—'

'She's talking nonsense.'

'Do you think so? I suppose she might be, but as I said the other day, she'll leave for her holidays in August and she's talking about moving in with her sister. We think Sir Christopher's dying, and once he's gone—well, you know what I mean, you're dealing with the case, but that doesn't alter the fact that if there is a big robbery there's still Giorgio who can be blamed and at the same time protected, so he'll keep quiet, or say what he's told to say. You understand me?'

'I . . . no. Giorgio's the boy from Kosovo who's cataloguing the library or something, is that right?'

'The collection. Theoretically, but his lips will be sealed on that subject, too. Yes, the boy from Kosovo. The last in a long line of boys.'

'I'd gathered that he was—though, surely, Sir Christopher, in his condition—'

'Oh, no. He just likes to have them around. A lot of them were pretty much saved from the streets, illegal immigrants, Italian kids with a bit of a record, you know . . . Just a bit of self-indulgent kindness on his part, really, and in this case he's on to a good thing. Giorgio speaks perfect Italian and good Russian and he's brainy. A medical student. He's willing to turn his hand to anything he's asked to do as well as the cataloguing and they pay him a pittance.'

'I follow you. He must be unhappy away from his home, though. He's very young.' Through the doorway, a weeping boy and Porteous's hand massaging . . .

'Unhappy? Away from Kosovo? An illegal immigrant rescued from the streets by a fancy lawyer? And now that he feels threatened because of the great hairbrush robbery, the same lawyer will be kindly offering to protect him.'

'I see. But the last big robbery? You told me the butler went. Surely, Sir Christopher—'

'Not Sir Christopher. Never Sir Christopher. It's the others, led by Porteous. They poison his mind, accuse whomever they want to be rid of. People who've been there too long, know too much. They'll be glad if the housekeeper goes now. She was born at the villa, you know. She and Sir Christopher are the same age exactly. Her mother was housekeeper to Sir Christopher's parents so she knows all about *that* story.' The young man, still leaning forward in his chair, just as he had in the garden, lowered his voice almost to a whisper. 'It seems James Wrothesly was a terror with the ladies and his *wife* caught him in flagrante in her garden when she came back a day early from a visit to England. She had this marble plaque put on the very spot and never went in there again. The staff all adored her, especially the gardeners. They still talk about her and keep her garden the way she liked it as though she were still alive.'

'Sir Christopher himself told me that. I saw the plaque, too.' The marshal glanced at his watch. He mustn't be late again and he still wanted to talk to Lorenzini, but the low, confidential tone and the image of a garden and a sad, dying man—

'That reminds me: The other day, when I wasn't allowed to see Sir Christopher, I did hear his voice beyond a door and I must say it crossed my mind that he might have had a drop too much. A bit slurred. Does he drink?'

'A glass of wine with his meals, delivered now by young Giorgio-whose-lips-are-sealed. Sir Christopher's bed's been moved to his mother's old sitting room on the ground floor since he got weaker, with Giorgio in the room next door so he's never alone. And he doesn't have a chat with the gardeners anymore as he's done every day of his adult life—even though he's always parked out on the dining terrace overlooking his mother's garden where we could easily go to him. We can see him from the kitchen garden in front of the lemon house. I've waved to him once or twice but he never waves back. It's not like him. The garden was always his first thought in the mornings.'

What on earth was the point of all this? The marshal stared hard, his big, slightly bulging eyes willing the young man to come to the point, if any. To no effect.

'Anyway, in a day or two it'll be August and we've been told to clean out the lemon house—of course, this is a dead period in the garden. The head gardener leaves for his holidays on the first . . . But you know about the big robbery so you can understand why I'm worried. Even the porter's being allowed to go away and I'm to stay in the lodge.'

'I see. Well, yes, it is a worry. Big houses are very much at risk in August but you can't take responsibility for that great place. You've said yourself that Sir Christopher hardly knows you exist.'

'I know. I just think he's a good man—kind of innocent, childlike in a way—and it pisses me off—sorry—that he should be betrayed. He doesn't deserve that.'

'You think he's being betrayed?'

'We know he is, and after all he's done for them. Porteous was a "Giorgio" too, you know, taken in off the streets, for all the airs he gives himself now.'

'You said the other day that Sir Christopher wouldn't recognise you if he saw you. So, your bothering to come here is . . .' What was it? The marshal searched for words and found none.

'Quixotic? That's what you're thinking, isn't it? When I think something's not right I speak up. I've got nothing to lose. They won't chuck me out as long as Sir Christopher's alive and they'll not have me back when he's gone, so what the hell.'

'You're not—I appreciate you'll be pretty much alone up there in the porter's lodge at night—you're not . . . afraid? I mean, afraid for your own safety?' It had suddenly occurred to the marshal that he didn't want a repeat performance of the Hirsch case, caused by his not paying enough attention. He was relieved when the young man laughed at the idea.

'I don't matter enough. I'm about as important as a slug in the garden—less important. Sir Christopher worries a lot about slugs. We've been known to have a half hour conference on the relative merits of pellets versus eggshells! You know . . . that day you came up, the day after he'd been taken ill? We've never seen him since. Giorgio says he can't walk at all now.'

'I see. Well, I'll report what you've told me to my commanding officer—and don't worry, the possibility of a bigger robbery is something he's mentioned himself. He's also a great admirer of the villa and its garden. We'll keep an eye on the place during August.'

'Thanks. Well, I'd better be getting back.' At the door he turned back to say, 'D'you mind if I ask you a question? I apologise in advance if it's indiscreet and you can't answer. We were talking about it when we started on the lemon house this morning so when I said I was coming to see you . . . Everybody wants to know, including me, and I don't think you can ever believe more than half of what you read in the papers. First there was this big story saying Sara Hirsch had her throat slashed and then half a paragraph saying it was a heart attack. Which is true? D'you mind my asking?'

'Not at all. The heart attack is true as the article said.'

'Thanks. I'm afraid the others will be disappointed—not out of any ill will to the poor woman, only because it would have been more exciting. Bye.'

He closed the door quietly behind him. The marshal murmured to himself, 'Something to talk about besides greenflies . . .' Poor Sara. The disinherited and the super-inherited. Oh well, he was gradually getting a hold on the day-to-day problems of a rich man if nothing else. Slugs . . . !

'Lorenzini!' The door opened as he called.

'I was just coming. There's something wrong with these dates.' Lorenzini plonked the Hirsch file back on the desk

'They're all correct. I've put nothing down on that list that's not documented. I've left out anything that's suppo-sition or that depends on Rinaldi's word alone.'

'That's good—as far as Rinaldi's concerned, at any rate. Not really true, though, is it? I mean, this note here says Rinaldi took over the antique business just after the war. Now, we can check, of course, because it'll be on his licence, and he knows we can check, but that's where your dates are a bit unconvincing.'

'There. I knew I was doing right to ask you.'

'You could have worked it out for yourself. You've got his date of birth on this rough copy of his statement. 'After the war' is a bit vague, admittedly, but even if we make it 1950 when Jacob Roth retired from business and Rinaldi took over, you've got Roth retiring at something like thirty-seven and Rinaldi in charge at nineteen. I'm not saying it's impossible but it's a bit unusual, wouldn't you say?'

'That's funny . . . I could have sworn I said the same thing to myself a while ago—but I'm probably imagining it with hindsight. Retired at thirty-seven, eh . . . ? Must have made a packet.'

'People did during the war.'

'Some people.'

'Yes. It's late, did you know?'

'Oh, Lord . . . Teresa will never speak to me again. Have you done the Daily Orders?'

'There. Just need your signature. I've got a wife, too, you know.'

The phone rang. Teresa.

'Am I to put the pasta on or not?'

'Yes—no. Have the boys had supper? Well then, eat with them. Sorry. I still need to talk to Captain Maestrangelo. I'm going to ring him now. No, no, because I might have to go over there. You know he will, he never leaves his office before nine-thirty or ten. You're right, he should . . .'

It was quiet over at Borgo Ognissanti Headquarters. As the marshal climbed the stone staircase someone came through the glass doors of the Operations Room, letting out the low buzz of a peaceful beehive. The doors swung shut and all was silence again. Upstairs, he walked alone along the polished red corridor. Through the windows on his left he could see, across the darkened cloister, a recreation room lit up and four lads in white T-shirts playing table tennis. Surely, even at this hour, it was too hot for all that bounding about. He stopped by a tall rubber plant and knocked on a pale oak door set in a stone arch. And well might the captain inhabit a monk's cell. It niggled him a bit when Teresa said he was good-looking but apart from that she was right about him. He'd end up a general, but he should enjoy himself a bit, smile now and again. Even the prosecutor had touched on the subject.

'Come in.' He wasn't smiling now. He was there, though, wasn't he? He was always there when he was needed. Solid as a rock, careful, serious, a good man. 'Ah, Guarnaccia . . . I was just thinking about you.' And for some unknown reason, his dark face lightened for the briefest moment like the sun breaking through banks of cloud and just for a second he smiled.

The marshal was still sitting there, hands planted on his knees, waiting for Maestrangelo to put the world right for him. Probably he shouldn't be taking up the captain's time like this but you can't see what people are really saying over the phone.

'I think you might be being overly scrupulous, Guarnaccia.'

'Do you? Perhaps I thought so, too, but I thought it best to tell you. Sir Christopher's an important foreign resident. If that young man's right and there is a robbery in August when we've just been up there for those knickknacks, and after this young man's warned us, too . . . What I mean is, if somebody's trying to pull the wool over Sir Christopher's eyes in some way . . .'

'They're doing it to us, too?'

'Well, yes. I must say I found the whole story a bit odd.'

'And you didn't like that man Porteous.'

'No, no . . . I'm not saying that. It's not a question of . . . No, you're right. I didn't. Anyway, that's one side of the thing. The other is that I feel . . . this Hirsch case—'

'Yes, I know the prosecutor's very pleased with the way you're handling that.'

'That's very kind of him but I don't think he realises that it was very bad that I didn't go round to see her before I did and I don't want to make the same mistake again.' The marshal rubbed at his face. He was tired and hungry. He shouldn't be here. What was the use?

'You surely don't imagine that popping round for a chat with the woman would have stopped whatever was going on?'

'No, of course not. I've said the same myself, no. Yes. It might have done. Rinaldi's in this. Maybe if he'd seen me going up there he might not have taken the risk. No, no . . . you're right. Only, I keep missing the boat or making the wrong decisions. That business with the Albanian girl, now, was very bad. If I'd—'

'If you'd done the right thing, whatever you imagine that was, the entire Albanian problem would have disappeared overnight, is that it? How is the girl?'

'They've operated again. Rinaldi hasn't called anybody?'

'Nobody. Nothing at all from the listening post, I'm afraid.'

'I thought as much. Has he been out?'

'No. Went back to the shop for a bit and then closed up. Our man saw him opening the shutters on the first floor. You'll be the first to know if he makes a move.'

'He's too clever for me.'

The captain sat back in his chair and looked hard at the marshal. 'The prosecutor doesn't think so, as I said.'

The marshal wanted to say, 'You shouldn't give the wrong idea about me, get up people's hopes. It's not right.' But he had too much respect for his commanding officer to openly contradict him. He frowned at the toe of his left shoe and said, 'He's going to interrogate Falaschi and Giusti, the two porters, tomorrow. I should think he'll be able to understand what's going on.'

'I thought you'd got the whole story out of them, that it was on Rinaldi's orders that they snatched the Hirsch woman's bag and got the keys copied, then went in there to frighten her.'

'Oh, yes. That, yes. They say he told them to frighten her into giving up the combination of the safe and they were to remove the contents, a file of documents with a label saying APT DOCS., her address book, and all videos they could find. There's an autopsy report on my desk that'll like as not provide a reconstruction of her accidental death at their hands . . .'

The captain waited a while and, when nothing more was forthcoming, said, 'I'm not sure I'm getting the point . . .'

'No, no . . . that's right,' the marshal said unhappily. 'It's all very well but what is the point? I mean, I do think that this morning those two told me all they had to tell. They're not bright, you see, and of course neither am I. So let's hope the prosecutor can make some sense of it all before . . .'

'Before?'

'Before whatever Sara Hirsch was threatening to mess up happens. I'll be too late again, you see. The secret's in the photographs. By God, I'd give a lot to see a photograph of Jacob Roth.' Detaching his morose gaze from the toe of his shoe he looked at the captain. He tried to concentrate but he couldn't get that picture out of his head. Not the picture of Jacob Roth, which he wanted to concentrate on, but the one that kept flashing in its place, that he couldn't fight

off. A small figure teetering on the verge of the motorway, stepping forward as she saw him, a trusting smile on her
face, into the path of a speeding car. Then that stomach-
tightening crunch. 'I've seen some terrible things in my time
but I don't mind telling you . . .' But he did mind, and he
couldn't tell. 'Have you found Lek Pictri?'

'Not yet but it won't be too difficult and I'm not even sure
I want to arrest him at this point. It won't help the girl and
if we leave him on the loose we have at least a chance of eventually getting to the bosses of this gang at national level.'

'That's true. She's become like a small child and no
mother near her . . .'

'You can't save everybody, Guarnaccia. The problem's too
big. And the worst of it is, every time something like this happens, racism increases a hundredfold. We've got law students
from Kosovo working as builder's mates, teachers scrubbing
floors, a displaced workforce doing all the dirty jobs we Italians don't want to do and they'll never hit the headlines.
They're invisible. People only know about theft and prostitution and episodes like the girl thrown out of the car. Let's
hope that sooner or later things will calm down over there.
For one thing, we've few enough men as it is, without having to police Albania as well. We have to pay extraordinar-
ily high salaries to get our men to go over there. Lord knows
where it's going to end. Guarnaccia, go home. Go home to
your wife and children. You're tired, that's all that's wrong
with you.'

So he plodded back down to the cloister, hearing only the
sound of his own breathing, his heavy steps on the stone staircase. He still hadn't got round to reading that autopsy report.
Tomorrow was another day . . .

'You're hungry, that's all that's wrong with you,' was Teresa's verdict. And that was certainly true. 'Shall I do you a slice of meat?'

'Just pasta.'

In the kitchen, showered and comfortable in T-shirt, ancient khaki trousers, and flip-flops, with a big bowl of pasta and a glass of red in front of him, Teresa chatting quietly as he ate, the world righted itself.

A one-edged cutting tool, possibly domestic, which has cut a flap of skin upwards almost as far as the left ear. Other small cuts under the left side of the jaw showing the probable angle at which the weapon was held by a right-handed person threatening the victim from behind. The flap effect due to the victim's sliding down through the attacker's grasp during the infarct, which caused collapse, followed at a short interval by death . . .

'Hello? Marshal Guarnaccia speaking. How are you, Signora? No, no . . . not at all. Tell me—oh, dear, dear, dear. These youngsters have no consideration—no, Signora, no! If anything had happened to him you'd have heard before this. Has he ever stayed out all night before or—no, well, I can tell you it happens fairly often. You'll find he's stayed overnight with some friend. You ring round his friends' houses, that's the best thing to do. He's a sensible lad and probably thought better of riding his moped home if he'd been celebrating a bit too much . . . good, good . . . passed with flying colours? Oh, Signora! Let him celebrate leaving school—is it?—it's him coming in? I'll ring off—and, Signora, don't let on you rang me. Congratulations!'

//

Followed at a short interval by death—

'Hello? Marshal Guarnaccia, Pitti Station. Mr. Prosecutor, good morning. I'm afraid I'm still reading the autopsy report.'

'That'll do any time. There's nothing in it you don't already know. I've just finished with Falaschi and Giusti.'

'And the lawyer?'

'Legal aid. Rinaldi hasn't coughed up for one, it seems. He's being very circumspect.'

'Yes . . .'

'That's not your view?'

'I just thought . . . well, it means he's not afraid of them. I thought that when I overheard them in his apartment. It was Falaschi, I think, who tried to threaten him—I suppose because he wasn't paying what he promised. It didn't bother him at all. I'm afraid they just don't know anything worth knowing. I got the impression they'd shifted some hot stuff for him but he couldn't care less.'

'Not being circumspect then? Just isn't bothered.'

'I'm afraid so. I talked to my second-in-command, Lorenzini, about him. His words were "He'd laugh in our faces." He reckoned we'd do well not to believe anything he says and I suppose he's right—'

'I'm sure he is. The trouble is, he's not saying much to believe or not believe, is he? Marshal? Marshal, are you there?'

'Yes. I have to find Jacob Roth and I was thinking . . .'

'Hello? Marshal?'

'Lawyers . . . excuse me, I'm looking in the phone book . . . Lawyers often go in families, don't they?'

'I'm sorry?'

'So the lawyer, Umberto D'Ancona, maybe had a son or a nephew and Sara Hirsch went to him . . . yes . . . here. Of course, the phone book's a bit out of date.'

'Not as much as the Land Registry. Have you found somebody?'

'Yes. An Umberto, too, so it's sure to be a relation. It's in Via Masaccio. I'll go over there right away if you'll excuse me. I'll telephone you the minute I get back.'

'Lorenzini! I need a driver. Look after things here. I have to go out.'

When they reached Via Masaccio on the other side of the city, the marshal, having deemed it appropriate to wear his uniform jacket, was miserably overheated. His driver—young, slim, and in shirtsleeves—double-parked and asked, 'Will you be long? Should I try for a parking space? I'd better stop in the shade at least.' He got no intelligible answer. The marshal got out, his eyes behind their sheltering sunglasses fixed on the town house of a sort common to this area. Iron railings enclosing laurel and oleander, not what you'd call a garden. Probably something bigger behind . . . U. D'ANCONA on the brass plate. He rang. A young woman, probably from the Philippines, opened up, took his name, let him in. In the entrance hall, dark, with fancy red, black, and white tiling, a short, dark young man, no doubt the maid's husband, looked out from a passageway on the right to check on him, then disappeared. The marshal was left waiting near an aspidistra in a huge majolica pot, and then shown into a room that seemed to contain more books than furniture but a lot of both. There were open French windows giving a faint breath of cool air though the dark green outer shutters were pulled almost closed against the heat.

A desk lamp was on. Behind the heavy desk in a big chair sat a small man. This was no son or nephew. This was the man himself. Great age had reduced his face to what seemed a skeletal form. His skin was bluish white where it was stretched over his temples and the bridge of his nose, and almost transparent except for the soft pale brown spots on his forehead.

He said, 'You'll excuse my not getting up,' and indicated a chair. 'I've been expecting you. I thought, to tell you the truth, that you might have come before this.'

'Thank you. I would have,' said the marshal, settling into a big, cool leather chair, 'but I was told that you were dead.'

'Not yet,' said the lawyer with a smile, 'not quite yet.' The smile faded. 'But poor Sara, now. Dead without really having lived. It's Sara you've come about, isn't it?'

'Yes, it's Sara,' the marshal said, 'and that's the impression I got of her, too, though I didn't know her at all well.'

'You didn't? I must say you surprise me. I understood you were a valued and trusted friend to our unfortunate Sara. You really do surprise me indeed.'

'No, no . . .' The marshal felt a bit embarrassed. He might have taken it as a compliment if he'd remembered to go and see her a bit sooner. If she weren't dead. 'I only met her the once. She came to me not long before she died and told me she felt . . . well . . . threatened. I'm afraid she didn't tell me much about her circumstances—in fact, nothing I could make any sense of at all. Sometimes you only realise when it's too late that if you'd trusted somebody they might have helped you. She did say, though, that she had a lawyer and I advised her to talk to him . . . to you. I thought that you, knowing more about her, would be able to judge . . .'

'Oh dear . . .' D'Ancona rested his head in his right hand for a moment in silence. He sighed and looked up at the marshal, a searching look; searching, perhaps, for the source of Sara Hirsch's absolute faith in this stranger. The marshal looked back at him, silent, troubled. At last the lawyer decided, 'You and I, marshal, should have met before this. Together . . . well, well . . . useless speculation.'

'Yes. I've thought about it a lot. As I said, I only met her once. She expected a lot of me, by the sound of it, but you could be wrong about her trusting me, unless it was with hindsight. That does happen. When it's too late we feel the goodwill, know we could have, should have spoken, trusted somebody more. Talking to you she maybe realised she could trust me but I'm here today because she didn't. I know nothing about her. I don't know why she died as she did, even though I've found the men responsible. I only know what was in two psychiatric reports, written by doctors she couldn't or wouldn't confide in, and what I found, or perhaps I should say didn't find, in her apartment.'

'I see.' The lawyer fell silent, thinking this over, looking at his hands, which rested now on the desk. They were pale, shiny, the joints a little deformed, perhaps by arthritis, large pale age spots on the backs.

So, was this going to be a repetition of his conversation with Sara Hirsch, though without the tears? Well, he would ask no questions. If the man wanted to talk, he'd talk, but the marshal had wasted enough time as it was.

'I can imagine,' the lawyer said at last, 'the difficulty Sara would have posed. She was afraid and she wanted your help, just as, when she lost her grip on life, on reality, she was afraid and needed psychiatric help, but she had a broader, more long-term agenda and so she wasn't open, frank, in either case.'

'And you? After all, she's dead now.'

'So whatever her agenda was I can tell you about it now? Yes. Yes . . . that's true as far as it goes and I can certainly unravel some of the mysteries of Sara's life for you.'

'Some.'

'I, too, Marshal, have an agenda, and a bigger, more global one than Sara's, though they touch at some points.'

He was going to be as secretive as Sara. He would yield a few facts with no reasons, the marshal could see it coming.

'Don't consider yourself unreasonably disappointed.'

The marshal wasn't having any of this. 'You said you expected me sooner and I told you I thought you were dead. I'm sorry to be blunt about this but you knew you weren't. You also knew that Sara Hirsch was. You knew she'd been to see me. Her death was in the papers as a murder story. Why didn't you come to see me?'

'A reasonable question. I waited, watched . . .'

'Murder investigations can't wait. After forty-eight hours they're cold.'

'But it wasn't, as I now understand it, a murder. Is that correct?'

'Legally, no. Morally—'

'Ah, morally . . . morally . . . there we are looking for what is good, true, rather than what is legally tenable. I can feel your resentment, your disapproval, even. You have a job to do, but I have mine and when you know what it is—and I will tell you—you'll understand me. First, though, we must think of you. I know from Sara that you realised at once how the threats directed against her had to do with her apartment.

You were right. The visits, the anonymous communication, were intended to frighten her into leaving. She had the usufruct of that apartment and the one below it, as had her mother before her, as long as she remained resident in it.'

'So if she left she lost her right to it?'

'Exactly. Also the income from the third-floor flat, whose tenant was paid off before the pressure on Sara began. She was in difficulty without that income but she had no direct control. The building belongs to a trust.'

'Was there a private contract, stipulating these terms, in her safe?'

'There was.'

The lawyer was hesitating but the marshal would not be stopped now.

'Was Jacob Roth Sara's father?'

'He was.'

'But he never married her mother.'

'No. He never married Ruth. Jacob had just gone to England on business in 1943 when the Germans occupied Florence. His father, Samuel, naturally afraid for his son's future, advised him to stay there. He left Sara's mother, Ruth, whose parents had sent her to the Roths in Florence for safety, already pregnant. She had told nobody. Who could she tell? Jacob was gone. Her parents had been taken away in Prague. Her survival depended on the Roths and they were now at risk from the occupying army. They saved her. They had her taken into a convent and baptised. They arranged an Italian passport for her through the Jewish community here. I myself had a hand in that. I was involved with the Delasem, in Via de' Rustici, an organisation set up to help Jewish immigrants. In the shelter of the convent the child, Ruth, gave birth to a child, Sara. The Roths saved what they could: their son, Sara, Sara's heritage—two valuable paintings which had arrived rolled up in her suitcase with some mementos of her family history—and the few pictures and objects of value they owned themselves, which we buried here in the garden at the back of my house. Having saved what they could, these good people were arrested by the gestapo and sent to Fossoli, from where Italian Jews were deported to Auschwitz.'

'And you? You were here then?'

'I was here. They came into this house as they did the others. There were sufficient objects of value to satisfy the exigencies of the officer in charge. They didn't touch my wife. I was very fortunate.'

'But . . .'

'But?'

'I've heard some of this already from the sisters in the convent, but what I can't understand is why, after the 1938 race laws, any Jews who, like you, could afford to, didn't flee.'

'Marshal, we are Italians, you and I. We both know, through the jobs we do, that passing laws is one thing, enforcing them another. Nobody ever believed those laws were anything other than a sop to Hitler or that they would be seriously applied. And remember, too, that Italian Jews are first and foremost Italians. It's not because we've been here for six centuries, which you could say of Jews in many other countries, but because Italy has only existed, politically speaking, for one and a half centuries, and we were instrumental in its creation. Being merchants, travelling freely and frequently, having contacts throughout the country and throughout Europe, who better to act as lines of communication, who more useful in bringing about the Risorgimento? And didn't we then fight for our country in the First World War?'

'I hadn't thought . . . I suppose I've never had occasion to give it much thought. Even so, I know that in the thirties, what was happening in northern Europe was known here, through those same lines of communication. People like Ruth Hirsch, the people you helped through this organisation . . . why here? This was a country under Fascist rule.'

'And one of the other things you've never had occasion to consider is that there were Jews here who supported the Fascist regime. That surprises you? It's true. They considered themselves perfectly safe and many of them were so. A lot of refugees, on the other hand, made this an intermediate stop, realised some of their assets, particularly those with artworks to sell, and moved on—to America if they could afford it.'

Why was it difficult to ask? Anyway it *was* difficult, and knowing the answer he was going to get didn't make it any easier. D'Ancona evidently understood.

'You didn't know Jacob Roth. He was a complicated man, a disappointed man, but he was not all bad.'

'None of us are that. He made a fortune during the war.' Not a question but a statement without a trace of expression in his voice or on his face.

'He made a fortune, yes. Quite a substantial fortune. Those who fled took what they could carry. Jacob's clients came, like little Ruth, with paintings rolled up in their suitcases. They sold them to Jacob and went on their way.'

'He made a fortune buying valuable paintings at low prices from fleeing Jews and presumably sold them at a huge profit after the war?'

'In any war there are those who make great profits, Marshal.'

'But he was a Jew!'

'And so must be among the righteous? And are all Germans wicked?'

'No, no . . . that would be ridiculous. There are good and bad people everywhere. No . . .'

'But it's easier for you to conceive of innocent Germans than of guilty Jews?'

'I . . . yes. If you mean am I shocked by what Jacob Roth did, yes.'

'Then, Marshal, you are a racist. Look, to be a victim is a tragic misfortune: it is not a virtue, a virtue which by some magical form of osmosis becomes an attribute of every member of the race. This is central to what I am trying to do. That is, it's my greatest problem. The emotional immaturity which will not allow Jacob Roth's sins to be as normal as any other man's. For me, Jacob Roth did a great wrong. For you, a Jew did a great wrong. We cannot easily understand each other. Consequently, I shall tell you only what is relevant to Sara's death whilst assuring you that Jacob did nothing that was illegal.'

The lawyer paused and bent to reach into the desk cupboard to his right. He seemed to be struggling.

'Can I help you?'

'No. It's just a bit cumbersome.' He managed to lift an oblong cardboard box onto the desk. 'These are the things Sara's attackers were looking for. The things you are looking for, too, I think. She brought them here for safekeeping, according to her, on your advice.'

'On my advice . . . Well, she did right. It's what I would have advised had I known then that they existed.'

'She really told you nothing? You might help me with the lid. It's close fitting . . . save my standing . . . thank you. Perhaps you're surprised to find the contents so unexciting.'

'No, no. I knew something about these things from a little girl, a neighbour's child. She was shown some photographs that she described to me.'

'Here.'

Then the marshal really was surprised. He was holding the photograph he had so wanted to see, the one of Sara's parents, Jacob and a very young Ruth. It was just as the child had described it, though she hadn't noticed, looking at the old-fashioned clothes and the mournful browns of the faded print, that Jacob was not only tall but very good-looking. Ruth, was thin and gawky, though her big dark eyes and fine features promised beauty. What was unexpected was that whereas he had thought of a snapshot preserved in a bit of tissue or an envelope, this photograph was an enlargement. It was framed, too, in a Florentine frame of the sort sold in Piazza Pitti. There was no mistaking that marbling.

'She didn't always keep this hidden, I see.'

'No, indeed. Ruth always kept that photograph in her drawing room. It was the only one of them together, you see. Sara hid it because of recent events. The ones in the envelope were always in the safe for obvious reasons.'

It was a stiff card envelope and large black-and-white photos carefully wrapped in tissue paper.

'The flowers.'

It was D'Ancona who was surprised now. 'She showed someone these pictures? Are you sure?'

'Quite sure, yes. To the same little girl. Everybody confides in someone, and a stranger, or at least a person not involved in our lives, is often the safest bet. Will you tell me about the flowers?'

'I think I must. As you say, we all confide in someone. But I must ask for your assurance that what I tell you goes no further.'

The marshal stared at him. 'I can't give you that. You know I can't.'

'But the men you arrested know nothing of this.'

'Or anything else. They did what they were told to do. By Rinaldi.'

'Ah, yes. Rinaldi.'

'You know him?'

'I knew him when he was a shop boy, working for Samuel and Naomi Roth. He has been very fortunate. The Roths befriended him when he was orphaned of his father during the war. He lived with his mother, who rented the first floor where I imagine he still lives. Jacob let him take over the business, said he had taste . . .'

'It was Rinaldi who told me you were dead. Does he know how Jacob made his money?'

'He knows something of Jacob's life but not that. He was a child in the thirties. Rinaldi is a problem and he certainly has something to answer for as regards Sara's distressing end, but if you will be patient with me I know we'll find a solution. Shall we first consider the painting? As I said before, Ruth arrived from Prague with two of them. They were her future. Her father trusted the Roths with them and the Roths in turn entrusted them to me before they were deported. They lay for some years, along with other pictures bought by Jacob and a few valuable pieces from the shop, in a safe buried in the garden here. When Jacob returned he took everything away. One of Ruth's paintings he sold for her then. A donation was later made to the convent which had sheltered Ruth and little Sara. The rest of the money was invested for their support.'

'Why didn't he marry her?'

'Don't be too quick to judge. Remember he knew nothing until he came home. He thought Ruth had been deported with his parents. He wasn't sure whether they were alive or dead. He came to me as his father's last letter had instructed him to do. Even I didn't know about Ruth's baby. When we first saw Sara she was about one. Jacob had become engaged to be married whilst he was away. What had happened with Ruth . . . they were young, they were thrown together. The war separated them. These things happened.'

The marshal couldn't accept this. 'No, no . . . Well, these things happen, I'll admit, but there was a child on one side and a fortune on the other, an ill-gotten fortune, too, whether he did anything illegal or not.'

'You are very pragmatic, but you are missing one vital piece of information. Ruth loved Jacob. She was in love with him until the day she died. He was a handsome young man, talented, tormented, complex. He fascinated her, body and soul, at that tender age and she never again met anyone who could replace him. I'm inclined to believe that happens more often than we care to think, to both women and men. Most people try to combat it with common sense, force themselves to accept a lesser relationship or maybe two or three or more. They don't "take". That's the only way I can, if not explain then describe it. If you add to that the circumstances, war, persecution, fear, loneliness, Ruth's isolation, trapped in a foreign country, a foreign religion, in motherhood . . .

What could ever happen to her afterwards of anything like a similar intensity? What could touch her? She had learned to love Jacob with what I can only call a purity that burned steadily and brightly in solitude, largely untended for a lifetime.'

'Largely . . .'

'Their relationship . . . did continue, yes. She lived on the crumbs from his table, if you like.'

The marshal frowned. The nature of love was another of those things he hadn't had much occasion to think about but he'd have felt more comfortable with something a bit cozier than what the lawyer was talking about. It reminded him too much of the lives of saints, their names long forgotten, recounted with bloodcurdling relish by the priest of his childhood. All that burning purity being offered up.

'Like he was some sort of god.'

'Oh, no. She knew his faults. They only seemed to bind her closer to him.'

'And what about him? I mean, while she was giving birth to his child he was piling up his fortune. So what was she for him?'

It had been a rhetorical question, really, since the man married somebody else, but the lawyer seemed to be giving it serious consideration. At last he said, 'His conscience, his truth. The man Ruth loved was the real Jacob Roth. He clung to that.'

The marshal looked carefully at the lawyer, thinking over what he'd said about how it happened to men and women. He was quite sure that D'Ancona had been in love with Ruth Hirsch and her pure burning flame for the whole of his life. Perhaps with both of them, with their story. After all, what could have happened since of equal intensity to this provincial lawyer? The only one left out of the story was Sara, who never lived. Sara, brought up on leavings to dream of greater things, who would have been satisfied with a sensible man and a couple of nice kids. Instead of which, blasted by war and greed, egoism and passion, she'd started life hidden in a convent with a lonely, frightened mother and ended it . . .

'May I ask what you are thinking that makes you frown so? You find my assessment of their relationship unconvincing?'

'No, no . . . I don't know anything about that, no. I was thinking that Sara died by accident and—oh, it's nonsense really but she never seems to have been important, does she? Not even important enough to have been murdered. Why did they want her out of the apartment?'

'I don't know but probably to sell it.'

'You said it was owned by a trust.'

'Set up by Jacob, yes.'

'Were you on the board of trustees?'

'Yes.'

'And Rinaldi?'

'Yes.'

'So he's an interested party.'

'I must ask you to be patient. When you know the full facts and can appreciate what I am trying to do I shall be able to help you.'

'I'm sorry. I'm here to listen to you, not interrogate you. It's just—well, what I said before—Sara never seems to have mattered.'

'She mattered to you. She told me that you were very kind to her and took her seriously. I have to confess to you that I didn't.'

'You didn't?'

'I'm sure you, too, must have had your doubts about whether these threats she talked about were real or imagined.'

The marshal was relieved. 'Yes. Yes, I did and I'd thought until now that it was because I didn't know her well enough to judge but if you say the same . . . I promised to go and see her and I left it too long. When I got there she was dead.'

'And you blame yourself.'

'Not exactly. I know that would be nonsense. It's just such a shame that she was never important enough. Some people can command attention for the most trivial thing while others . . .'

'Ah yes. That was the driving force behind everything Jacob did, do you know that? Some boys could study, but not a shopkeeper's son, some could choose their future, develop their talents but not a shopkeeper's son. Jacob had brains and skill. He wanted to paint but from the age of twelve he was working in the shop for his father. His parents had worked so hard and felt so proud of having created a thriving business, a secure future for their son. They could never have imagined the future that awaited them in Auschwitz or Jacob's future, that of a man so enriched by that same terror that he could practically give their little shop away. His intention was to make himself rich but, more than that, to belong to that class of people that treads on the rest, not to the class of people trodden on. He threw away his paints.'

'And might he really have been a great artist?'

'Might have been . . . I've never believed in "might have been", Marshal. Given the ferocity of Jacob's driving force he would have succeeded at whatever he chose to do—like Picasso, whose mother once said that had he been religious he would have become pope. But Jacob didn't use his force for art, he used it for himself, to make himself what he wanted to be in his own eyes and in the eyes of the world.'

'Yes, I can understand that. But could he paint?'

'Oh, he could paint. I have nothing here to show you—at least, nothing original. As a youngster he spent a lot of his spare time making copies from the great masters, as Florentine art students do. There was one in particular . . . I asked him to give it to me as a present. I was impressd by it. I still am. If you'd like to switch on the lights over there next to the French windows you can see for yourself.'

The marshal went, hat in hand, to the end of the over-crowded room. In the gloom he banged his hip on the corner of a table stacked with books and files. Just like the prosecutor's office, in which case there would likely be books piled on the floor too. Best tread carefully. The thin slash of brilliant light between the slightly open louvred doors only accentuated the dimness of the room.

'The switch on the left.'

The marshal looked at the painting and he, too, was impressed. *The Concert.*

'You know it—but, of course, being stationed at Pitti. You did say and I'd forgotten. You must know the galleries well.'

'No, no . . . Just a few pictures . . . This one I remember because there was a special exhibition for it when it was restored. I have to be at these events. But—the young one on the left, the one in the feathered hat—his face is blank.'

'Yes. If you look closely you'll see that the features are very faintly sketched. He left the faces until last, he said, because they were the most difficult part, and in the end he didn't finish that or anything else he was working on.'

'That's when he gave up?'

'Yes.'

'And did you hang this picture as some sort of reproach to Jacob?'

'I hadn't thought so but I suppose you could be right. Still, I was only about two and a half years older than he was, in my first years as a student of law. I was luckier than Jacob, you see. My parents had a little more money than his and ambitions for me that coincided with my own. I could hardly criticise him. I couldn't even understand him. I don't know if I ever did really understand, though, like we all do, I flattered myself that I was the only person in his life who came near to it, with the exception of Ruth. But then, she loved him.'

The marshal made his way back to the leather chair and hesitated, wondering whether to sit down again or whether it wouldn't be wiser to let the prosecutor talk to this man. He seemed to talk a lot but where were the facts, the facts about Sara's death? He was deciding to leave it to the prosecutor when he heard himself asking, 'That blank face . . . There's still one blank face in this family picture—I'm very grateful for your help, of course, but I'm wondering where the brother is. She talked about a brother. And where is Sara's other painting?'

The cages with their vertical iron bars were all empty. They stretched the opposite length of the courtroom from where the marshal stood at the press entrance looking for the prosecutor. He saw him at last to his right on the front row below the bench. He was very still, very quiet, which made him easier to spot since the lawyers were on their feet making a bit of a fuss about something. The hearing resumed. The marshal said to the official at the desk behind him, 'I thought that Mafia car-park trial was on today.'

'Next door.'

'Oh.' That would account for the empty cages.

'This is the joker who was allowed out of prison for a day, murdered a prostitute and set fire to her bed, then went back to his cell. The judge will adjourn after this witness. Should be a psychiatrist's report next but he's not here.'

'Thanks.' The marshal went in as soon as the court rose but just before he reached the prosecutor a plainclothesman got there first and engaged him in some complicated discourse in an undertone. The marshal stepped back and waited until it was over and the prosecutor turned to leave and saw him.

'Has something happened? How did you find me?'

'I rang your office.'

'He's adjourned till Monday. Let's go for a coffee.' The prosecutor's place at the long table was a miniature version of his office. He tipped the lot into his battered briefcase and pulled at the stock around his neck.

The marshal had told him most of it by the time they reached the bar across the broiling piazza.

'And did he tell you?'

'About the brother? There is a brother.'

'So he has the painting.'

'It's possible.'

'Two coffees! He could be behind the attack on Sara, then, if she wanted it back. What did he say about it?'

'Nothing really. He gave me this. He said now that Sara's dead it can serve no purpose.' The marshal produced a video-tape in its black cardboard sleeve from the pocket of his uniform jacket. 'He thought we ought to meet Jacob Roth.'

'Guarnaccia! You're not going to tell me he's not dead either?'

'No, no . . . He's dead. He left this for his daughter, Sara.'

'Come on. There's a video machine in the office next to mine—no, let me get this.'

They drank off the thick espresso in one swallow and pushed their way out through a horde of incoming tourists.

'Do you have your car?'

'Over there.'

'If you get there before me, it's the office to the left of mine.'

'My dear daughter, when you see this I will be gone, perhaps long gone. I shall give it to Umberto, who will keep it as a sort of insurance policy for you in case of difficulties. I fore-see no difficulties but most of what has happened to me in my life has been unforeseen.'

Jacob's face had become gaunt and his hair was white but he was recognizable in the photograph of Jacob as a younger man from the intensity of his dark gaze. He was seated in the very armchair that the marshal had occupied less than two hours ago.

'You know your name is not mentioned in my will. I owe you an explanation and you shall have it here. Your mother, my Ruth, never in her life wanted explanations, excuses, apologies. If I tried to give them she would place a finger over my lips and look deep into my eyes until she had qui-eted me. You have her eyes, Sara. The first time I saw you in that gloomy convent reception room, you looked at me with Ruth's solemn eyes in your baby's face. You seemed to be reproaching me for intruding on you and distracting your mother's attention. You hid your face in her hair at the sound of a man's voice and later you screamed when one of the nuns carried you away. Yesterday, as you left us, you had that same expression. I decided to prepare this message for you. I will tell you the truth about your painting, because it is yours and it will return to you and be a joy to you if you are married and financially secure, which I hope you will be, or a means of sustaining you if you are not.

'You know from your mother that she brought two paint-ings by Monet to us from Prague and that I sold one for her on my return to Florence. I settled some money on Ruth in addition to the proceeds of that sale and gave her the use of the second- and third-floor flats in Sdrucciolo de' Pitti so that she would have a home and a little income.

'Until then, those two paintings, and many others, had been hidden in Umberto's garden because of the Occupation. I took away a number of the paintings after the war and sold them. When I moved here with my young, ingenuous wife—the war to her had meant a shortage of food and stockings, girls instead of men working her father's land—she saw your painting. That was the first of a series of unforeseen disasters. She wasn't meant to, of course, but it was delivered with the rest of the things remaining with Umberto and she was there . . . Would it have made any difference if I had been ready with a story? That it was in safekeeping for a friend, anything? She said, "It's so lovely. They're my absolutely favourite flowers." She said, "Give it to me! Darling, let it be your wedding present to me, please!" I was afraid. I was a coward. I said yes. And she had it hung in the prettiest room in the house and loved it more than anything else in our home for the rest of her life. When I think of her life I think of light, serenity, and flowers. When I think of my own it is dark. Dark . . . a turmoil of nightmares just kept at bay. And not always kept at bay . . . Everything I did was an attempt to be part of that other world. I was bound to fail, I know that now. You have to be born into it, to be ignorant of anything else, to be like my wife.

'I told Ruth what had happened. I offered the price of the painting. I offered to sell another, more valuable one of my own for her. She refused. She didn't want money. She had lost her family in the camps, lost her home, lost everything but what she had carried here in a suitcase. She asked for nothing and she took nothing except what was necessary to secure your future. When I asked her why she hadn't told me she was pregnant before I left Florence to be stranded in England for the rest of the war, she answered me, "I was seventeen years old. Why didn't you ask?" She was proud, Sara, your mother. She loved me unconditionally. She never considered using you to persuade me into marriage, even though I was only engaged when I found her again. I think—no, I'm sure—that she knew from the start what my marriage was about. She knew, too, that I loved her and would never leave her. She was part of me. She was, in the end, the only part of me that survived. She and Umberto kept me alive.

'Well, your painting remained in my wife's room and it remained Ruth's property. Our decision was that it would return to her—or to you—on my wife's death. It was Ruth who died first, as you know. My wife survived her by only a few months. She left her favourite painting to our son. He paid the death duties on it from her estate. It was the one memento of happier times that she had clung to. Not because it was my wedding present to her but because I was able to assure her that it was not one of those . . . tainted ones, the ones that had made her despise me . . . How could I have told her it belonged to the woman I loved and to you, our daughter?'

Here Jacob interrupted. The direction of his glance changed and another voice murmured something in the background. Jacob looked to one side, said, 'Yes', and the screen filled with fuzzy white spots, then went blank.

'Damn!' The prosecutor got up and reached for the remote control. 'That can't be the end and it's obviously an amateur job. Let's hope it's not broken.'

It wasn't broken. Jacob's face reappeared. He was in a different chair, and the picture, which had been darkening as he talked, was now much brighter and clearer. Some leaves, tinged with rosy pink, were moving gently to the right and you could now distinguish the fine quality of Jacob's clothes, his long brown hands. Evidently, he'd moved out into the lawyer's garden, perhaps as the afternoon light faded in the big room.

There must have been a third person. Another voice said, 'That's fine. Don't touch anything. Give me a shout if there's a problem.' A young, cheerful voice that belonged to another world. Then a pause.

'Sara, the unforeseen . . .' He stopped a moment and closed his eyes, and when he went on they remained closed for the first sentence or two, as though he were unable to look at the camera, at an imaginary Sara. 'The unforeseen thing that happened to me . . . and to my wife is very hard for me to tell you. Even so, I am at the end of my life and the last thing that remains for me is to protect you by telling the whole truth and giving it into the safekeeping of Umberto in case you should need it.'

He coughed and murmured something, looking down. Someone gave him a glass of water from behind the camera. The marshal recognized the shiny, arthritic joints of the fingers, the age-spotted skin. Jacob sipped from the glass and, still holding it, forced himself to continue.

'Ten years after my marriage I received a letter from a man whose name doesn't matter. He is dead now. He had sold me a number of Impressionist paintings in the thirties for a very low price. Like your mother, he was fleeing from Nazi persecution. He and my father had dealt with each other for many years. He came back to me because he and his wife were old, sick, and penniless. I received him myself and took him to my wife's private room since she was absent and no servant would be likely to disturb us there. He was . . . agitated. When I offered him compensation—which he considered so insufficient as to offend him—he became more angry, angry and noisy. I was worried we would be overheard. I asked him to step out into the garden.

'"Afraid somebody might hear the truth about you? That's it, isn't it? Your parents died the worst of deaths but at least they didn't live to know how you stole from their trusted friends. How many of us were there? How many other desperate people did you cheat of their lives?"

'"I cheated no one. I paid. I paid for everything."

'"Paid a pittance! Paid an insult!"

'"Paid as much as I could afford at the time."

'"You'll pay the price of your actions yet! You remember that. You may not pay money but you'll pay, you'll rot! Under your fine clothes you are putrid!"

'"I have paid! My parents died in the camps. I was cheated out of my life in every possible way. I built another and you won't destroy it."

'"Give me what you owe me!"

'I gave him a cheque. It was for a large amount, for a credible amount . . .'

Did Umberto D'Ancona, behind the camera, say something they couldn't hear? Or just look at him?

'No . . . it wasn't the full amount, not even then when I had everything. It wasn't . . . I was afraid. How many others might appear out of the past?

'At any rate, this man had the satisfaction of not only making me pay him an acceptable sum—oh, I could see in his eyes that he knew I was still cheating—but also of seeing his bitter words become fact. My wife had returned and heard our raised voices. She had come out to look for me and had heard everything. My marriage ended that night. It was June 13th, my birthday. That's why she came back early. She didn't want me to dine alone on my birthday.

'If Umberto ever decides that you have need of this tape you will become the third person in this world to know the truth about me. Umberto always knew, your mother I told. She would have loved me with all the strength, all the fierceness of her generous spirit, no matter what I did. I think only women are capable of that kind of love and few even of them.'

Jacob reached out and unseen hands helped him to place the framed painting on his knees.

'This painting, Sara, is yours. Umberto tells me that we must now take a Polaroid photograph of it and me and today's newspaper, just like a kidnap victim. I suppose your painting is a kidnap victim. He also tells me that this has no validity in a court of law. It can only help protect you from any accusation of making a false claim. Umberto believes that I am doing it to ease my own conscience, that I should tell my son the truth now. I hope he is wrong in saying that my belief that Kista will do the right thing is an imaginative product of my cowardice. I think he will give you your painting when he receives my request after I'm dead. There is more of his mother in him than of me. I have no right to ask for your indulgence, Sara, but I must. The letter which my son will receive will tell him about Ruth, about you, and about the Monet. Unless you have need of this video, no one on this earth other than Umberto will ever know how I got the fortune which qualified me to marry into my wife's greater one. No one other than my . . . victims. We did everything possible to prevent Kista from knowing about our broken marriage. My wife always behaved impeccably. Her manners never failed her. Oh, Kista may have felt something of the truth, he must have, but he never saw any manifestation of it. The rest . . . my past is something I must protect him from. His mother suffered from it all her life. I feel it as some hereditary disease that I don't want my son to inherit. Sometimes he looks at me in a certain way, asks a question, and I think he suspects me, but he never insists. I know he doesn't love me. He belongs in her world and sees me as a stranger. I don't talk to him. What could I possibly say? I've heard it said that the degree of civilisation can be measured by the distance man puts between himself and his excrement. I believe that in the world's terms it is the distance between a rich man and the source of his wealth. A few generations and any stink will fade away.

'I hope that if you ever find it necessary to know this story, you will have something of your mother's strength and compassion, not for my sake but for your brother's. Try to love him. Loneliness is terrible . . . Loneliness . . .'

He sipped a little water. The hand that held the glass shook. A faint voice again off camera. Jacob shook his head and turned away. The screen went blank.

They waited but there was nothing more and the prosecutor pressed the rewind button. 'And he says he never let Sara see this?'

'No. When she went to him for help he told her what was on it but only the bit that concerned her—Jacob's admitting paternity—and her painting. He suggested she just tell her brother it existed.'

'So precipitating her death. Does he realise that?'

'Yes. Of course. But he said if he'd shown her the film the result would have been the same.'

'Not easily moved from his purpose, Umberto D'Ancona. Yet you think it's worth my talking to him?'

'Definitely, yes. It's not that I think you'll change his mind. What his organisation is doing is too important to risk and, as he says, it's too late to help Sara.'

'And have they succeeded in helping others?'

'Oh, yes. Quite a few. He told me about one French couple living out their last years in dire poverty and the woman suffering from cancer. One of their paintings that had been stolen by the SS was spotted by a member of the organisation in an exhibition in Paris. Of course, I'm talking about stolen paintings now, different from Jacob's thing, but it's still quite a business to get them back, especially if they've changed hands a few times, and the last buyer loses out.'

'Hm. They must have known of the dubious provenance.'

'It's still not easy.'

'No. And D'Ancona's right, of course. If Jacob Roth's story gets splashed all over the papers—not just his ill-gotten gains, but Ruth's story and poor Sara's death—it will get a lot harder. A gift to the racists: "They rip each other off and we're supposed to do the right thing." He's not going to change his mind for me, Guarnaccia.'

'If you could just talk to him. There must be a way. You would think of something between you.'

'Well, I'll give it a try.'

'Yes. We have to find the brother and find out where Rinaldi fits in and . . .'

'And?'

'There's something more.'

'You keep saying that. But surely, you already know from D'Ancona that Sara, infuriated by the way she'd been led on and wasted her life, was claiming more from Jacob's estate than just her painting. I'd say her mother had a lot to answer for myself, but, in any case, you've shown me the dates and it all fits. The business of Sara's needing psychiatric help after her mother's death but not immediately after. That odd gap. It was the death of Jacob's wife a few months later that did it. She thought she'd get her painting but Jacob held off, didn't want his son to know. And then her more recent relapse. That was Jacob's death. She inherited a brother and still no painting. She contacted him, she was seeing him. She wanted money; he, presumably, wanted her off his property. I agree that we need to find the brother, I agree that Rinaldi's interest needs clarifying but that said, what's happened has happened. The lawyer's right when he points out that as nothing can save Sara now, the problem's a judicial one. We want a conviction for the attack on her. The rest is history.'

'Yes, of course. You're right. I'm not competent to . . . So, you'll go and see him.'

'I'll go. And I'll see to it that in the meantime, a close eye is kept on Rinaldi. If we leave him in peace long enough, put it about that our case is sewn up with the arrest of the two porters—I'm going to let them out on bail—he'll get careless and use his regular phone. He'll probably even get together with them after a while. Why not? They work for him. People always get careless, fall into old habits. It's to our advantage that he thinks he can laugh in our faces, as your man Lorenzini said.' He got up and pressed the eject button. 'I'll have this copied and take it back to him.'

The marshal stood and picked up his hat. 'What do you want me to do next?'

'I don't know but I know what I'm going to do next: get back into my own shambles of an office and smoke a cigar. Better switch this thing off . . . Right, let's go.'

Out in the corridor he took a look at the marshal's face and said, 'Take a break from this business. There's not much you can do right now. Have you much else on at the moment?'

'No . . .'

'You don't sound very sure.'

'No, no . . . It's just a case I was involved in, not my case at all really but—'

'Come in and sit down a minute.'

Hadn't the marshal said it himself, on hearing that Sara Hirsch had talked about him to D'Ancona as a trusted friend, someone she'd confided in when really she hadn't? You only realise when it's too late that if you'd trusted someone they would have helped you. He sat with his hands planted on his knees, staring dumbly at the prosecutor, struggling with the idea of taking a bit of his own advice.

The prosecutor was determined to find an ashtray.

'It may look untidy but I know exactly where everything is as long as nobody moves anything . . . Ah!' He lit the tiny cigar and leaned back, contented. 'There was something I wanted to ask you about, now I think of it. I was talking to Maestrangelo about arrangements for the surveillance of Rinaldi this morning, very early this morning—does he ever go home or—never mind. Anyway, he mentioned you. He seemed a bit concerned about you. That's why I asked you if you had much else on at the moment. He was telling me about this latest Albanian affair, the young girl on the motor-way. You were there?'

'Yes, I was there. And if I'd . . .'

'How is she?'

'They had to operate twice. Now they've moved her to a place where they can teach her to walk but it's not going so well. She cries a lot for her mother.'

'I'm afraid her mother won't be crying for her, or if she is, she won't be looking for her. But they'll get her on her feet again, you'll see, and when they do—I think I told you when we met that I used to be a children's judge?'

'Yes.' The marshal's sad face brightened. 'Is there something you can do to help?'

'There is, yes. A good friend of mine—a very old friend, we were at elementary school together—runs a little home for children in distress out in the country. In my days as a children's judge I often had need of him. You know the sort of thing. A man murders his wife, he gets put away, and the children are orphaned of both parents. A lot of cases of children battered or sexually abused within the family, children stolen from God knows what country, escaped from their Gypsy captors and a life of begging and being beaten, all the usual things. They have about fourteen children there now. It's the first peace most of them have ever known. They go to school, do their homework together round a big table by a log fire, eat to their hearts' content, help feed the hens and rabbits, play. Have you ever seen children who've never played, Marshal?'

'I think Enkeleda might be one of them. She probably knows how to feed hens and rabbits, though. She's not a child, really, but the brain injury's left her with a mental age of about five.'

'I think she'll do all right with other children around. It's a lovely place, high up in the hills so it's cooler there. The only trouble is that, though it's healthy, it's a bit isolated and these are children who are already afraid of the outside world. It's good for them to have a variety of visitors, to learn a bit about life in the safety of their refuge. I go up there as often as I can. I suggest you and I pay them a visit one day, have lunch with the children. Wear your uniform and talk to them a bit about your job. Introduce Enkeleda to them.'

'Introduce her?'

'That's right. I'll have a word with the hospital social worker about it and we'll take her with us. Make sure she understands in a few simple words that if she learns to walk she can go and live there. She'll learn all the faster for it, you'll see. I'll give them a ring and we'll organise it as soon as possible. In the meantime, take a break from the Hirsch case until you hear from me that there's some development. I think I'll ring our friend Rinaldi up for a cheery, even apologetic chat. It occurs to me that I might remember now where we met at dinner.'

'You do?'

'No, I don't. I'm sure we never met at all, but if I choose a suitably illustrious name, titled, of course, he'll be quite happy.'

'Yes.'

'A little baroque curlicue. I'm learning from you.'

'Me?'

'Not as impressive as your off-the-cuff one about D'Ancona's name.'

'I'd have done better to ask Sara Hirsch his name, along with a few other things. I'd better go.'

'Take that break, Guarnaccia.'

He took a break. That is, he did nothing useful as far as the Hirsch case was concerned, which, in his opinion, was what he'd been doing all along. Not much of a break. He did come to the surface of life sufficiently to have a row with Teresa about Giovanni.

'Salva, you can't force children to do what they don't want to do.'

'Did I say anything about forcing him? I'm just saying we could have discussed it, that's all I'm saying!'

'Discussed it? *Discussed* it? I've been trying to get you to discuss it for the last month but I might as well have talked to the wall. I've been telling you about it day after day but the spoken word means nothing to you. You haven't heard a thing I said, have you? Well, have you?'

'Of course I have . . .' Out of the fog some sentences emerged, sentences he'd responded to with a grunt or a hug, according to mood. That night . . . that dreadful night after the motorway . . . he'd been so desperately grateful to her for talking to him long and quietly about the boys, soothing him until he fell asleep. Those floppy little limbs, a poor dead rabbit . . . but the prosecutor—

'Salva, for God's sake! You're not even listening to me now! If you can't be bothered to take an interest, then all right, but don't start giving orders when the war's over.'

'War? Orders?'

'You spend all day ordering those poor lads around and then you come home and start—'

'Poor lads? What do you mean "poor lads"?'

'Living in a barracks away from their families. And some of them not much older than Giovanni. I don't suppose you ever listen to them any more than you listen to your own children.'

'They're not in the army to be listened to!'

'Just as well. Do you want coffee?'

'Yes, but what do you mean "the war's over"?'

'I mean he's already made his choice. He's signed up for the Technical Institute.'

'But that means . . .' He knew by now he was on thin ice and prudence prevailed. 'He'd already decided at the end of the school year, before we went on holiday.' Said in a way that he hoped might sound somewhere between a question and a statement—in case she'd told him at the time. She had. He submitted to the ensuing tirade.

He was upset. He had left school at fourteen himself and he'd been looking forward to having his sons at the high school. The last he'd heard, or so he'd imagined, was that Giovanni was to go to the School of Science. The thought had given him enormous satisfaction.

'He said he was sure.'

'Well, he's changed his mind. At his age—'

'No, he hasn't changed his mind. Totò's changed his mind for him, preparing the way for himself! It's all the fault of that blasted computer!'

'You're the one who wants Giovanni to join the carabinieri.'

'What's that got to do with it?'

'These days they need modern skills, Salva. I bet you're the only person in your station who can't use the computer.'

'Well, I'm not. Lorenzini's fifteen years younger than me and he can't, either.' Lorenzini would have been surprised to hear this but Teresa didn't know any different and he clung to his traditional ally. 'Besides, Totò will have enough trouble getting through his national service, never mind joining up professionally, so he hasn't any excuse for not going to a good school just so he can type theft reports into a computer.'

'The Technical Institute is a good school and Totò wants to design software. I told you.'

'What does that mean—don't tell me! I don't want to hear any more about it!'

His heart was pounding. He could hear it in his head. Teresa got up from the kitchen table where they were having their coffee.

'Where are you going?'

She came round to him and drew his head close. 'Whatever's the matter with you, Salva? Why are you so upset?'

'I don't know,' he said, trying to swallow down the pounding that made it hard to breathe. 'I don't know what's wrong with me and I don't know how you put up with me. I'm useless. I should have helped you with this weeks ago, not now. It's too late now. I'm too slow. My mother always said I was and she was right.'

'Don't say that.'

'Why not? You always do.'

'Well, then. There's no call for you to be saying it, is there?' She held his head and looked down into his big, mournful eyes. 'What is it, Salva? It's not just the schools. You're really upset about something else, aren't you?'

'Just about being slow. What else is going to blow up in my face because I wasn't listening . . .'

As long as she kept hold of him and he could feel the vibrations of her voice it was all right. But the rest of the time he felt the cold fat toad still squatting in his stomach and he couldn't dislodge that feeling of apprehension.

Still, days passed and nothing happened. He listened with dogged attention to all the usual people with all the usual problems. Some of them were quite taken aback by the interest their lost passports, stolen mopeds, broken car windows provoked.

'You're not thinking it's connected with some bigger crime or something, are you?'

'No, no . . .'

With August came the first big exodus from the city. The evening news showed mile-long queues for the ferries to Elba, Sardinia, Sicily. The local news announced the death from a stroke of Sir Christopher Wrothesly.

'Sir Christopher had been ill for some time,' the announcer intoned.

Poor sad man. Still, it was one thing less to worry about. After all, if there should be a big robbery up there now, Sir Christopher wouldn't suffer from it.

The temperature in the city was 102 degrees. At the airport, the hottest place of all, it was 105.

More warnings were issued about going out during the middle of the day. The pollution alerts that had been flashing almost daily on the avenues went dark as the resident population deserted the city. Storms exploded in the north and south of the country but Florence lay in an unbroken breathless torpor, broiling the tourists so that they got tireder and hotter and more forgetful of their cameras and handbags. The marshal's office filled daily.

At last, after a few false alarms, the first August storm broke, plunging the city into afternoon darkness and washing it clean. Terra cotta roof tiles were soaked, white and green marble was refreshed, gilding glittered in the pink evening sunlight.

As usual, the weather continued unbroken along the coastline. The news showed beaches with people packed side by side, radios loud against a background of squealing children and the yells of soft drink vendors. A reporter asked a lithe young woman lying between other bodies, well oiled and browning nicely, 'People are starting to take their holidays in June or September these days, what do you think?'

'You're joking! And stay in the city in August? I'd die of the heat!'

'It's pretty hot here.'

'If I get too hot I jump in the sea.'

A shot of the sea with bodies packed as tightly as on the beach.

It was the morning after that report, which made the marshal and his wife grateful not to be at the seaside, that he received a phone call at seven-thirty just as he was sitting down in his cool office.

'Guarnaccia? Is that you?'

'Speaking. Who . . .'

'I don't know whether you'll remember me. Brogio, Antonio. We were at NCO school together.'

'I don't think . . .'

'It's all the same. Long time ago and I wasn't in the army above ten years. I left when my father died. Took over his undertaker's business.'

'Ah! Brogio, yes. I've got you placed now. It must be . . . I don't know how many years.'

'Too many to think about, don't dwell on it. Listen, this is a business call, I didn't ring you up to waste time chatting.'

'Business? No, listen—'

'No, no, no, no, no! Nothing like that.' Undertakers were known for paying bribes to policemen and emergency ward staff for directing business their way. 'No, it's your advice I want. I mean, it's a bit of a funny business. Hardly the sort of thing you can ring 112 for so I thought, since we knew each other, you could tell me who I should call. The thing is, I've got a body here I can't bury.'

'Why ever not? The prosecutor told me—'

'Somebody else might have done it and thought nothing of it, but after ten years as a carabiniere nobody can pull the wool over my eyes, know what I mean?'

'I . . . no.'

'There should have been an autopsy done.'

The marshal knew that the prosecutor had released Sara Hirsch's body for burial the day before and for one sense-less moment his stomach tightened as it flashed on him that he had never read the second part of that autopsy—hadn't the prosecutor said there was no need? In any case—

'Are you still there?'

'Yes. Yes. I'm still here.' He got a grip on himself. 'There was an autopsy done. I have a copy of it here in the file. Besides, you can see for yourself—'

'I can see a left arm broken at the shoulder and four bro-ken fingers on the left hand is what I can see.'

'An arm . . . ? No, no, I don't think . . . If you want, I can read you—'

'I know my business, Guarnaccia, and I can read a corpse with or without an autopsy. I've got this left arm, right? And what I've also got is a wound to the back of the head. And before you tell me that could have happened when the body hit the ground at the moment of death—'

'Yes. That's right. I saw the body and I remember a head wound . . .' The marshal had grabbed the file and was trying to extract the autopsy reports from it with the receiver jammed under his chin. A broken arm? Maybe in the second one . . . 'The attack was pretty brutal and the reconstruction . . .' Damn! There were pages and pages . . . 'An arm twisted behind the back isn't unlikely . . . If you'll just give me a minute.'

'As many minutes as you like but I'd say you've got your wires crossed somewhere. I'm not saying he didn't die of a stroke like the death certificate says. Even I can see from his face that he has had a stroke. All I'm saying is I can't bury this chap until there's an autopsy done because, whatever he died of, I'd say he had a bit of help and if you've got a file open on the business you'd better get round here.'

There. It had happened.

Eleven

It was raining in the garden. The afternoon storm was over and the sky had lightened but it was still shrouded in mist and weeping softly on the wet earth and leaves. The marshal stood behind the French windows of the small sitting room and looked out, watching the rain, waiting for it to stop. Once or twice he thought it had but when he stepped outside and left the shelter of the porch he realised that he was wrong. Looking up, he could see only a misty haze, but the fine drops were touching his face and dampening the dark shoulders of his uniform, making them darker. The marshal, catlike, didn't care for rain. A man obliged to be out all day in uniform never does like rain. No umbrellas, no taking your jacket off and borrowing something until it dries. He gets wet, he stays wet.

So the marshal waited, looking out, and every so often he went as far as the path to check again. He was anxious to get to the lily pond. A few birds were beginning to sing but in the garden it was still raining.

The visit to the Medico-Legal Institute that morning in stifling heat seemed like days ago. Sir Christopher's body had been delivered there the day before. His own physician, contacted by the prosecutor, had been immovable.

'Certainly the contusion on the head was pointed out to me. Sir Christopher suffered a number of very minor strokes and, some months ago, a rather more serious one which paralysed his right side and impaired his speech. I suggested a clinic but the idea distressed him. He could hardly be forced. He had a young man, a medical student I was told, who was in constant attendance. Sir Christopher was confined to a wheelchair of late and the only autonomous movement of which he was capable was that of transferral. In other words, getting himself from his bed to the wheelchair, from wheelchair to armchair and so on. For anything more complicated or potentially dangerous—the bathroom, for instance—he required assistance. I understand he attempted something of the sort alone and fell, hitting his head. The wound had been dressed and I removed the dressing to examine it. I found a very superficial excoriation, irrelevant as far as the cause of death was concerned—by all means, ask me anything you wish.'

But the questions led nowhere.

'No, I did not examine the left arm and hand since I had no reason to do so.

'I would say that he had been dead for approximately twelve hours.

'I was called by Sir Christopher's secretary a little before eight and, since I had two urgent house calls to do, I arrived at L'Uliveto at about nine-thirty.

'He was in his bed, where the boy who looked after him found him when he came into the room as usual at around seven-thirty A.M.

'The body was composed and the bed tidy. The final stroke would seem to have occurred during sleep.

'I saw no suspicious circumstances whatever. I would have alerted the appropriate authorities had I done so. Sir Christopher had been a very sick man for some time and his death was in no way unexpected.

'You will find that an autopsy will confirm the cause of death as an ischaemic episode, possibly accompanied by some haemorrhaging, given the somewhat hardened condition of the arteries.'

And it did. The pathologist had looked at Maestrangelo and the marshal across the half-exposed corpse. The sawn-off circle of skull had been sewn back in place with large black stitches.

'What about the head injury?' Maestrangelo asked.

'Superficial.'

'And the arm? The fingers?'

'That's your department. He didn't do that falling out of bed.'

With the cautionary tale of Sara Hirsch in mind, the marshal said, 'He was meant to keep calm and quiet because of the risk of more strokes He'd had rheumatic fever as a boy. If somebody attacked him, twisting—breaking—his arm, could that have . . . you know . . .'

'Upped his blood pressure, increased his heart rate, precipitated the blockage of the artery and its rupture? That what you're after?'

'I . . . yes.'

'No.'

'No . . . ?'

'Not a chance. Look here.' The pathologist lifted the cold, waxy limb. 'What you can see on the underside is post-mortem lividity—'

'Just a moment.' The captain looked at the mottled red patches, then at the pathologist. 'You can confirm that he died on his back?'

'I can confirm that he was lying on his back for many hours not long after he died but postmortem lividity takes time to become visible and if the body's moved in time and the process is not too far along, gravity will do its work and blood will settle according to the new position. Be that as it may, my point is that there's no real bruising on the dislocated shoulder or broken fingers. These are *postmortem* fractures. Why would anybody twist the arm of a dead man? It's an undertaker's trick.'

'No, no . . .' Those big stitches reminded him of that hair-dresser . . . he hadn't seen her since they moved Enkeleda. 'No. He called me to tell me about it. Refused to bury the man. He's an ex-carabinieri, you see . . .'

'Then I can't help you. Undertakers sometimes have to do it, as you know, if the limbs aren't composed immediately after death and rigor mortis causes difficulty in dressing the corpse.'

'He didn't dress it,' the captain pointed out. 'He just called us. And the man supposedly died in his bed, most likely in his sleep. The body was composed when his own doctor examined him and wrote the certificate.'

'As I said, it's a job for you.' He had pushed the drawer back into the refrigerator.

It was still raining. The marshal stood outside the French windows, sheltered under the porch, waiting. He found that if, instead of looking up at the misty, deceptive sky, he watched the leaves of the climbing roses and wisteria framing his view he could detect the tiny movements as fine raindrops touched them.

A job for the carabinieri. One that could get you in real trouble if you didn't do it thoroughly and even more trouble if you did.

Well, it wasn't the marshal's responsibility and Captain Maestrangelo was just the officer for it. 'Acting on information received, they were obliged, given the standing of the subject, to go through the proper motions to establish the circumstances of his death. An HSA report'—homicide, suicide, or accident, but he didn't spell that out—'a routine procedure,' with apologies to all concerned. The right man for the job. The marshal could have done without being there at all. Waiting for the captain to pick him up after lunch, he'd had a call from the prosecutor's office. Rinaldi had gone out and was being followed in an unmarked car on Viale Petrarca.

The prosecutor himself had come on the line when he'd explained his problem.

'Don't worry. I'd prefer to leave him on a long leash. Call me when you get back and I'll let you know where he goes.'

Up at the villa, the young gardener had opened the gates, acting as porter, this being August, as he'd explained.

He said, in lowered tones, 'There's quite a crowd here. I'm glad to see you. I thought, to be honest, that they'd have had the decency to wait until he was dead—but then, they had no scruples last time, when his father was in hospital, so I shouldn't be surprised, I suppose.'

This time, it was the marshal who said, 'We'd better have a talk later.'

'Just give me a shout. They've told me to open up the lemon house again. Opening the stable door rather than shutting it. They didn't do him any harm, did they?'

'I don't know.'

'I'll ring up to the house to announce you. Go in at the central door. Naturally, there isn't a servant in the place. You'd better get inside quickly, there's another storm brewing.' Thunder was rumbling around the hills and there was a hot, damp wind blowing. When they got out of the car outside the house it was very dark.

They were inside the mosaic hall with its dusty fountain when, with a deafening crack, the storm broke and the deluge began. Even in the gloom they had no need of any directions. There might have been no servants but there was a single light coming from a room to their left, the one where the marshal had glimpsed a boy in tears and Porteous's hand slowly massaging.

Men's voices were loud beyond the open door, not raised but loud with authority and self-importance. It was the captain who asked permission and entered, the marshal following and remaining a step or two behind.

The rain beat on the tall windows as the men in the room fell silent, a questioning silence on the part of the officials from the tax department and the men from the ministries of fine arts and of monuments, a silence of fear on the part of the thin, fair boy standing a little apart from them. But neither the captain nor the marshal looked at these people. The three men in the centre of the group drew their attention, the space around them electric. The eyes of Porteous and the smooth young lawyer were alert but confident, those of Rinaldi defiant. He'd had the time it took for them to

come along the drive to prepare his expression but his face
was red.

'Good afternoon, Signor Rinaldi,' the captain said.
'Gentlemen . . .'

One way or another, they all made some answer. Or did
Rinaldi not speak? The marshal didn't really notice. His big
eyes had registered the long sitting room, its dusty brocaded
chairs, its tapestries. But Rinaldi only made a fleeting impression, that of a long-sought-for road sign in the dark, pointing . . . Renato Rinaldi . . . *Dear Renato, whose taste for fine
paintings and statuary has always guided my own—more so than
my father's'* . . . pointing to a fourth face, the face that held
his attention as the captain began his discourse. Next to the
beautiful woman, painted full length in oils, in her garden.

*'When you go into the house, look at her portrait in the long draw-
ing room . . . the most beautiful woman I have ever seen . . . there's
a portrait of my father, too . . .'*

This one, too, full length in oils. Indoors in evening dress.
The father. That was who held the marshal's gaze. Young still,
handsome, James Wrothesly, in his prime. There was no mistaking those eyes, that black determination, that unwavering
stare. It was Jacob Roth.

Now Rinaldi was talking.

'The tax office asked me to assist with the valuation since
I'm familiar with the collection so, naturally—'

Unthinking, his eyes never leaving Jacob's, the marshal
touched the captain's sleeve, interrrupting. 'We need to call
the prosecutor.'

The captain looked at him. It was enough. Without a
flicker of change in his habitual grave expression, he asked
that they be shown to the room in which Sir Christopher was

found dead and, once they were there, that they be left
alone. Porteous, who accompanied them, was clearly unwilling to go but, if he had thought to protest, one look at the
marshal's face sufficed for him, too. He went, closing the
door.

The marshal was breathing heavily. Smells, sounds,
images filled his head. Faces staring at him with intensity in
life, faces mutely, blindly reproachful in death. The dark
stink of a death camp, the perfumed light of a garden . . .

And the captain needed explanations, logical connections,
words, so many words . . .

He did his best as his eyes photographed this new picture,
the invaded room, its pretty furniture pushed aside, the big
oak bed with the covers tossed to the foot, the imprint of its
grave burden still visible. A wheelchair parked nearby. And
the painting! Sara's painting, no longer diminished to flat
black and white strokes and patches but alive and dazzling.
Water lilies . . . 'And if I watched them long enough . . .'

'Guarnaccia . . .'

'Yes. I'm still trying to take it in myself. My son once
showed me something in one of his schoolbooks. A sort of
trick picture. You could either see it as an orange-coloured
silhouette of a chalice or else the black ones of two faces.
You were always looking at the same thing, only it depended
how you looked at it but, anyway, you could never see both
at once, even for a split second. I don't know if you follow
me . . .'

The captain looked desperate.

'I'm sorry. That painting in the drawing room came as a
bit of a shock to me but I realise it probably shouldn't have
done. When people change their names they always cling to

something, don't they? Sometimes the same initials, a middle name. You probably understand that better than me.'

'Guarnaccia, before the prosecutor gets here, I need—'

'Yes. Wrothesly. It's a bit difficult for me to get my tongue round it but if you see it written down—and, after all, I did see it written down—it's there, isn't it? His real name. James Wrothesly, Sir Christopher's father, was Jacob Roth. He made a fortune taking advantage of his fellow Jews fleeing from the Nazis in the thirties. Then he changed his name, perhaps in England, and married a rich young woman, brought her here, and had a son by her. But he had left a young Jewish girl pregnant in his father's house above the shop in Sdrucciolo de' Pitti. Sir Christopher and Sara were half brother and sister. There was trouble over the inheritance. We know what happened to Sara but . . .' He went close to the big bed, staring down at the imprint. 'What happened to you?'

Once the prosecutor arrived, Porteous and young Giorgio were called in to describe the events surrounding Sir Christopher's death. It was clear from the start that Porteous had no problems about this at all. Only the boy was nervous and careful to speak only when spoken to. For the rest of the time his eyes were fixed on Porteous as he talked smoothly on. They were all on their feet. No one seemed inclined to sit down in this room.

There was very little to recount, it seemed. Sir Christopher had spent the last day of his life in much the same way as many preceding ones. He rose early, helped, as was usual, by young Giorgio, and spent the first part of the morning on the dining terrace overlooking his late mother's garden, his favourite spot and conveniently close to this room. When it became too hot outdoors he was brought inside and the boy read the daily paper to him. He ate very little lunch but otherwise appeared quite normal. He lay on the bed and slept for a while. There was a storm brewing in the afternoon which prevented his being outside. Again the boy read to him from the newspaper, which Sir Christopher, having lost the full use of his right hand after the last stroke, could not manage alone. After looking through some business papers between six and seven, as he generally did, he had a light supper and was helped to bed. He didn't complain of feeling ill. On coming into the room at about seven-thirty the next morning and opening the outer shutters and the French windows, the boy discovered that Sir Christopher was dead. He called the secretary at once. Of course, there had been some deterioration recently, but naturally Sir Christopher's death, coming as it did without any immediate warning signs, was a terrible shock.

'Naturally,' the prosecutor agreed.

'I should imagine it was,' the captain said, and they both looked at the marshal.

What did they want him to say? All this talk and the boy's face . . . he'd been watching the boy's face, remembering how that day he had cried. He was afraid now, afraid and distressed. Not the other fellow, though, talking and talking, sure of his ground, confident. So why lie, then? The boy knew.

'When you left him that evening, what was he doing?'

'He was'— a glance at Porteous—'he was sleeping, I think.'

The marshal, too, turned his attention to Porteous.

'And what about during the night?'

'I'm sorry?'

'I should be asking . . . Giorgio, isn't it? I should be asking you. I imagine Sir Christopher relied on you if he needed to get up in the night.'

'Yes.'

'How was it managed? Where do you sleep?'

Giorgio pointed out a servants' door, camouflaged with the silk hangings on the walls. 'In the corridor out there. There's a small room where I sleep and a bathroom.'

'And that's the bellpull there near the little desk? So far from the bed?'

'No. I mean yes. That rings in the kitchen. Sir Christopher used a brass handbell. I could hear it easily. He kept it with him outside, too, in case he needed me.'

'And that last night, did he need you?'

'I . . . no . . . not that I remember.' His face flushed, his eyes again seeking those of Porteous but no help was forthcoming there.

'Isn't that a bit odd? Or did he never get you up?'

'Usually he did, yes.'

'Once a night? Or twice, usually?'

'Twice.' It was almost inaudible above the noise of the storm.

'Did you say twice?'

'Yes.'

You could tell his mouth was dry. The marshal loosened his hold a little. 'Well, the doctor said he'd been dead a good twelve hours when he saw him so that would explain it, wouldn't you say so, Captain?'

The boy let out a breath more audible than his answers had been.

'Thank you very much, both of you,' the captain said. 'Now we can leave the marshal to check over the room so he can write the required report, unless you . . .' He raised his eyebrows at the prosecutor.

'No, no, everything seems clear to me. Let's get out of the marshal's way and let him get on with preparing the report. Bureaucracy, the bane of our lives.' They moved towards the door, Giorgio in the rear. As they reached it, the boy felt a heavy hand fall on his shoulder.

'Giorgio? Can I call you Giorgio?'

'Yes . . .'

'You'll forgive me but I can't remember your surname— or the proper way of pronouncing your real first name, if it comes to that—let them go, let them go. You're not in a particular hurry, are you?'

'No.'

'Stay and give me a hand here. Show me that bell you were telling us about.'

The boy's eyes went straight to the bedside table. An inlaid box, a bedside light, a full water carafe with a glass upside down over the stopper.

'Yes . . . that's where I thought it would have been but it's not. I wonder where it's got to. D'you think it got moved in the confusion?'

'Yes. Yes, it must have . . . Excuse me, I—I need to go to the bathroom.'

The marshal lifted his hand but as the boy went towards the small concealed door it was easy to see that he could still feel the weight of it on his shoulder.

'Just a minute—sorry, but if you could just tell me one small thing—what papers was Sir Christopher looking through that last evening? I mean, I know what it means to lose the use of your right hand, my mother was the same. Couldn't manage the newspaper, couldn't gather papers together. You need two hands for that sort of thing. I suppose you tidied stuff like that up for him.'

'Yes.'

The marshal wandered over in the boy's direction and planted his large hand on some papers lying on the little desk. It was too dark, anyway, to see what they were. 'I suppose it'd be this stuff here, this insurance policy . . . well, in his state of health . . . was it this?'

'Yes. The insurance policy.'

'All right. Off you go. I'll be waiting for you.' He lifted his hand and switched on a small desk lamp. The papers were bank statements. He left the room, confident that the boy would be some time in the bathroom. Poor lad looked as sick as a dog. Fortunately, the others had paused in the central hall and were talking near the dry fountain.

'Excuse me.' The conversation stopped dead. 'I have a question for you.' He stared straight at Porteous. What did he have to be amused about? Well, the marshal didn't much care if Porteous thought him funny. He wanted an answer. Simple enough. 'I was wondering . . . you said Sir Christopher was looking through some papers that evening and the lad can't remember what they were. Being his secretary, I thought you likely tidied up that sort of thing—private matters and so on. So, was he looking through those old letters of his mother's that are lying on the little desk there? The lad thought he was but I thought I should check with you.'

'You did right. Yes, his mother's letters. We thought we should look through them and decide what should be kept. Given his deteriorating health, Sir Christopher was trying to put everything in order.'

'Good. Right.' He walked away. He was aware of the silence he left behind him and it crossed his mind that he should have excused himself . . . or had he?

He was back in the small sitting room before the boy reappeared, his face damp, blue eyes tiny in his drawn face. He was much fairer but, perhaps because he was thin, he reminded the marshal of Totò when he knew he was in serious trouble.

The hand that descended on the trembling shoulder now was a gentler one.

'It's all right. Don't be frightened of me, there's no need. Do you believe me? Look at me. Do you believe me?'

'Yes.'

'Then, for goodness' sake, tell me what happened.'

It was getting lighter and yet the soft rain was still falling. He tried stepping outside again, liking the smell of wet earth and what he thought were camomile flowers somewhere not far away in the long soaked grass. His mother had collected them from the fields and hung the bunches up to dry before picking their daisylike heads to make camomile tea. Teresa bought it in tea bags and put honey in it when he felt offcolour. You need somebody. It's not right to be alone. You need a family. And the sad thing about Sir Christopher Wrothesly—the saddest thing—was that, if his view hadn't been blocked by the so-called friends who wanted to isolate him for their own purposes, a family would have grown around him—a sister who was so in need of someone to look after once her mother had died that she 'borrowed' a neighbour's child; a poor relation who respected him and cared for his garden; young Giorgio, so grateful to be rescued from the horrors of Kosovo, the only one distressed by Sir Christopher's death. Well, he knew now the reason for that distress. He would be glad to finish with all this and get away from the oppressive weight of sadness, the soft insistent wetness on his face. He should go in and wait for the rain to stop, think over what Giorgio had told him.

'When I left him that evening, he was ill.'

'Giorgio, wait. Sit down. You're shaking. There, at the little desk. No. I'm all right.'

'He didn't want me to go. He . . .'

'Go on, I'm listening.' He didn't want to stand over the lad, oppressing him, or sit in front of him as though it were an interrogation. Besides, wandering about, he could reconstruct the story as it was told him. He stood now looking down at the depression in the pillow on the empty bed.

'He reached for me with his left arm, trying to speak, but he couldn't make any words. I knew what he wanted to say. The secretary made me go. He pushed between us and got hold of his hand but it was me he needed. I was the only one who always knew what he was trying to say.'

'You liked him.'

'I did like him, yes, because he was kind to me. Before the stroke he talked to me a lot, asked me about my childhood. When I told him about my father being killed he seemed really moved. My mother spent everything she had to get me out of the country. The last thing she said was, "Forget. Walk away. Start a new life." I wanted to, I still want to, but it's . . . lonely . . . I've heard nothing from anyone at home since the bombing.

'I applied for asylum. A nice policewoman asked me about my background. My Italian's good and I know some Russian.

I had been studying medicine in Belgrade until the troubles started and I rushed home . . . The policewoman gave me the number of Sir Christopher's lawyer. She said they'd taken in boys before. She warned me they were taking advantage of the situation of people like me. They'd pay me almost nothing for long hours of work but they would legalise my being in the country. It would be quicker and easier than trying for asylum and I could look about me for something better.

'Before I came up here I was washing the floors and cleaning the toilets in a dancing school.

'It was nearly a year and a half ago. I can't go back! Will they send me back?'

'Don't worry about that.'

'I didn't steal the cuff links they found in my room, I swear. I know some of the staff believe I did. The housekeeper, for one, and a few of the gardeners. I heard one of them say I was Albanian and that Albanian is just another word for thief. And that was even before the secretary said that some of the things had been found in my room when the carabinieri came the second time, the day after you talked to Sir Christopher. They might have found them but I didn't put them there.'

'No, no . . . They didn't find anything at all.'

'They took my fingerprints, though, and then, that day you came back with a warrant—a warrant for my arrest, that's what I was told. Sir Christopher's secretary told me he'd got rid of you, told you that Sir Christopher wouldn't press charges because he'd never know, that telling him would upset him too much and he was ill. He told me not to worry, that he and Sir Christopher's lawyer would look after me.

'The only person I told was Jim, the English boy who works in the garden. We're the same age and sometimes we go down to Florence together.

'He said they were just trying to frighten me so I'd keep my mouth shut about what was going on around here. He said if you'd really found the cuff links in my room you'd have said so and asked me about it.'

'We would.'

'He said you were all right. But he thought, and the head gardener thought, that what that robbery was really about was the hairbrushes because of Signora Hirsch, Sir Christopher's half sister. They thought she might have been inventing it, that there was no proof and a few hairs from the brushes could be tested for his DNA. They could do it without telling Sir Christopher and that would frighten her off if she was a fake. Then they seemed to give up on it. Of course there was no point when she died.'

'That's all nonsense, gossip. They stole those bits and pieces because someone in your position could easily have got rid of them. They needed you, do you understand? They wanted Sir Christopher at home where they could manipulate him as he got weaker. They didn't want a nurse, an outsider who might testify against them. They wanted to keep you here and keep you frightened.'

'But the housekeeper overheard . . .'

'Perhaps. Perhaps they thought of it once they had the hairbrushes. It's still no more than gossip. They knew Sara Hirsch visited here. Sir Christopher would have told them she was really his half sister. They must have realised she was unlikely to be a fake. Did you ever see her here?'

'We all saw her. She used to come and have tea in the garden. I was with him when he saw in the paper how she'd been found dead and it was right afterwards that he had the stroke. He took a few steps away from his garden chair with the help of a walking stick and I was bringing the wheelchair nearer. He lost his grip on the stick and then he fell. He was conscious and trying hard to say something but he didn't seem to be able to breathe properly and his face was twisted. After a few days he could manage to talk a bit better but he never mentioned his sister again. He did talk about his parents to me sometimes.'

The marshal came closer to him, looking at a photograph in a silver frame on the desk.

'Those are his maternal grandparents. They were English. The day I told him about my father he told me that his father never talked to him much. I think he talked to me because there was never anybody else around much except for business things. After the big stroke, the secretary and the lawyer and that man who sometimes comes to look at the pictures and statues only came in here when there was something he had to sign. I suppose it was because he couldn't speak properly anymore. I understood him most of the time. I couldn't make out all the words but I always knew what he wanted. They moved his bed downstairs then because of the noise from the top floor.'

'What noise?'

'We had to move some of the statues and pictures from up there. We took them to the lemon house because it opens on to the road and they had to be taken away. They said they were going to be restored.'

'I see. And you must have suspected that they were steal-ing from him. There's no point in distressing yourself about that now. It can't hurt him anymore.'

'That's not the point. The problem was he needed me and I always had to be helping them. I used to take him out on the terrace or down to his mother's garden in his wheelchair every morning and leave him there . . . they made me. He was quieter in the garden than anywhere, staring across at the lily pond. It was when I had to leave him indoors after lunch that he used to get agitated. It's a nice view from here but there isn't much light in the room, not in the afternoons. It's cooler that way, I suppose, but it looked so sad. He couldn't do anything, read, or . . . nothing at all. Just sit in the wheelchair all the afternoon. It's not true about reading to him either. I would have done it but they said they needed me . . . and . . . You won't tell anyone? He was so upset at the idea that his mind would go before he died. No one has to know and *they* didn't want anyone to know. They kept mak-ing him sign things. He couldn't read and he was only lucid at odd moments. When he was, he cried. I think it was because he couldn't speak. You can't imagine . . .'

'I know. My mother was the same after her stroke. She cried all the time, wanting to be taken home. She'd lived in that house over sixty years but it was her childhood home she remembered, I think.'

'What Sir Christopher tried to ask for most often was to be taken out to where he would be quiet near the lily pond. He couldn't understand when I tried to explain about the heat. He would reach out his left arm to point at that pic-ture, trying to say something. They're water lilies, that's why.

A Monet. He liked it a lot. I think when I left him alone he'd stare at it for hours and hours. Often I'd make an excuse, taking him to the bathroom and so on, and come back to see if he was all right. Sometimes he was sitting where I'd left him two or three hours before, not sleeping, just staring at the picture. Or at the wall. Once I found him over there. He was struggling to open the French windows with his left hand but that bolt's a bit stiff and you have to be standing. It had gone dark because there was a storm coming, like today, and he was sobbing, perhaps with frustration, or else he was frightened. That's when I started leaving a light on. One day he must have pulled himself to his feet with that brass knob on the bolt and managed to open it up in the middle of the storm. He had wheeled himself outside and soaked his shoes and socks in a puddle of rainwater. He was giggling. Sometimes he was like a child.'

The marshal walked to the French windows. 'He could push the wheelchair himself?'

'Oh, yes. It's a left-handed one. He just had to turn that outer ring. Those are the marks where . . . those scratches . . .'

'Go on.'

'They said, "Take the night off. Go down to Florence." It was an order. It was true that I hadn't been out for over a month. The secretary said he'd stay with Sir Christopher and he was here in the room with him when I left. I went down on the bus. I didn't do anything much. Ate a pizza, wandered around for a bit. I haven't seen that much of Florence and lately I'd got used to just looking down at it from up here. It felt odd, maybe because it's so sticky and warm down there at night, or because of the floodlights, all the tourists strolling about . . . there was a fire-eater in Piazza della

Signoria . . . I don't know, it just didn't seem real. Every now and then the scene was lit by sheet lightning. I drank a few beers with my pizza so maybe I was a bit light-headed, and I was very nervous.'

'Why were you nervous? Did you realise he was sicker that night?'

'Yes. He'd eaten nothing all day. He hadn't let me dress him. He didn't want to go out. At breakfast time and lunchtime he'd cried and held on to my arm trying to tell me something was wrong. All he could manage to say was, "Pain . . ."'

'When I asked him where the pain was he just cried. I don't think he knew. He didn't feel things in a normal way on his right side. You see how on his wheelchair there's a padded support for his right arm? Once I found him near that table there. His hand, bound to the support so it wouldn't drop and get hurt, was trapped under the edge of the table. He was sweating with pain but he didn't pull his hand out because he didn't understand where the pain was coming from. I told the secretary that day that he was ill. I told him twice. But the doctor didn't come. I don't know if he called him.'

'He didn't. Tell me what happened when you came back.'

'I knew they wanted me to stay out late but it started raining and, besides, the last bus is at one ten. When I was coming back on the bus I saw the lights on in the lemon house and a three-wheeled truck parked outside. I realised then what a stupid thing I'd done. I'd warned them that he was dying and that made them rush to get the stuff away. If I'd said nothing . . . Yes, I know he'd have died anyway but not like that, not . . . No! No, I should—I should have—'

'It's all right. It's all right. Calm down. Breathe properly. Breathe. That's better.'

'They wanted to be ready when he died, you see, for when those men out there came in and asked for the inventory and started checking. I keep thinking that if I'd thought of telling Jim—he wasn't one of those who say all Albanians are criminals. He was always friendly to me. If I'd thought—'

'You were in no position to do anything. Don't torment yourself.' How easy it was to say.

'Yes, I'm sorry, I know you're right. Jim let me in without getting up. He heard my voice and pushed the button. I came into the house by the kitchen door. They didn't notice me. I saw them down in the lemon house, the secretary and the lawyer and the two porters who always come. I used the servants' passage and came in here through the small door. I thought he might have been ringing for me, he might have needed to get up. He wasn't here. I'd left his wheelchair parked to the left side of the bed but that wasn't here either. The French windows were open. It was still raining hard. I knew right away where he would have tried to go. Perhaps he wanted to die there, near the lily pond where he was always peaceful. But he didn't get that far. He must have gone out on the dining terrace instead of keeping to the path that leads to the garden below it.'

'Show me.'

The boy didn't want to go out there but the marshal got him to his feet, insisted. Much as he disliked going out in the rain himself, it had to be done and done now before the reappearance of the prosecutor, the captain, the secretary, anyone, could interrupt the story. Their feet crunched on wet gravel and wet leaves slapped at their shoulders as they went in silence under the rose-covered archway. They came out on the open dining terrace. To their right a soaked figure in billowing marble drapery held up a hand in the mist as if trying to stop the rain, or stop something else. The shiny laurel leaves nodded and dripped.

'He was lying here like a cat that's been run over and left to stiffen in the road. The rain was pelting down on him. The wheelchair was on its side facing across at the lemon house. All the lights were on down there. He saw it all.'

'Yes.' The great doors of the lemon house were open. It was a fair distance but you don't need to make out faces to recognise people you know well. Your friends. 'Yes, he saw.'

'All that time afterwards, shut in my room while they were . . . messing with him, I tried to tell myself that he was in one of his childish states, like the last time he'd opened up the windows and got his feet wet and laughed. It's not true. He knew he was ill. He knew I was out. He took his bell because it's gone, I don't know where. He must have heard something. He was in too much pain to sleep. He went out and he must have seen them. His friends. I know his mind was clear, you see. To stand up from a wheelchair, especially with only one hand to push you forward, you have to lift the footrests to set your feet on the floor and you have to put the brakes on. He did everything properly. He died standing up, watching his friends. He must have grabbed at the left arm of the chair as he fell. You can see the scratches on the guide wheel where he pulled it over with him. He was still gripping it. I didn't find the bell, it was too dark. He was wet and stiff.'

'Did you touch him?'

'Just his neck for a pulse but I knew—and his hand, his left hand. It wouldn't let go of the wheel. I felt for his eyes. They were open and it was raining in them, so I closed them.'

'You didn't try and move him?'

'No. I knew how heavy he was even when he was alive. I went and told them. They were carrying a painting to the lemon house. I think they were furious about being seen. They left me standing there while they talked in a whisper about what to do. I was scared myself but they were in a real panic. They told me to go to my room and to come in as usual at seven-thirty in the morning.

'They were a long time getting him in and messing with him. I covered my head with the sheet, trying not to hear. I lay awake all night. I felt cold and stiff. I was wet, I suppose because I got in bed without getting undressed. I just took my shoes off.'

The marshal interrupted him. 'You're frozen now. Come on back inside.'

The room seemed even darker as the skies outside cleared.

'Isn't there another lamp you could switch on? Oh, thank goodness for that. You should change your shirt.'

'It doesn't matter.'

The marshal opened the door of the corridor leading to the bathroom and Giorgio's bedroom. 'How much could you hear of what went on in this room when you went to bed? Did you understand what they were doing?'

'I suppose so. That's why I kept my head under the sheet, trying not to hear. I could make out their voices but nothing they said. Then they went away. I stayed under the sheet and my ears buzzed in the silence. Then the birds started singing. After a long time the alarm went off. Everything sounded normal but I knew it wasn't, like in a nightmare. I didn't come in here, I went to the kitchen and waited, looking out of the window. The kitchen maid arrived. She said, "You're early. Have I to make his tea?"

'I said, "No. He's dead." So that she would be the one to call the secretary. I didn't steal his father's things.'

The marshal said, 'No.'

'Afterwards I sat next to him until the doctor came. They'd put his blue pyjamas on. He didn't like them.'

Those last minutes before the rain stopped, the marshal spent alone in the sitting room, thinking, not about Sir Christopher's death but about his mother. It was true that this pretty sitting room was designed to keep out the heat, that porch arrangement with its thick foliage especially so. But that did make it sadly dark on a rainy afternoon even with the lamps on. He saw a big standard lamp and switched that on, too. He looked at Sara's water lilies first. Much good had the painting ever done Sara. But what about the young woman who unwittingly robbed her of it? What was her name? Wasn't it Rose? Or was that some connection in his mind with the garden? No, it was Rose. The silver-framed photograph of her parents had a dedication which confirmed it. On the wall near the small writing desk was a simpler wooden frame with a child's effort at depicting the lily pond. An early effort by Sir Christopher before he could spell, write letters of even height, pronounce his own name. 'To mumy from Kista.'

Baby abbreviations often lasted a lifetime. His own Totò would never be Antonio except to strangers.

Perhaps only the housekeeper who had been born here and shared Sir Christopher's childhood knew that name, but she was a servant and must have called him Sir Christopher.

His own sister probably never knew it. His friendly poor relation probably didn't know it. They should have known. They should have been near him at the end. They would have known which pyjamas he didn't like.

When it stopped raining he went out. He returned to the dining terrace where Sir Christopher had died. Stooping, he soon discovered the brass bell where it had rolled behind a terra cotta urn spilling wet pink geraniums. He picked the bell up. The mist on the garden was dissolving and he felt the heat of the sun on his head and shoulders. Over by the lemon house a familiar figure was moving among the big pots. He rang the brass bell and the figure stopped, looked up, and waved in recognition. The marshal pointed and began making his way down the staircase to Rose's secret garden.

They met at the lily pond.

'How's it going? Have they shown you the will?'

'You're not going to tell me you've seen it?'

'Two of the gardeners witnessed it. Had to be nonbeneficiaries and they didn't want anybody from outside. It's a fake, of course—well, he signed it after a wobbly fashion but no one will question that since he'd lost the use of his right hand. He couldn't read, though. You ask Giorgio. The will's a fake.'

'It could have been drafted before. You don't know—'

'There was nothing for the gardeners, nothing for the household staff. He would never have done that.'

Of course. 'The small bequests . . .' Sir Christopher's pleading voice, unable by then to articulate. *The small bequests particularly . . . pe-ic-yery . . .*

Don't worry. I'll have everything drafted for tomorrow.

'They left him to die alone like a dog, but he was a gentleman. Is there nothing you can do to them for leaving him alone like that?'

'There is, there's a law against failure to assist a sick or helpless person . . . but those two, Porteous and the lawyer, they're not family. If anything, the blame would fall on Giorgio. Their word against his.'

'Not just his. We all know what's been going on. We always hear things—'

'I believe you, but this'—he indicated the marble plaque at their feet—'is an example of how gossip invents the wrong reasons for the right facts.'

'You mean Rose didn't catch him here?'

'Yes, she did, but not with another woman. James Wrothesly's wife found out something worse.'

'He must have had a woman, though. Sara Hirsch was his illegitimate daughter. We all knew that. She used to come here, so she was real.'

'Yes, Sara Hirsch was real.'

'And will it come out now, the real secret?'

'No.'

'The story will go down in history as it is then.'

'I expect so. That's the way history is.'

'I suppose you'll want me to tell you all about the will.'

'No. I want you to tell me what she wrote here, if you understand it. Rose, the lady who loved her garden.'

'And abandoned it. I don't know Latin but we all know what that says.

> In the midst of this fountain of delights
> Wells up some bitter taste to choke us
> Even among the flowers.

'We're going to have to do some weeding in here, after all this rain.'

The evening sun beamed down from a warm blue sky. The last clouds were vast, dazzling puffs of white touched with gold and pink, cushions for rosy cherubs with gilded wings, a suitable frescoed ceiling for the city below.

Twelve

The Appeal Court confirmed the sentences of the porters, Gianfranco Giusti and Piero Falaschi, who got fourteen years each. Rinaldi had been convicted with them in the first instance but without the information about Jacob Roth and the photographs of the Monet painting, the porters' claim that he was the instigator was unconvincing and on appeal the judgment was overturned.

'I don't suppose it came as any surprise to you,' the marshal said. The prosecutor was driving them out to the country and he was very cheerful.

'First rule of a happy life: Forget a case once it's out of your hands. You can't have been surprised yourself. We were lucky to get a conviction in the first instance. He had a good lawyer and we had precious little—in particular, no motive. I thought we were all agreed that the pleasure of putting Rinaldi behind bars was minor compared to that of Umberto D'Ancona's success. They've done a lot, you know, his organisation. I may not have followed the appeal but I've been very interested in following that. Didn't you see the article in last Friday's colour supplement—"Cézanne returned to collector's daughter"? I can't imagine having D'Ancona's energy should I ever reach his age. I haven't got it now. Anyway, I don't know about you, but publicising Jacob Roth's sins wouldn't have been as satisfying as finding out from a grateful Rinaldi just what was going on up at that villa all these years. What a triumvirate! Porteous, Rinaldi, and that smooth young lawyer. All wriggling their way onto the board of trustees so as to inherit control of the villa, plus Sir Christopher's mother's estate.'

'We don't know it all, though,' the marshal pointed out. 'Nobody will ever know how much stuff never made the inventory and vanished, some when Jacob was dying, the rest when Sir Christopher was moved downstairs, not to mention the famous "big robbery". I remember, the first time I went up there, Sir Christopher told me it was like Aladdin's cave, that top floor.'

'Did he? Well, it wasn't when Maestrangelo and I went up there. Of course, there were signs. The pictures on the walls were none of them the same size as the fade marks behind them—bit amateurish that, I thought.'

'They didn't care. Porteous had a free hand to move stuff around as he pleased. The tax people haven't given up yet, though, and, of course, the young gardener was a big help.'

Jim had turned up at Borgo Ognissanti Headquarters, bright as a button and as full of stories as ever.

'Well, *I* think, and *the head gardener* thinks . . .'

And with the help of the captain's fancy coffee-table book they were able to identify some urns and statuary that, if not listed in the inventory, had certainly once been in the garden. The photographs had been taken several years before when Jacob was still alive.

'Of course,' observed the captain, 'we don't know what Jacob and/or Sir Christopher sold and what was stolen from them by the people to whom they had been more than generous.'

'The stuff filled the lemon house twice over,' Jim said, 'and the *head gardener* says that Sir Christopher was bound by the terms of his father's will that gave Rinaldi usufruct only, though he would have liked to leave Rinaldi his flat and shop. *So* . . . when Sir Christopher was gaga, the lawyer and the secretary sold it to him for a pittance. Wobbly signature on unread contract as on fake will and their fence's lips are sealed.'

And they believed him but where was the proof?

Still, the prosecutor's curiosity had been, in some measure, satisfied and so had the captain's.

'He actually smiled,' remarked the prosecutor to the marshal now, 'not there and then but afterwards—I mustn't take the wrong turning here, like I'm always doing . . . is this it? Yes—did you see how pleased he was? I think he actually touched the frame with one finger. Do you remember?'

'Well,' murmured the marshal, feeling in his pocket for dark glasses as a lively spring gust drove off a rain cloud and the sun appeared, 'not every day do you see a drawing by Leonardo in private hands.'

'No,' admitted the prosecutor. 'It's not the same, is it, as seeing one in the Uffizi? I don't know why . . . At least they couldn't make that disappear. Tagged by the ministry, it would attract far too much attention. Did you ever wonder what would have happened to Ruth and to the children, if Jacob had spent his energies and manic determination on being a painter?'

'They'd have been just as badly off,' said the marshal firmly. 'Ruth would have taken second place to his painting instead of to Rose. She would have sacrificed Sara to Jacob's demands and Sir Christopher would have still been a fourth-rate amateur painter. Only he'd have tried to get attention through his father's reputation instead of through his fancy, titled friends.'

The prosecutor lifted one hand in surrender. 'Forget I asked.'

The marshal himself had been satisfied on one point. He had an inkling now of what a rich man's daily problems might be, first among them being money worries. Jacob's grandiose ideas had been all very well at the outset. He'd bought that place for a song in the years under the postwar republic when the Florentine nobility had started to unload property in the face of new taxation and the confiscation of neglected land. He married the money to maintain it all but by the time he died it was no longer enough and, in recent years, Sir Christopher had started eating into his mother's capital to keep his standard of living up to the level of his expensive guests. Lapsing into full-time invalidism was the only alternative to ruin. The triumvirate had been wresting from Caesar an empire with just about enough money to keep it ticking over and nothing for the massive restoration needed after years of neglect. And they'd be bound by law to carry out the restoration because the villa was a registered building. The situation had long been desperate. They needed to liquidate everything possible, including the flats above Rinaldi's in Sdrucciolo de' Pitti and, especially, whatever they could subtract from what Sir Christopher had inherited from his mother, including the Monet. The last thing they needed was a daughter making an unexpected claim on the estate. The prosecutor had said that their

Machiavellian minds would find a way, now they were rid of the problem of deceiving Sir Christopher and frightening Sara, and he had turned out to be right. Jacob's trust stipulated that, after Sir Christopher's death, the villa must be used for educational purposes. That was a broad term. It stretched easily to expensive residential courses taught by famous names to those rich enough and idle enough to populate the villa with the sort of people it was used to accommodating. As regards the clause mentioning the education of Jewish boys of talent, especially in the arts, D'Ancona, the only surviving Jewish trustee, had been outvoted and the clause was forgotten. It was good to think of Jim, a survivor if ever there was one, and the head gardener, of course, still caring for Rose's garden, weeding it after the rain. She had loved her garden and, despite what she had suffered there, had left it in the care of those who loved it and her.

'Do you think the car smells of cigars? Only, my wife thinks I've given up . . . We're nearly there. I must say, you don't seem too put out about that villainous trio getting away with it. After all, you did all the hard work.'

'Me? No, no . . . Besides, God doesn't pay on Saturdays.'

'What? Do you know something I don't know?'

'Oh, no. Nothing really. I hear a bit of gossip from up there now and then. I gather they still employ a few boys in straitened circumstances for a pittance. I also gather that they're chosen for their looks rather than their clean records and that there's been a lot of quarrelling about it. If the weather stays fine they'll soon be wheeling out the lemon trees . . .'

'Wheeling out the . . . Oh, I see. You think they'll get theirs without any help from us.'

'They shouldn't have thrown that young Kosovar boy out. He was worth his weight in gold.'

'Where's he gone, do you know?'

'I don't. I only know he was upset that they didn't let him stay for the funeral.'

They drove through a village and took a small road dropping into a valley, then an unmade one rising high into the hills.

'At this time, the younger children, at least, will have eaten.'

They had. The well-settled ones ran to the car, shrieking, took their hands, and pulled them in six directions at once—to see the new dog, the baby rabbits, a broody hen, a school report, a new television. The recent arrivals watched, wary but interested.

The prosecutor greeted his old friend, 'father' to this big family, and asked, 'Where's Nicolino?' He'd talked about this seven-year-old as the car climbed the hills. A child sexually abused by his stepfather, who then murdered his mother. The little crowd opened up. Nicolino appeared and said, 'Who are you?'

The prosecutor told him and said, 'I heard you'd arrived here yesterday and thought I'd come and see how you were getting on. This is Marshal Guarnaccia.'

'I'm stopping here.' At the sight of a uniform, the little boy backed up against the 'father', who put a hand on his shoulder. 'And this is my dad now.'

'Good. We came to see Enkeleda, too.'

'I know where she is. I'll take you, if you want.'

'Thank you.'

He led them along a path and then down a grassy bank, telling them this was a shortcut and offering a helping hand to them both. Very proprietorial. Wild daffodils bobbed in the wind and you could see for miles across the valley. On the lower path, Nicolino paused to warn them in a whisper, 'She's cleaning out the rabbits. She doesn't like it if you make a noise because of the babies.'

The prosecutor whispered back, 'We won't, don't worry.'

The rabbit hutches were ahead to their left in a long line. They had to go forwards in single file. They didn't see her at first, crouching there in darkish clothes, very still. Then the prosecutor stopped and turned, waiting for the marshal to catch up with him.

'Look at her . . .'

The claw-footed stick which had replaced a walking frame was parked by the first hutch in the line. Enkeleda was farther on. Her dark hair had grown back nicely and hung in soft childish curls on the back of her collar as she bent over something held in her two hands. It was a moment before she noticed the interruption. Then she turned and saw them. Her eyes were alight with wonder at the tiny brown-and-white rabbit quivering in the palm of one hand held close to her chest. She wobbled a bit as she turned, and the marshal, seeing her on uneven ground, put out a protective hand. She misunderstood and held her tiny burden out for him to see. With care—but it was only care for the baby rabbit—she began to walk towards the marshal, smiling.

What with one thing and another, it was a little after five when he got back to his station. He unlocked the door and then stood there in the waiting room, keys in hand, staring.

'Yes, it's me. It's been a long time. Don't you recognise me?'

How could anybody fail to recognise Dori with her dazzling blond hair and her shapely red lips—even with her amazingly long legs hidden by jeans.

'Of course I do, but what are you doing here? Come on, come in my office.'

When she was sitting in front of him, offering no explanation, he asked, 'What about the baby? Boy or girl?'

'Dunno. Lost it at five months. I was ill for ages. Never again.'

'I'm sorry to hear that—but don't say 'never again'. It'll pass, you'll see.'

'No, it won't. I can't have any more and just as well. Listen—can I smoke?'

He gave her an ashtray. Once she'd lit up, she looked at him with a mixture of wariness and affection.

'You're the only person who's ever been nice to me . . . so I wanted to tell you because if I don't somebody else will. You're bound to find out. I'm going back on the game.'

'What? You're *what*? And Mario?'

'Oh, Mario . . . Jesus . . . I mean, he trotted off every morning at a quarter to eight and I was supposed to clean up his crumbs and wipe the floor over and then he'd come trotting back again and I was supposed to have the water boiling for his pasta and then it was one long whinge—there are no clean shirts, have you seen the fluff under this bed? Where's the other sock to this? You've forgotten to get milk again . . . No, no, I couldn't stand the boredom. So I upped and offed.'

'Back to Ilir?'

'Why not? He's out now and he wants me back. Nobody ever earned him as much as me and he kept me in style. We ate in a restaurant every night. I like a good time and I get clients who give me a good time, you know what I mean? I like champagne and a few presents. I'm not spending the rest of my young life washing the floor of some poky little kitchen for a boring spotty clerk who thinks he's earned the right to have his socks washed for a lifetime because he's been good enough to *save* me from the streets.'

'But what about when you're not young anymore?'

'Well, it's all over then, isn't it? Get it while you can, I say. I just . . . I wanted to tell you myself. It's not that I'm not grateful to you. I know you meant well. Are you pissed off with me? You are, aren't you?'

'No, no . . .'

'You've every right to be. I'd better go. I'm sorry. Because of you, I mean, not that little prick Mario, only because of you. I know you did your best.'

Carve it on my tombstone, thought the marshal, watching her leave through a skein of cigarette smoke.

He wished that Giorgio had come to see him instead of disappearing. Gjergj, that was his real name. Nothing was ever heard of him again but the marshal never forgot him. For some reason, that one remark stayed in his mind. *'They'd put his blue pyjamas on. He didn't like them.'*

Had he gone home to Kosovo? They were still fighting there. Wherever he was, the marshal wished him well.

OTHER TITLES IN THE SOHO CRIME SERIES

JANWILLEM VAN DE WETERING

Outsider in Amsterdam   *Just a Corpse at Twilight*
Tumbleweed   *The Streetbird*
The Corpse on the Dike   *The Hollow-Eyed Angel*
Death of a Hawker   *The Mind-Murders*
The Japanese Corpse   *The Rattle-Rat*
The Blond Baboon   *Hard Rain*
The Maine Massacre   *The Perfidious Parrot*
The Amsterdam Cops: Collected Stories

SEICHŌ MATSUMOTO
Inspector Imanishi Investigates

PATRICIA CARLON
The Souvenir
The Whispering Wall
The Running Woman
Crime of Silence
The Price of an Orphan
The Unquiet Night
Death by Demonstration
Hush, It's a Game
Who Are You, Linda Condrick?

PETER LOVESEY
The Vault
The Last Detective
On the Edge
Rough Cider
The False Inspector Dew
Diamond Solitaire
The Reaper
Diamond Dust
The House Sitter

JOHN WESTERMANN
Exit Wounds
High Crimes
Sweet Deal

MAGDALEN NABB
Death of an Englishman
Property of Blood
Death in Autumn
The Marshal and the Murderer
The Marshal and the Madwoman

CHERYL BENARD
Moghul Buffet

QIU XIAOLONG
Death of a Red Heroine
A Loyal Character Dancer

J. ROBERT JANES
Stonekiller
Sandman
Mayhem
Salamander
Mannequin
Carousel
Kaleidoscope
Dollmaker

AKIMITSU TAKAGI
Honeymoon to Nowhere
The Informer
The Tattoo Murder Case

STAN JONES
White Sky, Black Ice
Shaman Pass

TIMOTHY WATTS
Cons
Money Lovers

PENELOPE EVANS
Freezing
First Fruits

CHARLOTTE JAY
Beat Not the Bones

MARTIN LIMÓN
Jade Lady Burning

CARA BLACK
Murder in the Marais
Murder in Belleville
Murder in the Sentier
Murder in the Bastille

TOD GOLDBERG
Living Dead Girl

REBECCA PAWEL
Death of a Nationalist

MTP
OCT 09 RECD